Dead Ends

Emilia G Collins

Copyright

Copyright © 2025 Emilia Blandino

All Rights Reserved.

No portion of this publication may be reproduced, distributed, or transmitted in any form or by any means, including photocopying, recording, or other electronic or mechanical methods, without the prior written permission from the author, except as permitted by UK copyright law.

Cover Design by Emilia Blandino ©

Author portrait photography credit: Apollo Flux

Emilia Blandino asserts the moral right to be identified as the author of this work.

This novel is entirely a work of fiction. The names, characters and incidents portrayed in it are the work of the author's imagination. Any resemblance to actual persons, living or dead, events or localities is entirely coincidental.

All rights reserved under International and UK Copyright laws.

ISBN: 9798288301087

Paperback book edition © June 2025

Dedication

To my mum, Jane – for your brutal honesty, unwavering love, and for always keeping me grounded (whether I liked it or not).

To Paul – my kind and quietly resilient stepdad, who somehow puts up with us all.

To Carmela and Louise – thank you for surviving my chaos and still speaking to me. That's love.

Louise – I can confirm you are in no way affiliated or similar to the Louise in the book. Soz for the name choice.

To my husband, Ryan – for your endless patience, support, and for pretending to listen to all my plot ideas.

And to Ellis and Noah – my amazing little humans. Thanks for the cuddles, the giggles, and occasionally letting me write a sentence in peace.

Couldn't have done it without any of you. Seriously.

A special thanks to Michael Knight for being the kind of man people can truly aspire to be.

"The past can tick away inside us for decades like a silent time bomb, until it sets off a cellular message that lets us know the body does not forget the past."
– Donna Jackson Nakazawa, Childhood Disrupted.

Chapter One

The House on the Hill

Emily paused by the kitchen window, half-hidden behind the curtain. The evening light was golden, soft, casting long shadows across the back garden. Her mum was out on the patio again, sitting in the faded green chair beneath the pergola, legs stretched out, her slipper dangling off one toe. A bottle of wine sat on the table beside her, already half empty. Her glass, stained dark red, glistened in the fading sun.

Emily didn't need to count how many glasses were gone. She just knew.

The rule was simple: **don't go outside**. Not when the bottle's out. Not when the glass isn't full anymore. Not when Mum stares out into the garden like she's watching a war play out in the bushes.

She crept away from the window, careful not to let her bare feet squeak on the lino. The last thing she wanted was to catch Andrea's attention. When her mother was drinking, her mood was a coin toss—sharp, sudden, and always landing on something that cut.

The house was too quiet. Always was around this time, when everyone was playing invisible. Upstairs,

Cynthia's bedroom door was shut as usual, the faint hum of music leaking through like a distant memory. She hadn't come down for dinner. Probably wouldn't. She rarely did.

Emily padded into the lounge. The curtains were still open, and the telly was on mute—some nature documentary playing to no one. She sat on the edge of the sofa, hugging a cushion to her chest, letting herself listen to the small, familiar sounds of the house: the distant creak of Louise moving around upstairs, the gentle clink of Mum refilling her glass outside.

This was the in-between time. Before Dad got home. Before Louise thundered down the stairs and turned the TV up too loud, pretending not to care that Mum would scowl at her or that Cynthia might come down and glare before disappearing again. Emily liked this time least. It made her feel hollow. Like she was just waiting for something to go wrong.

She was thirteen. Old enough to understand things without being told, but young enough that no one ever explained anything properly. She had long brown hair that always needed brushing, olive skin that turned gold in the summer, and a heart that felt like it beat too loudly in her chest sometimes. People said she was mature for her age. Teachers liked her. Strangers called her "sweetheart" and "clever girl." But none of them knew what it was like to live in a house where everyone had their own escape plan.

Louise was fifteen and took up all the space in a room. Big voice, big laugh, big personality. She acted like she didn't care about anything—school, family, what anyone thought—but Emily had seen the way her eyes darted toward the back door when their mum was drinking. She noticed how Louise always made sure Emily stayed upstairs when Andrea got into one of her moods.

They shared a bedroom. Emily loved that, even if it meant chaos—makeup wipes on the floor, fizzy drink cans on the nightstand, loud phone calls with friends. Louise could be annoying, loud, even mean—but never cruel. Not really. She looked after Emily in her own weird way.

Cynthia didn't. Not anymore.

At seventeen, Cynthia was a ghost in her own house. She drifted from room to room like she was walking on glass. Always quiet, always watching. She barely spoke to Louise, never smiled at Emily. She'd once been warm, years ago—read bedtime stories, braided their hair, made up dances in the living room. Then something happened. Or maybe nothing did. Maybe she just got tired of the noise, the pretending.

Emily missed her, even if she didn't say it.

Their dad, Mike, would be home soon. She imagined the sound of his van pulling into the driveway—the heavy sigh of the engine, the rattle of his keys as he came through the door. He'd smell of sweat and dust and whatever takeaway he'd grabbed from the garage shop on the way back. He'd call her "Em," ask about school, maybe tickle her ribs if he wasn't too tired. He always smiled. Always laughed. But he never asked the important questions.

He didn't help with dinner. Didn't fold laundry or go to parents' evenings. He worked six days a week and left early, came back late. He was *nice*—that was the word people used. But Emily had learned that "nice" wasn't the same as *safe*.

A sharp clatter outside made her flinch. She glanced toward the kitchen—Mum had knocked her glass over. The red wine spread like blood across the patio table, dripping onto the concrete. Andrea didn't react. She just watched it, like she was mesmerised by the mess.

Emily swallowed hard and stood up.

She knew better than to go out there.

Instead, she crept upstairs to her room and closed the door behind her, letting the soft hum of Louise's music muffle the silence in her head. She flopped onto the bed, stared up at the ceiling, and let her thoughts scatter like leaves in the wind.

She didn't know who she was becoming yet.

But deep down, something told her this year was going to change everything.

Emily lay on her bed, arms folded beneath her head, watching the ceiling slowly fade into darkness. Louise's music drifted softly from the speaker on the windowsill—low enough not to carry, loud enough to blur the silence. It was one of her moody playlists, full of echoing guitars and sad boys murmuring about things that felt important when you were fifteen and angry at everything.

Downstairs, she'd heard the familiar thump of their dad's boots when he came in—his usual route straight through the hallway, a grunt of greeting, then the creak of the armchair in the living room. The TV would be on now, probably something pointless, with the sound turned up just enough to drown out the things no one wanted to hear.

Louise sat cross-legged on the floor by the mirror, untangling her hair, eyes narrowed at her reflection like it offended her. She hadn't said much since they came upstairs. But she didn't need to. The air was already heavy with things unspoken.

Then came the first sound—glass on glass. Not alarming on its own. Just a clink. A signal. A start.

A few seconds later, their mum's voice followed—flat, slightly raised, slipping into that familiar, bitter rhythm. Their dad replied, but his words were muffled, tired, and too calm for how sharp her next sentence cut through the floorboards. Then a scrape of furniture, something knocked or pushed aside, and another laugh from Andrea that sounded close to crying.

Emily sat up slightly, pulse thudding, gaze fixed on the door.

Louise reached over and turned the music down. Not off. Just enough to feel the shift.

"She's not even properly pissed yet," she said, flicking her hair over one shoulder. "Give it an hour."

Emily didn't answer. She knew how this went.

The shouting always came in waves. Not every night, but often enough that it had become part of the house—like a leaky pipe or a stain in the ceiling you couldn't scrub out. Their dad didn't shout back. He sighed, deflected, said the wrong thing at the wrong time, and left the rest spiralling.

There'd be no dinner now. No one would say it, but they all knew. Cynthia wouldn't come out of her room, and Louise would pretend not to care while secretly watching the stairs. Emily would stay quiet, heart rattling behind her ribs, praying it didn't get worse and knowing that praying had never helped.

Still, she listened because that's what she did. Not for the words—they were always the same, old wounds reheated and served up like leftovers—but for the spaces between them. The warning signs. The shift from drunken ramble to something darker.

Louise leaned against the bedframe and exhaled through her nose. "She's in one of those moods."

Emily nodded, curling back onto her side, blanket pulled up to her chin.

And tonight, didn't feel different. It felt familiar. Like most nights—quiet in all the wrong ways, full of unspoken rules and measured breaths, the kind of night that wrapped itself around your shoulders like a blanket that looked soft but scratched where it touched your skin, the kind of night where nothing terrible had happened yet, but you already knew exactly how it would go.

Chapter Two

Fault Lines

The weekend came with pale grey skies and the kind of steady drizzle that soaked you through without ever turning into proper rain. Emily sat on the windowsill in the lounge, her knees drawn to her chest, watching the raindrops collect and race each other down the glass. Louise's music thudded softly through the ceiling above, a muffled bassline that never seemed to stop.

It was Saturday. Which meant no school, no bus, no Chloe or Nia. Just the house. And the people inside it.

Andrea was still asleep—or pretending to be. Her bedroom door had been closed all morning, and no one had dared knock. A half-finished mug of tea sat forgotten on the kitchen counter, and the recycling bin outside overflowed with wine bottles from the previous nights.

Emily heard the stairs creak. Cynthia.

She glanced back as her oldest sister crept through the hallway, hair pulled into a low bun, sleeves of her hoodie pushed up to her elbows. Cynthia didn't look at her as she passed, just drifted into the kitchen searching for something. A few moments later came the sound of a cupboard door opening, the kettle boiling, the clink of a spoon in a mug. Then, silence again.

Emily slipped off the windowsill and lugged herself into the hallway. Cynthia was leaning against the counter, arms crossed, staring at the floor.

"Morning," Emily offered.

Cynthia didn't respond straight away. Just sipped her tea.

"You sleep okay?"

"Fine."

Emily shifted her weight awkwardly. "I thought maybe we could do something today. Just us. Like we used to."

Cynthia looked up, surprised. Then her expression folded inward, like she was suddenly exhausted. "I've got a lot of coursework to do."

"We could go to the library. Or just... walk."

"Em," Cynthia said gently. "Not today, okay?"

Emily nodded, heart sinking. "Okay."

Cynthia reached for the bread bin and took out two slices of white bread. She didn't ask if Emily wanted any. Just made her toast and walked out of the kitchen, tea balanced in one hand, toast in the other. Emily watched her go. Cynthia didn't look back.

Upstairs, Louise's door burst open. Her footsteps pounded across the landing before she clomped down the stairs two at a time. She wore leggings, a hoodie that wasn't hers, and headphones around her neck. Her phone was in one hand, her mood already crackling.

"Oi," she said, not unkindly. "You eaten?"

Emily shook her head.

"Well, I'm starving. You making toast or what?"

Emily shrugged and moved back to the counter. Louise leaned against the fridge, scrolling.

"Mum still dead to the world?"

"Yeah."

"Classic."

Louise made no move to help. She just talked while Emily worked the toaster and buttered slices as they popped.

"I messaged that girl from history. You know the one with the massive hair? She proper blanked me yesterday. Just left me on read. So I told her she could stick her group chat up her arse."

"Nice," Emily muttered.

"Also," Louise added, "you left your PE kit in the bathroom again."

Emily flinched. "Sorry."

"If it starts to smell, I'm chucking it out the window."

"Okay."

They sat on the stools at the breakfast bar, chewing in silence. The butter was too cold, so it tore the bread. Emily didn't care.

"You should stop trying with Cynthia," Louise said suddenly.

Emily blinked. "What?"

"She doesn't want to be part of it. Just let her go be mysterious and tragic. She clearly prefers it."

"She used to care."

Louise rolled her eyes. "Yeah, well, I used to want a pet rabbit. People change."

Emily didn't laugh.

Louise sighed, her tone softening. "Look, I know you miss her. I do too. Kind of. But she doesn't want anything to do with us anymore. Or Mum. Or Dad. She's already halfway out the door. Just counting down the days 'til uni or wherever she's running off to."

"She could take us with her," Emily said. It sounded pathetic the second it left her mouth.

"Yeah. In her handbag. Right next to her self-loathing."

The toaster clicked again. Another round. Louise took both slices this time.

Emily watched her eat, then asked, "Do you think Dad knows what it's like? Here?"

Louise shrugged. "He knows. He just pretends not to. It's easier that way."

Emily wanted to argue, but the words stuck in her throat. Of course he knew. But he left them here every morning and returned too late to notice the damage. He smiled, he laughed, and played the man of the house.

They spent the morning half together, half apart. Louise stayed on the sofa watching a film Emily wasn't interested in. Cynthia remained upstairs. Andrea didn't stir. Emily read for a bit, cleaned the sink because it bothered her, then went to her room and laid on the floor.

It wasn't even lunchtime when the doorbell rang.

They all froze.

Emily was closest, so she opened it. A man stood on the step, holding a clipboard and wearing a navy blue jacket with the gas company logo.

"Hi there. We're just doing a round of meter checks. Mind if I take a look at yours?"

Emily blinked. "Uh... one sec."

She turned. Louise had appeared behind her, arms folded.

"What?"

Emily whispered, "Gas guy. Wants to check the meter."

Louise took charge instantly. "Mum's not feeling well. Can you come back Monday?"

The man looked surprised but nodded. "Sure thing. Have a good day."

They closed the door.

"You can't just let people in," Louise hissed.

"I didn't! I was going to check with Mum."

"Yeah, because she's in such a good state to talk to strangers."

They glared at each other until the tension cracked, and Louise walked off.

The rain had stopped. Everything outside looked soaked and shiny. Emily sat by the window again, her reflection faint in the glass.

She heard Cynthia come downstairs. Not quietly this time. Not a wisp. She went into the kitchen and opened the fridge. A pause. Then:

"Where's the milk?"

Louise yelled from the lounge. "We're out."

"Of course we are."

Emily waited. Then went to join her sisters in the kitchen.

"I'll go to the shop," she offered.

Louise looked at her. "Take money from Mum's purse."

"I don't like doing that."

"Then we won't have milk."

Cynthia sighed. "Here."

She reached into her hoodie pocket and handed Emily a five-pound note. Their fingers touched briefly.

"Thanks," Emily said quietly.

Cynthia didn't reply.

Emily slipped on her trainers and stepped into the weak sunlight. She strolled to the corner shop, breathing in the damp smell of wet pavement and cut grass. She liked the shop. It was small and predictable.

When she returned, the house was louder. Louise had put music on properly, not through headphones this time, and Cynthia was shouting at her to turn it down.

"It's Saturday!" Louise yelled.

"Mum's sleeping!"

"She's always sleeping."

Emily put the milk in the fridge and stepped into the lounge. Her sisters stood at opposite ends of the room, both tense.

"She doesn't need an excuse to scream at us," Cynthia snapped.

"Oh, I forgot. You're the expert on disappearing when things get hard."

"At least I don't act like it's a joke."

"And you think sulking in your room counts as courage?"

"Girls!"

The voice silenced them. Andrea stood in the doorway, pale, eyes bloodshot, her dressing gown sagging off one shoulder.

"Do you have to shout like animals? Some of us are trying to sleep."

Cynthia looked away. Louise muttered something under her breath.

Andrea stepped further in. "What was that?"

Louise said nothing.

"That's what I thought. Useless, all of you. Like a fucking zoo."

She disappeared back upstairs. Cynthia followed, muttering something about studying. Louise slumped onto the sofa, arms crossed tight.

Emily remained standing. Frozen.

"You okay?" she whispered.

Louise didn't answer.

Emily walked over and sat beside her. Slowly, carefully, she leaned her head on her sister's shoulder.

For a moment, Louise didn't move. Then she let out a long sigh and rested her cheek against Emily's hair.

They sat like that, the house creaking around them.

Broken. But together.

The screaming started just after dinner.

Emily had been in her room, sketching on the back of a school worksheet she wasn't planning to finish. The shouting was sudden, sharp. Her mother's voice was high and desperate. Her father's, low but rising with each word like a sink just starting to overflow.

She moved into the hallway, heart ticking fast. Cynthia's door was already cracked open. Louise appeared a second later, pulling her hoodie tighter.

"Again?" Louise whispered, more tired than surprised.

Emily nodded. Together, they drifted to the top of the stairs. Louise hovered near the bannister but didn't sit. Emily lowered herself onto the step, tucking her feet beneath her. From here, she could see through the gaps between the spindles.

Downstairs, their parents stood in the lounge. Andrea's arms flailed as she shouted. Mike's fists were clenched at his sides. Then he reached forward, grabbing her wrists.

"Let go of me!" Andrea cried.

"I can't do this anymore," Mike snapped. "I can't live like this."

"Then go!"

"What are you hiding? Why can't I see your phone? Why are you lying to me?"

"I'm not lying!"

"Let me see it! Just give it to me!"

He wrestled with her hands as she tried to pull away. A dark wine bottle wobbled dangerously on the coffee table. Andrea screamed, not in pain but in rage.

Then Mike cracked. Not violently, but completely. His body sagged. He dropped her wrists and stepped back, crumbling into the armchair like he couldn't stand. His hands covered his face. A sound escaped him—half-sob, half-sigh.

"I can't do this," he muttered. "I don't know who you are anymore."

The girls said nothing. Cynthia had slipped back into her room. Louise stayed put, arms crossed, expression blank.

Andrea stood frozen for a moment, then stormed out of the room. She pushed past Emily on the stairs slamming the bedroom door shut.

Mike didn't follow.

That night carried on as usual. The performance played out in front of them was a regular occurrence. Cynthia didn't come out. Mike stayed in the lounge with the TV on, just sitting, not really watching.

Emily crept quietly through the house after filling a tumbler with water at the sink. Her father hadn't moved. The dim glow of the hallway light reflected off his glasses. He looked asleep, but she wasn't sure.

She climbed the stairs in socks, every creak making her wince. At the top, she paused. Andrea's door was closed, but she could hear it—the sobbing.

Soft. Ragged. Hidden behind the noise of her sisters' music and the house's breathing. But it was there.

Emily hovered, then inched warily to the door. She raised a hand and knocked gently.

"Mum?"

Silence. Then a shaky breath.

"What is it?"

"Can I come in?"

A pause. Then: "Yeah."

Emily pushed the door open. The room was dark except for the dull light of a lamp. Andrea was curled on her side, her eyes puffy, and her cheeks streaked.

Emily approached slowly, unsure.

"You okay?"

Andrea gave a short, humourless laugh. "No."

"Can I... stay for a bit?"

Another pause. Then Andrea lifted the blanket. Emily slid in beside her. For a moment, they just lay there. Andrea's hand trembled slightly as it rested on Emily's arm.

"I'm sorry," she whispered.

Emily said nothing.

"I just... I can't keep doing this."

"Then don't."

Andrea sighed. Her breath smelled faintly of wine. "It's not that easy."

"You should just leave him then."

Her mum flinched, like the words had weight.

"If I leave him, he'll fall apart. He'll be all alone."

"But if you stay," Emily said softly, "*you'll* fall apart."

Andrea went still.

Emily looked at her, really looked. At the woman who had once been her safety. Now, a shadow of herself. Still beautiful, still fierce in her way, but tired. So tired.

"You're a good kid," Andrea murmured, brushing Emily's hair from her forehead. "Too good."

Emily didn't answer.

They stayed like that. Quiet. Breathing in time.

Eventually, Andrea's tears stopped. Her breathing slowed. Sleep took her in waves.

Emily stayed awake longer, staring at the ceiling, feeling the weight of a house that never quite settled. Walls too thin and emotions too loud.

But for once, her mother let her stay and she was happy to embrace a warmth she once knew.

Chapter Three

Musk

The next morning began like most did—Emily waking to the smell of toast and Louise cursing about something she couldn't find. Their shared bedroom was a mess of school shirts, mismatched socks, and open drawers. A half-empty can of hairspray sat precariously on the nightstand beside Emily's homework folder. She rolled onto her side and blinked the sleep from her eyes.

Louise was already half-dressed, struggling to tug her blazer over her arm while holding her phone under her chin, muttering into it. Her hair, a wild crown of black curls, was pulled into a messy bun, and her school trousers were creased from where she'd slept in them the night before.

"You going to stare all morning or actually get ready?" Louise grinned and tossed a crumpled white shirt in Emily's direction. It missed by a mile, landing on the floor in the corner.

Emily yawned. "I've been awake longer than you."

"Lies. I've heard your snoring. Sounds like a fat old man."

The usual teasing. Safe, familiar.

Downstairs, there was no sign of Mum. Her bedroom door was closed. That usually meant she'd been drinking until late and wouldn't reappear until mid-afternoon. Emily's dad had already left for work—he was always gone before sunrise—so the house felt still, but peaceful in a way.

By the time the girls were ready, Cynthia had already made her escape. As usual, she'd slipped out early, barely making a sound. Emily hadn't seen her properly in days, just a blur in the hallway or a shadow behind a door. She always took the early bus, always walked alone.

The morning air was crisp but warming, and the streets of North London buzzed with the usual start-of-day energy—cars lined the driveways, buses groaned to a halt at the corner, and kids in identical uniforms spilled out of front doors, shouting over one another. Emily tugged at her blazer sleeves and adjusted the strap of her backpack as she stepped onto the school bus.

School was the part of the day that felt normal. Predictable. A world where she wasn't the youngest sister, dodging moods or managing silence. In English class, she answered every question with ease.

Her teacher, Mr. Lacy, gave her one of those approving nods that made her chest feel warm. They were doing creative writing this term. Emily loved it. She could disappear into stories where she was someone else entirely.

At lunch, she sat with her friends, Chloe and Nia, in their usual spot by the benches near the art block. They chatted about the latest drama on facebook, flicked through each other's phones, shared crisps and half-finished sandwiches. Emily laughed easily, though her eyes occasionally flicked across the courtyard, watching people move in and out of view.

That's when she saw Louise.

Louise was surrounded by a cluster of older kids, loud and full of aggressive confidence. She spotted Emily and beelined toward her, smirking.

"Oi, rat!" she called, loud enough for nearby tables to hear.

Emily rolled her eyes. "Here we go."

"Who's this, your new skank club?" Louise said, grinning as she looked at Chloe and Nia. "Hope you told them you're a little thief. I know you took my fiver"

Emily flushed, glaring up at her. "Shut up, Louise."

"Aww, don't cry, sis. Just saying hi." Louise leaned down, pinched Emily's cheek, then strutted off with a cackle. Her friends hooted and followed.

"She's awful," Chloe muttered, clearly unsure whether to laugh or not.

"She's not that bad" Emily said quickly, even though her heart thudded in her chest. "She's just… like that."

Later, in History, Emily found herself sitting next to Connor Matthews. He had warm brown eyes, a quiet voice, and a habit of tapping his pen against his notebook when he was thinking. He didn't say much to her, just nodded as she sat down. They worked on a group project, writing notes in silence. Occasionally, their shoulders brushed when they readjusted in their seats. Each time, Emily's stomach did a small somersault.

Did he like her? She wasn't sure. He'd smiled at her once in assembly. But then, he smiled at most people. He was just nice. That didn't mean anything, did it?

By the end of the day, the sun had pushed through the clouds, casting a bright, sticky heat over the pavement. Emily sat by the window on the bus, blazer clinging to her back, her hair frizzing from the humidity. Louise climbed on halfway through the journey and slumped into the seat beside her with a groan.

"I hate summer. You fucking stink," Louise muttered.

"You're sweating more than me," Emily shot back.

They sat in silence for a bit. Not hostile, just tired.

When the bus dropped them off at the bottom of the hill, they walked side by side up Wakemans Hill. The pavement shimmered in the late afternoon light. Emily loosened her tie and fanned herself with her hand. The houses looked too perfect—like dollhouses arranged in rows, each with trimmed hedges and shiny cars in the drive. Their house sat near the top, tall and red-bricked, with its big windows and the tallest tree in the front garden that no one could trim anymore.

"I think Cynthia's already home," Emily said, spotting a shadow behind the curtain upstairs.

"She always is," Louise replied, kicking a pebble down the road. "Weird little hermit."

They reached the front door. Emily hesitated with her key.

"Reckon Mum's up yet?"

"No idea," Louise said. "But if she is, we'll know soon enough."

Emily opened the door.

The hallway smelled faintly of wine and last night's air freshener. It was quiet again.

She stepped inside, shrugged off her blazer, and glanced around.

Another normal day.

At least, on the surface.

Chapter Four

The Empty Room

Cynthia appeared like a ghost in the hallway.

Emily didn't even hear her come down the stairs. She just looked up and there she was, hovering at the edge of the kitchen, her eyes wide behind a long curtain of hair.

"Mum's not here," she said quietly.

Louise glanced up from the sofa, where she was scrolling through her phone, and frowned. "What do you mean?"

"I went into her room," Cynthia said, picking at a thread on the sleeve of her jumper. "We haven't got anything in. I wanted to check if she left money or something."

Emily stood still. The words took a moment to settle in her chest.

"You went in her room?" Louise said, standing. "Is she asleep or something?"

"She's not there," Cynthia repeated.

Louise didn't wait. She pushed past her older sister and marched up the stairs, Emily trailing behind. Cynthia followed last, quietly.

The door to their parents' room groaned open.

Emily wrinkled her nose. The smell hit her first—stale wine, musty curtains, something rotting faintly sweet in the air. Mum's room always had a sort of static buzz, like time didn't move properly in there. But today, it felt worse. Abandoned.

The floor was invisible beneath piles of clothes, flattened cardboard boxes, screwed-up receipts and paper bills. A single slipper was by the door, the other lost somewhere beneath the mess. An old fish tank sat on a low table at the foot of the bed, long dried up and slimy with a film of green algae. Something black and shrivelled sat at the bottom of it—Emily didn't want to know what.

"I forgot we had a fish tank," Louise muttered.

"I forgot we had a floor," Emily replied, her voice tight.

They picked their way through the room, searching—but there was no sign of their mum. The curtains were half open, light spilling across the crumpled duvet. No handbag. No phone. No coat on the hook. No movement.

"Maybe she went to the shop?" Emily offered, though she didn't believe it.

"She wasn't here when I got back, seems like a long time to be at the shop?" Cynthia asked. "And she left the back door unlocked. She never does that."

Louise spun on her heel and stomped downstairs. Emily heard the jangle of the house phone being pulled off the cradle.

She punched in the number quickly.

"Pick up," Louise muttered.

The dial tone rang and rang. "Bitch." No answer.

She tried again—still nothing.

The third time, it rang once, then cut off completely.

"She hung up," Louise said, stunned.

"She might be somewhere with no signal," Emily suggested. "Or... her phone's dead?"

Louise didn't respond. She sat on the stairs and stared at the phone in her hands. Then she opened a message and typed something quickly. Emily peeked at the screen:

Where are you? We've got no food in. Are you ok?

They waited.

Ten minutes. Then twenty. Cynthia wandered back upstairs. Louise lay stretched across the sofa, tapping her foot. Emily sat at the kitchen table, chewing the edge of her thumbnail, refreshing the messages. Her heart jumped every time the phone buzzed—but it was never Mum.

By the time the front door clicked open, it was nearly eight.

Their dad shuffled in, wearing the same stained navy overalls and steel-toe boots he always came home in. His skin glistened with sweat, and his forehead was shiny under the crystal chandelier in the hallway.

He set his keys down on the counter. "Evening, girls."

Emily rose to her feet. "Dad… Mum's not home."

He paused. His hands dropped and his arms hung heavy by his sides. "What do you mean?"

"She wasn't here when we got back," Cynthia said from the doorway. "She didn't leave a note. Her phone rang once, then cut off. She's not answering. We don't know where she is."

Their dad blinked at them like they were speaking another language.

Then, without saying anything, he pulled out his mobile and dialled.

It rang out.

He called again, pacing. Again. Again.

"Come on... come on, pick up," he muttered.

His voice cracked on the fourth attempt.

Louise hovered in the doorway. "We tried already, Dad."

"I know, I know," he snapped, voice rising. "But maybe—maybe she'll answer *me*."

The girls stood silently as he continued calling. With every attempt, his frustration built, his body shaking. Eventually, he threw the phone onto the hard floor and sat down, head in his hands.

"She can't do this to us," he whispered. "I can't live like this."

Emily froze and stared at her father, unsure how to help.

"She's gone off. Disappeared." He looked up at the ceiling, jaw trembling. "Always when I'm working. Always when I've got nothing left in the tank. She's killing me, girls! She's killing your Dad!"

"Do you know where she'd go?" Cynthia asked, her voice level.

"No," he said. "I don't… I don't know who she is anymore."

And then he broke.

He collapsed to the floor, curled up on the cold wooden boards in the living room, sobbing. Big, gulping sobs. He clutched his head like he was trying to hold himself together. He rocked back and forth, repeating the same word:

"Devil… devil… she's the devil."

None of them knew what to do.

Emily stood frozen in the doorway. Louise stepped forward, then stopped herself. Cynthia vanished into the hallway again, maybe unable to watch.

Eventually, the sobbing quieted.

The house fell into silence.

That night, they went to bed with empty stomachs and heavier hearts. No one said goodnight. The air felt too fragile for words.

Emily curled under the covers beside Louise, staring at the ceiling. Her stomach growled, but she didn't move. The darkness felt thicker than usual. She was so tired.

Chapter Five

Not Normal

The room was dim, the curtains still half-closed from the night before. The only sound was the slow creak of the floorboards as Louise paced back and forth like a lion in a cage.

Cynthia stood by the window, arms folded, her expression unreadable. She hadn't said anything since last night—not really. Her silence felt heavier than ever.

On the living room floor, their dad hadn't moved.

He lay where he'd fallen, curled on his side like a child, his arm across his face. His body shook now and then with shallow, broken sobs. Occasionally, he whispered something—sometimes it was "I can't," sometimes just "Please."

Emily stood in the hallway, peering around the doorframe, watching.

Louise exploded first.

"This is pathetic!" she shouted, kicking the base of the armchair. "You're the adult! Do something! What's wrong with you?!"

Their dad didn't answer.

"Get up!" Louise yelled again, louder this time. "We've got nothing in the cupboards, Mum's vanished, and you're lying there like a fucking baby!"

Still, nothing.

Louise stormed out, shoving past Emily on the stairs.

"Don't follow me," she snapped.

The door to their bedroom slammed hard enough to make the frame shudder.

Emily flinched.

She turned back to the scene before her. Her dad, the man she'd always known as 'a bit unusual', was unrecognisable. He looked so small. His big arms, the ones that used to toss her up in the air when she was little, now hugged his sides tightly like he was afraid of himself.

She crept into the room, slow and careful, and sat down on the arm of the sofa.

"Dad?" she whispered.

No answer.

Her eyes flicked over to the empty coat hook, the dent in the floor where his work boots usually sat, the photo of all five of them from their trip to Thorpe Park years ago, still framed neatly on the wall. They all looked happy in that photo. It felt like another life.

He suddenly spoke.

"I'm going to die," he muttered hoarsely. "I swear I'm going to die."

Emily felt a strange, dark twist in her chest.

She stared at him, really stared. For the first time, she didn't see him as *just Dad*. She saw the man. The frightened man. The messy, broken one. And behind her pity was something else—anger? No. Not quite. Something harder to name. Something heavier.

She thought about when she was eight, and Mum had gone to a job interview for a cleaning company. She had been gone forty minutes. He'd called her a dozen times in a row, pacing the living room with a look in his eye that made Emily feel like the air was cracking. He'd muttered things under his breath, things like "She does this on purpose," and "She wants me to lose it." Then she came home, and he'd screamed at her before crying into her shoulder.

She thought about how, once, he'd banged on Cynthia's locked door in the middle of the night because he heard crying and wanted to *know what she was crying about*. He'd apologised the next day, but Cynthia had looked smaller for weeks afterwards.

She remembered the tantrums. Rare—but real. He'd once thrown a whole dinner plate at the wall because there wasn't enough gravy. How he'd cried so loud in the bathroom once that Louise turned up the TV to drown it out.

It had always been painted as stress. Just stress.

But stress wasn't supposed to feel like this.

Emily swallowed hard. "Dad," she said again, firmer this time. "We need food."

He didn't respond.

She reached out and touched his shoulder.

"We need to eat," she said, more gently. "We don't have any money. Please."

For a moment, he didn't move. Then slowly, with the stiffness of someone waking from a nightmare, he rolled onto his back and looked up at her. His eyes were red and wet. His face pale. He looked like he'd aged ten years overnight.

He didn't speak. Just stared through her.

He pushed himself up, groaning. His hands trembled as he sat on the edge of the sofa.

"I'll go," he said, voice cracking. "I'll get something. Just… just stay here."

Emily nodded.

He stood, wobbling slightly, and grabbed his keys from the shelf near the door. He didn't put on a jacket. Just opened the door and walked out into the morning light like a ghost.

Emily sat still for a long time after the door closed.

She didn't move until she heard Cynthia's soft voice behind her.

"You okay?"

Emily shook her head, but didn't speak.

Cynthia sat down beside her, close but not touching.

They stayed like that, two girls in a silent house, wondering who would come back through the door— and what kind of person it would be when they did.

Chapter Six

Empty Spaces

By the third day without their dad, the silence in the house had changed. It wasn't heavy anymore—it was brittle, like glass stretched too thin. One loud sound and it would all shatter.

Emily pressed her school shirt between her knees, trying to flatten the deep creases. She tugged it over her vest and buttoned it wrong the first time. Her trousers were still damp from a half-hearted rinse in the sink. She couldn't remember if they had detergent. She couldn't remember if they ever had.

Downstairs, Louise banged around the kitchen.

"Do we even have bread?" Emily called.

"No. Just pasta," Louise shouted back, her voice already annoyed.

Cynthia appeared at the top of the stairs, silently brushing her hair. She didn't look at either of them as she walked down, grabbed a cereal bar from her stash in her school bag, and left through the front door before anyone could say a word.

She was always first out the door now.

The bus ride was quiet. Emily sat with her friend Yasmin, but didn't speak much. She could feel the heat rising from her unwashed uniform, feel the oily shine of her unbrushed hair sticking to her scalp. She kept pulling at the sleeves of her blazer. She didn't want anyone to smell her. Didn't want anyone to ask.

At lunch, her stomach growled audibly. Yasmin offered her half a cheese sandwich, but she refused with a polite smile.

"I'm not hungry," she lied.

Later that evening, Louise's boyfriend Callum brought them chips. A small gesture that felt euphoric in the moment. He didn't come in, just passed them through the front door in a greasy paper bag.

"I'll be out later," Louise said, already halfway out the door with her portion. "Don't wait up."

Emily sat on the back step, eating slowly. The house behind her smelled like bin juice and old milk. The pile of dishes in the kitchen sink had started to sprout mould—green and fluffy, like tiny gardens growing on old plates. No one dared touch them anymore. The smell was unbearable.

That night, Emily lay awake until 2 a.m. scrolling aimlessly on her cracked phone screen, the Wi-Fi still somehow working. She wasn't tired. She never was now.

Louise didn't come home until nearly four. Emily heard the key in the lock, the careful way her sister tried to tiptoe upstairs, then the creak of her bedframe.

The next morning, Emily found a carrier bag dumped on the kitchen table. Inside: a loaf of bread, two packets of instant noodles, and a dented tin of baked beans.

"You stole this," she muttered to herself.

She didn't ask. She didn't have to.

By Friday, Emily had stopped brushing her hair. Louise had started wearing crop tops to school under her blazer and chewing gum in lessons. Cynthia barely spoke to either of them and had stopped eating at home entirely. Her side of the fridge had gone untouched for days.

That night, Emily heard shouting through the walls—Louise on the phone, arguing with someone. Maybe Callum. Maybe one of her friends. She said something about being tired of "playing mum." Emily felt the sting of that one. So did Cynthia, apparently. Her door slammed a moment later.

The dishes kept piling up. The bins overflowed. The fridge was empty again. Mould climbed the walls around the sink. No one cleaned it. No one even acknowledged it.

On Saturday morning, Emily snapped at Cynthia for taking the last piece of bread.

"You don't even talk to us and now you're eating our food?"

Cynthia didn't answer. Just stared at her, dead-eyed, before walking away.

Later that afternoon, Emily picked a fight with Louise in the hallway about toothpaste. It ended with Louise slamming the bathroom door and shouting, "You're turning into Mum!"

Emily stood frozen for a long time after that.

She stared at herself in the mirror. Her reflection looked unfamiliar—her eyes puffy, her cheeks hollow, her long brown hair matted and wild. Her school badge was barely hanging onto her blazer by a single thread.

Outside, the sky was a flat grey. Inside, the house felt smaller than ever. Every room held an echo of the people they used to be. A shadow of a normal life.

Emily didn't cry. She just sat on the bottom step of the stairs and let the silence wrap around her like a coat. She didn't even notice when Cynthia slipped out the front door. Or when Louise slammed hers shut upstairs.

She was alone. And for the first time, she realised what that truly meant.

Chapter Seven

Cracks in the Mask

Time passed, but Emily wasn't sure how much. The days blended together—school, home, silence, hunger, mess, repeat.

Their dad came by now and then. Every couple of weeks he'd show up in the early evening, usually on a Thursday, a supermarket bag in hand like some strange ritual. Inside would be a random assortment: a few ready meals, crisps, sometimes a loaf of bread or milk if they were lucky. Once, there were two cans of cat food. The cats devoured them in seconds.

He never stayed long.

He looked tired. Greyer. Like something inside him had been switched off.

"Everything alright?" he'd ask vaguely, eyes darting around like he didn't really want the answer.

Louise never replied. Cynthia stayed in her room. Emily gave a small nod. Then he'd leave again, the front door clicking shut behind him like the lid on a coffin.

They knew he was living at his mum's. They'd overheard him on the phone once, whispering in the hallway about "space to clear his head" and "needing to rebuild slowly." He said the word "rebuild" like they were some broken project, a crumbling shed at the bottom of the garden he might get around to fixing one day.

Cynthia had pulled even further away. She moved in secret now, quiet, still, and hollow-eyed. Emily had no idea what she ate. Maybe she had her own stash. Maybe she ate at school. Maybe she didn't eat at all. She barely looked at them anymore. Just floated in and out like a memory.

Emily and Louise, on the other hand, were surviving in their own way.

They'd gotten good at it—stealing, mostly. It started as a mistake, a moment of desperation and opportunity. But it had become something else. A routine. A thrill. A necessity. Emily hated how normal it felt now to slip a multipack of crisps into her school bag or walk out of the corner shop with bread stuffed under her coat.

The cats had started leaving the house more, and Emily guessed they were begging from neighbours. They came and went, thinner but alive. Still, they left little piles of faeces on the living room carpet now. The litter tray hadn't been cleaned in weeks.

The whole house stank of rot and cat piss.

The kitchen was barely usable. Plates were stacked high in mould, and something was growing behind the bin that nobody wanted to touch. A single towel had been reused by all three girls for far too long. The hot water had gone out once, but had mysteriously come back. Emily figured Dad must've paid the bill remotely.

One Thursday, Emily sat on the stairs with her head between her knees, cramps doubling her over. She thought at first it was food poisoning or stress. Then she checked her underwear and panicked.

"Dad," she said when he arrived that evening, clutching her stomach. "Can you take me to the shop? I need… pads."

He blinked at her for a moment like he didn't understand. Then he nodded.

"Yeah… yeah, alright. Go get your shoes."

The trip was quiet. He didn't ask her anything. Just waited by the car while she ran into the shop. She didn't want to think about how humiliating it was to buy them herself, how her hands trembled at the till.

Back at school, things were getting worse.

Emily had started skipping lessons, just disappearing for hours. Sometimes, she went to the library, and sometimes, she sat in the toilets. Once, she went to a park nearby and stared at the ducks until the school day ended.

A kind teacher, Miss Ahmed, noticed. She'd pull Emily aside now and then, gently, without pressure.

"Did you have lunch today?"

Sometimes she'd hand her a sandwich from the staff room. Emily always took it, always said thank you, even when her throat was too tight to speak.

But other people weren't so kind.

Her friends had stopped talking to her. One by one. First Yasmin, then Chloe, then Hannah. Their parents had caught wind of something. Maybe the dirty uniform. The bags under her eyes. The smell. The stories they brought home.

"My mum says I'm not allowed to hang out with you anymore," Yasmin had said one day, awkwardly, avoiding eye contact. "She says you're... not a good influence."

Emily hadn't said anything back. Just smiled tightly and nodded, like it didn't matter.

It did.

That Friday, it all came to a head.

Cynthia had stayed behind at school. Emily and Louise didn't think much of it. But when they arrived the next Monday morning, the receptionist stopped them at the gate.

"Girls," she said. "You're needed in the office."

Their stomachs dropped.

Inside, Dad was already there. He looked rumpled, unsure, and out of place in the school corridor, his coat draped over one arm and a worried look plastered across his face.

Cynthia sat beside him, arms crossed. She wouldn't look at either of them.

The head of the school, a woman named Mrs. Lane, motioned them inside with a warm but firm voice.

"We need to talk," she said, shutting the door behind them.

Chapter Eight

The Performance

The pastel blue walls of the school office were meant to be calming, but Emily sat rigid in her chair, pulse thudding in her ears. Louise tapped her fingers against her thigh rhythmically, gaze fixed on the floor. Cynthia sat furthest from them all, still and silent, as though her presence alone had fulfilled her obligation.

Their father sat across from Mrs. Lane, legs crossed like he was there for a job interview, not a welfare meeting about the crumbling remains of his family.

He smiled politely. His voice was calm. Warm. Measured.

"It's been a tough time," he began, sighing as though the weight of it all still sat fresh on his shoulders.

"Their mother—well, she left. Disappeared. It's... it's been devastating, of course. For the girls, especially. But we're managing. I'm doing what I can. You know, keeping things afloat. Being a single dad is not easy, but I've adjusted my work schedule. Trying to make time."

He ran a hand through his thinning hair, pretending to collect himself.

"They've been through a lot. I think Cynthia's just feeling overwhelmed. She's always been a sensitive one."

Emily stared at him.

She blinked. Once. Twice.

Had she misheard? Imagined it?

She glanced at Louise, who was now openly scowling.

Even Cynthia looked up, her expression unreadable.

The truth was gone. Erased in seconds. A new story planted in its place, watered by charming tone and carefully chosen words.

Mrs. Lane gave a sympathetic nod. "I understand this must be hard for you, Mr. Spencer. Cynthia's told us a little about the situation at home. We're just trying to get a fuller picture."

He smiled again. Nodded. Faked emotion in his eyes like he was playing a role in a drama written just for him.

"Oh, absolutely. I get it. I really do. But I think some of this might have been exaggerated. Kids talk, right? And emotions are high. But there's food in the house, I make sure of that. I pop in every day. I just didn't want to disrupt their routines too much."

A pause.

A small silence, the kind that hung heavy in the room.

Emily's hands clenched in her lap. Her nails pressed into her palms.

He hadn't been home in a week.

He hadn't called in days.

The cupboards were nearly empty again. The dishes had developed moss. The cats had stopped coming back altogether.

But she didn't say a word.

Neither did Louise.

Because what could they say that would matter? Who would believe them now?

Even Cynthia didn't speak up. Whatever courage she'd found to confess in the first place had clearly vanished now in the suffocating presence of their father's act.

Mrs. Lane looked at each of them in turn. "Girls? Is there anything you want to say?"

Emily felt her mouth open slightly, then close again.

She stared at the man across from her—the man who once held her on his lap and sang made-up songs, who had sobbed on the floor calling her mother the devil, who abandoned them in a house with nothing but cat shit and silence—and she saw him now, reborn in that chair, polished and practiced.

And she knew something with absolute certainty.

He would never tell the truth.

They left the office with promises of "follow-ups" and "checks" and "support options being explored." But Emily knew better. People like her family slipped through the cracks all the time.

The school bell rang, and life resumed.

That evening, as they pushed open the front door to their sagging home, Emily took a deep breath and prepared herself for the stench.

There was no sign of Dad. No note. No money. No groceries.

Cynthia vanished into her room.

Louise slammed the bathroom door so hard the frame cracked.

Emily stood alone in the dim hallway, blazer still on, her school shoes tight and scuffed.

Something inside her shifted.

Something hardened.

She walked into the kitchen and turned the tap on. It groaned and spluttered, then let out a thin stream of water that splashed into the kettle's base. She filled a bowl with the boiled water, dumped some dry noodles in, and placed the bowl on the counter.

She wasn't hungry. Not really.

Not in the way she used to be.

Emily walked upstairs to the room she shared with Louise, stepping over a pile of laundry, past the missing bannister rail, and sat on the edge of the unmade bed.

Her phone buzzed. It was a message from a girl at school she used to sit with, but she didn't open it.

What was the point?

Her friends were gone. Her family was disappearing piece by piece. Her education was a sinking ship, and she had no one throwing her a rope.

But she did have one thing.

She was learning.

She was adapting.

Surviving.

And when the time came—when it all truly fell apart—she'd be ready.

She wasn't going back to who she was before. That girl was gone now.

She sat back against the pillow, the mattress springs poking into her bum, and stared at the cracks in the ceiling.

Outside, the cats cried into the night.

Chapter Nine

A Year Gone

A year passed like water through open fingers—never slow enough to grasp, never fast enough to forget.

Emily was different now. Her blazer didn't fit anymore. She'd stopped wearing it anyway.

She'd grown into her edges. Sharper. Louder when she wanted to be. Quieter when it counted. She'd learned how to disappear in a crowd, how to spot the shopkeeper who wasn't watching the bread aisle, how to stay just drunk enough to laugh and just sober enough to run.

Her new friends didn't ask questions. They never mentioned school unless they were bragging about skipping it. They came from the estates, from flats with black mould, broken lifts, and mums who didn't care where they were or when they'd be home. Some of them still turned up for exams like nothing was wrong. Some of them didn't even pretend.

There was Miah, who always carried a blade despite never using it. There was Kai, who could charm free chips from any chicken shop worker in town. And there was Daz—eighteen, dumb as bricks, but kind, in a messed-up older brother sort of way. He was the one who bought them cans of cider and lit their smokes when their fingers shook too much in the cold.

They spent evenings under bridges, in parks, tucked behind garages at the edge of the estate. They laughed like everything was fine. Like they weren't the leftovers of a world that never made room for them.

Back at the house, everything was held together with tape and silence.

Cynthia stayed locked in her room most days. Still at school somehow. Still surviving, but hollow.

Louise had become a stranger in a denim jacket. Some nights she didn't come back at all. Others, she stormed in with bags of cheap groceries or stolen make-up, reeking of perfume and adrenaline. Her boyfriend was older. Always older. And no good.

The house was still a mess. Worse, maybe. The bathroom, now, essentially out of bounds.

Once a month, an envelope arrived.

Handwritten in soft, curvy letters.

To My Girls. I'm Sorry. I Love You.

Inside, three crumpled tenners or on a birthday, twenty, like that could make up for the year she vanished without a word.

Emily never wrote back. Never called. Never texted.

None of them did.

Their mother was just a ghost now. Another liar. Another coward.

How could a woman like her walk away from her children and sleep at night? How could she save herself and leave them behind in the wreckage?

She was as good as dead.

Emily had had a couple of boyfriends. Loose, fast, nothing real. They kissed under stairwells or behind corner shops. No one ever meant anything. She didn't let them.

She'd learned not to.

Until one afternoon, when the sun was low and the sky was red with warning, her phone buzzed in her coat pocket.

LOUISE: *Come home. Now. Dad's gone mad.*

Her chest tightened.

For a second, her feet froze in place, caught between staying and running.

Then she moved.

She left behind Miah's laugh and the half-smoked cig she'd been saving. She jogged the cracked pavement, cutting through the alleyways she knew like the back of her hand. Her lungs burned, not from exertion, but from dread.

She didn't know what waited at the top of the hill.

Only that Louise had messaged. Only that Dad had "gone mad."

And when Louise said it like that, she meant it.

The house appeared at the road's crest like a monument to decay—paint flaking, garden wild, curtains closed even though the sun still hung in the sky.

Emily stopped at the front door.

Took a breath.

Put her key inside the lock.

Chapter Ten

The Fire

The smell of smoke hit Emily before she opened the door.

She burst into the hallway, the front door slamming shut behind her, rattling the frame. The sharp sting of wood burning mixed with something fouler—plastic, fabric, ink.

Louise stood frozen at the bottom of the stairs, hands clenched into fists. Her face was pale but her jaw was locked, eyes narrowed in fury.

Above them, their father's voice thundered through the house.

"**Liar!**" he bellowed. "**You little bitch!**"

A crash followed—glass, maybe a lamp, maybe something worse. Then came the sound of Cynthia's voice—shaking, small, trying to be calm. Trying not to cry.

Emily ran up the stairs two at a time.

Cynthia's door was wide open.

The room, normally dim and hidden away, was lit in angry yellows and reds. Her shelves were empty, the books ripped apart, pages scattered like feathers across the landing. Her mattress had been flipped. Clothes dumped into bin bags and torn open. Drawers smashed. One of her posters had been ripped from the wall—just a piece of cellotape still clinging to the paint.

Their father was dragging her schoolbag out of the room by one strap. Cynthia stood in the corner, arms wrapped around herself, face white.

"You've been talking to *her*?" he spat, turning toward her with a wildness in his eyes that Emily hadn't seen in years—but remembered.

"You've been texting your mother? After everything she did? After what she left *us* with?"

"I only said—" Cynthia tried, her voice barely audible. "I just wanted to know if she was okay—"

"OKAY?" he roared. "SHE ABANDONED YOU! And now you're what? Playing happy families behind my back? You fucking traitor!"

He yanked open her wardrobe and began pulling everything out in clumps—coats, socks, her old school jumper. He grabbed a pile of it and shoved past Emily and Louise on the landing.

They followed him.

Down the stairs.

Out the back door.

Into the garden.

The fire was already burning in the metal bin they used to store garden clippings and rubbish. But now it roared tall and orange, licking the air and spitting sparks across the overgrown grass.

He flung the clothes in, then stormed back into the house for more.

Louise finally moved, storming after him, yelling, *"Are you mad? What the hell are you doing?!"*

Emily hung back.

Cynthia was still in the hallway, looking so small, her arms now limp by her sides.

The front of her hoodie was damp with tears.

More of her things landed in the fire. A notebook. A pillowcase. A shoe with the sole barely hanging on.

"Don't you ever speak to her again!" he shrieked. "You hear me? She's poison! Poison! And you'd rather choose her over *me*? After everything I've done for you ungrateful—"

"Everything you've done for us?" Louise shouted, shoving his shoulder hard enough to make him stumble. "What *exactly* have you done for us?"

But he didn't listen.

He kept feeding the fire. Kept shouting.

Emily stood with her back against the garden wall, arms around her stomach, trying to stay invisible.

This wasn't just rage. This was unravelling.

Eventually, there was nothing left to throw. Only smoke and ash, and Cynthia standing by the hallway door like she was already halfway gone.

She left that night.

None of them saw it happen.

When Emily woke up the next morning, the house felt quieter. Her shoes were still at the door, but her coat was gone.

Louise found her note on the bathroom sink. It was just one line:

I'm going somewhere safe. Don't look for me.

That was the last day they saw Cynthia in that house.

Emily didn't cry.

She just stared at the empty bedroom with its torn carpet and cracked walls.

And she wondered—was there any point in trying to find out where she'd gone?

Or was she the lucky one.

Chapter Eleven

Cider

The night felt thick—warm air that clung to the skin like sweat. The streetlights buzzed above them, throwing orange halos onto the cracked pavement. Emily and her friends walked shoulder to shoulder, laughter trailing behind them in uneven bursts. The smell of cheap cider floated up from the tins clutched in their hands, and the estate behind them pulsed with low music and raised voices.

It was nearly midnight.

Emily had one trainer on the curb and the other in the road, sipping from her can, barely listening to whatever story Miah was telling.

Then Daz stopped walking.

"Oi," he said, pointing across the road. "Isn't that your mum?"

Emily's head snapped up.

There, outside the corner shop, beneath the flickering fluorescent sign, sat a woman hunched on a wooden bench. A man slouched next to her, and both held crumpled paper bags like they were sacred relics. The woman's legs were folded underneath her, hair hanging limply across her face.

But even through the mess, Emily knew.

Her stomach dropped like a stone.

It *was* her.

"Jesus," Daz muttered. "She's smashed."

Emily could feel every set of eyes shift to her.

This was a test.

The girl with the missing mum. The one who lived in the house no one wanted to walk past. The one who wore the same hoodie for days and never invited anyone over. The one everyone said was 'off the rails' now.

She walked into the road without thinking.

Crossed straight over.

Didn't check the traffic.

Didn't say a word.

Her friends followed, but kept their distance.

She stormed right up to the bench.

Her mum looked up, her eyes glazed and twitching, then softened into something almost like recognition. Her lips curled weakly into a smile. "Emi—baby…"

Emily didn't stop.

"*What the fuck are you doing here?*" she barked. "You're disgusting."

The man next to her mum turned, squinting at her. "What's your problem?"

Emily pointed straight at him. "Shut your fucking mouth, you crackhead freak."

Her mum blinked. "Don't talk to him like that, he's—"

"*No!*" Emily shouted. "Don't you dare defend him! You left us. You walked out on us for *this*. This is what you are now? Sat on a piss-stained bench getting drunk with some scabby old bloke while your kids starve?"

"I'm sorry..." her mum slurred, trying to stand up. "I didn't know how to fix it—I wanted to—"

Emily shoved her. Hard.

Her mum stumbled backwards and nearly fell over the bench, grabbing the back of it to steady herself.

"You don't get to say sorry. You don't get to *want* anything. You left. You abandoned us. You let him destroy everything."

The man rose halfway from the bench. "You touch her again, I swear to God—"

"*Touch her again?*" Emily sneered. "What are you going to do? Pass out on me?"

Her mum reached into her coat pocket, hand shaking.

"Wait—please, Em. Take this," she mumbled, pulling out a crumpled £20 note. She held it out with both hands like it might change something. "Just… take it."

Emily snatched the note.

Looked at it.

Then at her.

"I hope you rot in fucking hell," she said quietly. "You owe us more than this."

Then she turned and walked away, her spine straight, eyes burning.

Daz caught up to her. "You okay?"

"I'm fine."

But she wasn't.

She felt defeated.

Like the inside of her had been scooped out and filled with smoke and static. Her heart pounded and her throat burned.

She shoved the twenty into her pocket and didn't look back.

But something was new in her mind now.

Now she knew her mother wasn't a ghost. Just a figment of her memories.

She was a breathing, broken thing with money in her pocket and piss on her shoes.

And Emily?

She was owed.

That much, she was sure of. And she damn well was going to get it.

Chapter Twelve

Bloody Boundaries

Emily didn't ask about her mum anymore.

She just *demanded*.

Texts were short, blunt:

"Got any money?"
"Need cash."
"Send £10. Now."

And somehow, her mum always did.

Maybe it was guilt. Maybe she was scared of Emily now. Maybe she just didn't want to deal with the confrontation. Whatever the reason, it worked. Every so often, Emily would walk to their designated meeting spot: a street corner near the canal, under the flickering blue glow of a dodgy streetlamp. Her mum would be there, waiting, alone or with that same damp-looking man.

Emily would take the cash wordlessly, maybe call her a bitch, and leave without looking back.

And so, she had money.

Not much—but enough to not starve. Enough to be less reliant on the man in the house. Her father.

But things at home were disintegrating.

Dad had become paranoid—watching them constantly, like they were suspects in some crime he had invented. He accused them of contacting her—*that woman*—nearly every day now. His eyes were bloodshot more often than not, and the way he paced the living room, muttering to himself, made Emily feel sick.

He stopped giving her money completely. Refused to buy her anything—even basics like toothpaste or pads.

"You can bleed all over the floor for all I care," he spat one night, tossing a half-eaten sandwich on the kitchen table.

He said she wasn't allowed out anymore.

Emily stared at him. "Try and stop me."

His voice dropped, ice cold. "Watch me."

She started hiding the little cash she got from her mum under a loose floorboard in the bedroom she shared with Louise. They rarely spoke now. Louise had retreated into her own space—still around, still present, but quieter. Like she was watching a movie and wasn't sure if she should be rooting for anyone in it.

Then came the boiling point.

It was a Sunday. Emily tried to leave the house, bag on her shoulder, laces double-knotted. She got as far as the hallway when her father appeared like a bad spirit summoned by thought alone.

"Where the *fuck* do you think you're going?"

Emily didn't flinch.

"I'm leaving," she said. "I'm going out."

"Not anymore, you're not."

"I don't belong to you," she snapped. "I'm not a prisoner."

He stepped closer, red in the face. "You're a lying little snake. You've been seeing her, haven't you? TAKING MONEY FROM HER."

Emily's chest heaved. "At least she gives a shit if we eat."

That's when he *lost it*.

He lunged—hands grabbing for her arm.

Emily screamed, yanking herself free, stumbling out into the garden. She heard the back door slam open behind her and his footsteps heavy and fast on the patio.

She turned—and saw it.

He was holding a sharp garden tool—something long and rusted, the kind you'd use to cut thick roots.

"I swear to God, I'll kill you!" he bellowed.

Emily ran.

Down the garden, heart crashing against her ribs. She fought through the back gate, feet barely touching the ground. Down the hill behind the houses, past the bins, the green fencing, the patch of grass where old mattresses had been dumped.

Behind her, the sound of his feet. Shouting. Threats. Fury.

But he was slower.

He was *always* slower.

Emily kept going, lungs burning, the cold air slicing into her throat.

She didn't stop until she was seven streets down, knees aching, breath ragged.

Then silence.

He hadn't caught her.

She pulled her phone out and turned it off.

She stood there, alone, near an old lamppost with paint peeled down to metal. Her entire body shook—not from the cold, but from the fear.

She knew one thing:

She *couldn't* go back.

Not ever again.

So what now?

She had nowhere safe to sleep.

No clean clothes.

A few crumpled notes from her mum in her coat pocket.

But she had her life.

And that… for now… would have to be enough.

Chapter Thirteen

Goodnight

The sky was dimming when Emily found the bench.

It was in a corner of the park where the streetlights barely reached. Half-shielded by low trees, tucked behind an old, rusted playground. It smelled like damp leaves and old beer cans. She sat down slowly, her legs sore, her chest still aching from the run.

She had escaped.

But she didn't feel free.

Not really.

The air pressed on her like a weight. Every distant sound made her flinch—a car door slamming, footsteps crunching gravel, foxes screaming like babies in the dark. She pulled her hood up and wrapped her arms around herself, trying to disappear.

She had nowhere to go.

No plan.

Just the clothes she had on her and a phone she wasn't ready to switch back on.

She watched the shadows. A fox slinked across the playground, pausing to sniff an empty crisp packet. Another one darted out behind it—smaller, younger maybe. They moved in silence. Wild, dirty, free.

Kind of like her now.

Emily blinked back tears.

Then—voices.

Four of them.

Male.

She sat up, alert.

They were laughing too loud, swaggering, their footsteps uneven and sloppy. The smell of beer reached her before they did. They spotted her instantly.

"Oi, oi—what we got here then?" one of them grinned.

Emily didn't respond.

"Cold out, love. Want me to warm ya up?"

The others laughed.

She stood quickly, backing away. "Please just leave me alone."

"Oh come on, don't be like that," another said, stepping in her path. "You out here all alone? That's dangerous."

They closed in.

Emily tried to dart to the left. A hand grabbed her arm.

"Get off me!" she shouted, twisting away, panic rising.

One of them shoved her back onto the bench. Another leaned in, his face too close, breath sour.

"Bet you're not so mouthy when you're on your knees."

She screamed, thrashing, kicking.

"HELP!" she shouted, lungs tearing.

But no one came.

The hands were rough. They laughed at her fear. She clawed at one of their faces, and he slapped her hard across the cheek. Her ears rang.

She realised then—*she wouldn't win this.*

Her body stiffened. A slow numbness started to creep in, like her mind was closing its own curtains. She let herself go limp.

She was giving up.

And then—
A voice behind them. Low. Deadly.

"Let her go."

Everything froze.

Emily blinked. A silhouette stood at the path's edge, blade in hand, the glint of a knife catching in the dim light.

Daz.

He was older than the lads—taller too. Known around some of the estates for being quiet, odd, dangerous if crossed.

"I said let her *fucking* go."

The lads hesitated. The one holding her dropped her arm.

"We're just messin', mate."

Daz stepped forward. His face was unreadable. "Mess somewhere else."

They backed off slowly, muttering threats under their breath. "You wanna watch yourself, freak. Ain't over."

But they left.

Daz didn't move until they were long gone.

Emily sat frozen, fists clenched, eyes wide.

Then he turned to her, crouched down beside the bench.

"You alright?"

She couldn't speak. Could only nod, barely.

"Come on," he said. "You can't sleep out here tonight."

She followed him. Silent.

He took her to a run-down hostel near the high street. Paid cash at the desk. Didn't ask her any questions.

The room was small, but warm. One bed, clean sheets, a lamp with a broken shade.

They sat on the edge of the mattress.

He handed her a bottle of water.

"Didn't think I'd see you like that," he said eventually.

Emily looked at him. "Why did you help me?"

Daz shrugged. "Didn't like what I saw."

She wanted to ask more. She didn't.

They talked for a while about nothing—music they liked, weird things foxes do, the best chicken shops. She started to feel her body come back. Her cheek throbbed where she'd been slapped, but she was alive.

Eventually, she laid her head on his chest.

It was solid—broad and strong beneath his thick hoodie, the kind of chest that made her feel, for the first time in days, like maybe she wouldn't have to keep holding herself up. His arms rested gently at his sides, but she could feel the tension in them—corded muscle under skin that was pale from too much time indoors or under streetlights. There were freckles across his collarbone and neck, scattered like soft stains on paper, and a faint trace of an old scar by his jawline.

His hair was dark brown, cut short but messy, like he never bothered with a mirror. It curled slightly over his ears and caught the light in copper strands when he turned. She could feel his pulse—steady. Quiet.

He didn't move. Just let her rest there.

Didn't ask for anything.

Didn't say a word.

Just let her breathe. Let her be.

Her eyes closed.

And for the first time in a long time…

Emily slept.

Chapter Fourteen

The floor

In the morning, Daz walked her as far as the high street. He didn't ask for anything, didn't say goodbye with expectation. Just handed her a croissant from the corner shop, nodded, and said, *"Take care, yeah?"* Then he was gone, just like that.

The minute he disappeared from view, the weight of reality came crashing back. She was alone again. Alone in yesterday's clothes, yesterday's pain. No one knew where she was. No one cared, except—

She hated herself for even thinking it.

But there was nowhere else to go.

Her thumb hovered over her mum's contact for what felt like forever. Then she sent the message:
"I've got nowhere to go."

The reply came quicker than expected. A location. No words. Just a dropped pin on the map. Emily stared at it for a long time before setting off.

Her mum looked different when she saw her. Thinner. Greasier. Eyes dulled by exhaustion and too many nights she wouldn't talk about. She wasn't alone either. Cynthia was there—quiet, tired, but alive.

They had been renting a room in a run-down terraced house illegally split into four flats. Emily could smell the mildew before she stepped through the door. The hallway carpet was worn to its threads and sticky underfoot. A toddler's screams echoed behind one of the doors, and a man cursed behind another.

Inside their room were two single beds pushed against opposite walls. A cracked mirror. A pile of secondhand clothes. A kettle balanced on a stack of books. No food in sight. The air was heavy, muggy, and thick with cigarette smoke. Cynthia nodded when Emily walked in, but said nothing. Her mother didn't explain. She just motioned to the small bit of floor between the beds.

"This is all we've got for now," she said.

Emily curled up that night on a blanket too thin to count as bedding. Her mum handed her a t-shirt—stained, oversized, with a faded band logo across the front. It smelled faintly of her, mixed with smoke and old perfume. Emily didn't say thank you. She just changed and lay down, arms crossed tightly over her chest.

The floor creaked when someone moved in the hallway. She didn't sleep properly, just drifted in and out of that half-conscious haze, ears tuned for danger, back aching. She didn't feel safe—not really. But it was better than a bench. Better than what might've happened last night.

In the dark, she listened to the rise and fall of Cynthia's breathing, slow and measured like someone forcing herself into sleep. Her mum snored lightly, turned toward the wall. Emily stared at the ceiling, tracing the damp stains that bled across the plaster like ink in water. She wondered if they'd been there when the house was whole, or if they were new— leaks that no one bothered to fix anymore. Maybe no one cared. Maybe they never had.

Her stomach growled, sharp and hollow. She pressed her arms tighter against it, as if she could smother the sound. The croissant was long gone, a soft blur in her memory. Hunger was something she'd gotten used to—not the sharp pangs, but the slow fatigue that followed. It wasn't just the lack of food. It was everything. Having nowhere to go. The way her mother didn't ask how she'd been, didn't even look at her properly. The way Cynthia lit a cigarette without offering one.

The next morning, no one talked about the plan. Her mum mumbled something about the council. Cynthia sat on the bed rolling a cigarette. There was no breakfast, not even a cup of tea. Emily left before either of them could ask where she was going.

She wandered the streets in her mum's too-big shirt, shoulders swamped by fabric, the same trousers from days ago stiff with dirt. She met up with some of the older kids at the park—kids who didn't ask questions. They passed around a joint and some corner-shop snacks. She smoked until her thoughts dulled, until the edges of her life didn't feel quite so sharp.

She didn't talk about where she was staying. She didn't want to hear herself say it out loud.

For now, it was just a place to sleep.

Just a place to hide from the cold.

Later, when dusk crept over the rooftops and the wind began to sting, Emily found herself back on that same cracked doorstep. Her mum hadn't messaged. No one had. But her feet had brought her there anyway. When the door opened, no one looked surprised. Not even her.

Her mum was on the bed in her coat, shoes still on, eyes open but blank. Emily stepped over a puddle in the room that hadn't been there earlier—something dripping from upstairs, maybe. She didn't ask. Cynthia had the kettle plugged in, making a cup of tea with no milk, no sugar, just a stale teabag bobbing on the surface like it wanted to sink.

That night, Emily didn't change clothes. She just curled up on the floor again and pulled the damp-smelling blanket over her shoulders. This time, she faced the wall.

She thought about Daz. About his silence. His patience. The croissant in his hand, flaky and buttery, even if he hadn't said it, even if he didn't need to. He'd cared. It made her chest hurt, worse than hunger, worse than any bruise.

She didn't want to sleep. But she didn't want to stay awake either.

In the quiet, her mum coughed, a dry rasp that echoed off the walls like a warning.

Emily closed her eyes and breathed through her nose, slow and steady. She pretended she was somewhere else. Somewhere clean. Somewhere with silence and security.

Chapter Fifteen

Still Here

The shelter was colder than Emily expected. Not just in temperature, but in atmosphere. The walls were painted in chipped, government-issue magnolia. The lights flickered, too bright to sleep under. They had been given one small room—three single beds squeezed in like a hospital ward. No decorations, no curtains, no privacy. A thin sheet and a blanket on each. The communal bathroom was down the hall and always reeked of bleach and damp.

Cynthia barely spoke. Their mum muttered a thank-you to the key worker, then sat down on the edge of her bed and lit a cigarette at the open window, even though the sign said no smoking.

Emily stood awkwardly in the doorway, her rucksack—still filled with the same few things—dangling from her shoulder.

That first night she lay on the mattress fully dressed, arms folded over her chest like she was bracing herself for an impact. But it didn't come. Just silence, interrupted only by the distant sound of someone crying in the hallway and the occasional shouting through paper-thin walls.

She only stayed there two nights that week.

Over the next month, she barely returned. The place didn't feel like a home, not even close. She found other ways to get by—sofa surfing with friends, crashing on floor cushions or battered mattresses in living rooms, spare rooms, sometimes just a coat on a carpet. No questions asked.

Money was harder. She hadn't eaten in a day when her mate Mason told her about bin diving.

"Tesco round the back," he said. "They chuck out stuff that's still good. Just a bit bruised or past the sell-by."

She followed him through the alley, the stink of bins sharp in her nose. They pulled open the lid and rummaged through crates of overripe fruit, bread in clear bags with orange 'Reduced' stickers, cracked eggs, dented tins. Emily gagged at first, but hunger drowned out disgust.

That night she ate a slightly stale cheese sandwich in a stranger's lounge while someone's older brother played FIFA and passed her a bottle of cider.

She returned to the shelter a few days later to grab some clean clothes and shower. Her mum looked up from the bed, eyebrows raised. Cynthia crossed her arms.

"You smell like weed," Cynthia snapped.

"I don't smoke weed," Emily muttered.

Her mum narrowed her eyes. "You off your head or something?"

Emily shook her head. "I'm not on anything."

They didn't believe her. She could see it in their eyes. It didn't matter what she said—she looked like a statistic now. She *felt* like one. Rough clothes, dry lips, shadows under her eyes, and calloused fingers from carrying her life on her back.

She didn't stay that night.

The party was in someone's garage. A few crates of beer, the light from someone's car headlights, and music thumping through a Bluetooth speaker.

She wasn't meant to be there. She didn't even know whose party it was. But she followed some mates in and blended into the crowd, keeping her hood up, her eyes low.

That's when she saw **him**.

Daz.

Standing near the back wall, beer in hand, talking to a girl with dark eyeliner and ripped jeans.

He looked the same—freckles, pale skin, brown hair falling into his eyes. Strong arms, sharp jaw. Still that quiet power about him. Emily's heart thudded.

He noticed her.

Their eyes locked.

And just like that, the chaos of the party faded. For a moment, she wasn't hungry. Wasn't tired. Wasn't broken.

She walked over, unsure what to say.

But he spoke first.

"Didn't think I'd see you again."

Emily shrugged. "Didn't think I'd still be around."

He smiled—small, crooked. Then tilted his head slightly.

"Wanna get some air?"

She nodded.

Anything to get away from the noise. Anything to feel seen.

Even just for a night.

Chapter Sixteen

Ash

They stepped out into the night, leaving the muffled bass of the party behind. The air was sharp and cool, a welcome change from the sweat and noise of the garage. A streetlamp buzzed above them, casting shadows on the pavement as they walked a little way down the street.

Daz pulled a crumpled packet of cigarettes from his pocket and offered her one. Emily hesitated—she didn't usually smoke—but took it anyway. Her fingers brushed his as she did.

"Got a light?" she asked.

He struck a match and held it steady. She leaned in, lips on the cigarette, eyes on his. The flame flared, and for a second, the warmth of it seemed to reach her chest.

They stood in silence, blowing smoke into the night. She watched it swirl and vanish. There was something comforting about the way he didn't rush to fill the silence.

"Did you get sorted?" he finally asked.

"Kind of," she replied. "I've got a place to sleep now. Just not really a place to live."

He nodded, like he understood without her needing to explain further.

"I've been there," he said. "Still am, some days."

Emily looked at him. He wasn't dressed like he had much—ripped jeans, worn boots, hoodie pulled tight around his lean frame. But he carried himself like someone solid. Like someone who'd been through things and come out the other side, even if only barely.

They talked more—nothing deep at first. Favourite music. The worst corner shop sandwiches. That weird fox with one eye that always hung around the park bins.

But as the cigarette burned down, so did their defences.

Emily told him about Cynthia leaving, about her dad losing it, about the garden tool and the chase and the gate slamming behind her.

Daz listened. Didn't interrupt. Didn't ask why she hadn't called the police. Didn't ask why she went to her mum. He just let her speak, nodding gently like he already knew the kind of fear she was talking about.

"I've never had someone chase me with a weapon," he said eventually, flicking ash onto the curb. "But I've had someone make me wish they would. Just to get it over with."

Emily glanced at him, startled. Then looked away, letting out a long breath.

They finished their smokes and went back to the party, but only physically. Their heads were somewhere else. They sat together on the broken sofa in the corner. She tucked her legs under her, and his thigh pressed gently against hers.

At one point he put his arm across the back of the sofa, not quite around her, but close enough that she could feel the heat from it.

She didn't say anything. Didn't pull away.

Later, when her head started to feel heavy and the noise dulled into a steady hum, she leaned against his side. He didn't move—just let her rest there, like he had that night in the hostel.

His chest was strong beneath her cheek. Solid. He smelled faintly of smoke and sweat and something familiar she couldn't place. His hoodie was soft from too many washes. His pale skin stood out under the dim garage light, dotted with freckles along his neck. His arms, folded across his stomach, were firm and steady.

She closed her eyes. Just for a moment.

They sat there in silence for a while, the thud of the bass pulsing through them. Emily felt still for the first time in weeks—not safe exactly, but steadied. Grounded, somehow.

Daz tapped the side of his shoe against hers, a quiet nudge. "Wanna grab a drink?"

She glanced at him, a small smile tugging at the corner of her mouth. "Yeah. Let's go."

They stood, brushing down their clothes, and walked side by side back into the blur of music and bodies and noise.

They re-joined the party, and for the rest of the night, Emily didn't drift through it alone.

Chapter Seventeen

Different

Two years had passed, and Emily looked different now.

At sixteen, she moved like a woman. She was taller, her frame slim but strong from years of walking everywhere and living on little. Her features had sharpened into something striking—dark eyes that had seen far too much, a softness in her mouth that rarely smiled, and long tangled hair she now made an effort to straighten or braid on the days she worked. People looked at her differently now, even if they didn't know why.

She had a job now, weekends only—selling merch from a flimsy stand outside Wembley Stadium on event days. She didn't love it, but it was cash-in-hand and kept her out of the flat. The council had finally given them somewhere semi-decent: a tired, top-floor maisonette with flickering lights in the hallway and a front door that stuck. But it had three bedrooms. She had her own now, which felt like a kind of victory. A tiny square with a mattress on the floor, a second-hand chest of drawers, and a window that rattled when it was windy. But it was hers.

She barely saw her mum or Cynthia—when she was home, she kept to herself. She avoided staying there most nights anyway, crashing at mates' places or riding buses to nowhere with a pair of headphones and enough battery to make it through the night.

She hadn't spoken to her dad since that night. She hadn't spoken to Louise either. She tried. Every few months, she'd send a message—"Hope you're ok" or "Just thinking of you x"—but they went unanswered. She was blocked on Facebook now. She didn't blame her sister. Not really. But it still stung.

Eve made the job bearable. She was seventeen, blonde, loud, and completely magnetic. Everything Emily wasn't. She talked nonstop and told Emily all about her sixth form drama club, her annoying brothers, and the lad she fancied who worked in Foot Locker. She had a stable home. Parents who actually came to pick her up from shifts sometimes. It was a life Emily watched from the outside, amused and envious in equal parts.

They were working a concert that day. One of those big stadium pop shows where fans wore glitter on their cheeks and sang in the queue. The sun was hot, and the stand was already half-empty by mid-afternoon.

Eve nudged Emily with her elbow, grinning. "He's here," she said under her breath.

Emily raised an eyebrow. "Who?"

Eve waved over someone just approaching. "Thomas! I told you about him. He's starting with us today."

He was tall, with clear blue eyes and neatly styled brown hair that swept just slightly over his forehead. His uniform looked too clean, and he moved with that quiet confidence of someone who hadn't had to worry much about life yet. There was something crisp about him—like his clothes had never been slept in, his phone never cracked.

"Hi," he said, smiling as he stepped behind the stall. "Thomas."

"Emily," she replied. She wasn't used to boys like him. Polite. Handsome. Well-spoken. She felt rough around the edges next to him. But he didn't seem to notice. Or if he did, he didn't care.

They spent the rest of the shift selling cheap hats and overpriced lanyards, teasing customers, and laughing at the ridiculous things people would buy. Thomas kept making quick, clever jokes that made Eve cackle and even got Emily to smile—properly—for the first time in days.

It was hard to pinpoint the moment things shifted for Emily. It wasn't sudden. It wasn't dramatic. But looking back, she could see the slow turning of the tide, the way certain days folded into each other and brought her further from what had been and closer to something new.

She still woke up some mornings with the feeling like there was a bag over her head. That the air wasn't quite enough. Despite its modest improvements, the flat still carried that stale smell of old smoke and damp carpets. Sometimes, the creak of a floorboard outside her door at 2 am was enough to keep her awake the rest of the night. She kept a small pocketknife under her pillow, not because she thought she'd need it, but because it helped her sleep knowing it was there.

She started carrying a little notebook with her. At first, it was to track her shifts and wages. Then she began jotting down thoughts, snippets of things she overheard on the bus, or something a customer said that made her laugh. It felt strange at first, like she was stealing bits of the world and tucking them away. But it became a comfort. A way of marking time.

School had long since faded into the background. She'd stopped going regularly just before her fifteenth birthday. Nobody really chased her up. She got the odd letter, a few calls. But eventually, they stopped. She wasn't missed, not really. Her mum had shrugged when she found out. Cynthia hadn't said a word.

And yet, there were days Emily missed it. Not the lessons, not the teachers, but the routine. The idea that she could just be a teenager for a while. Normal. She'd pass schools sometimes and slow her steps, watching girls in blazers and ponytails squealing over TikToks, or hunched together around their phones. It felt like a world she'd never fully belonged to but still missed like an old friend.

Emily hadn't seen Daz in weeks. Their reunion at that party had been a flash of something—nostalgic, raw, complicated. They texted a few times. He even met her for chips once near the canal. But it felt like two different versions of themselves trying to fit back together, and the edges didn't quite match.

It hurt a little. But not like it used to.

And then there was Thomas.

He made bad jokes and didn't try to impress her. He listened more than he talked, and when he looked at her, it wasn't with pity or fascination. Just... interest.

After their first coffee-and-noodles hangout, he messaged her the next day.

Thomas: You left your straw wrapper in my noodle carton. That was rude.

Emily: You left half your food untouched. That was ruder.

Thomas: Next time, I'll eat yours too, then.

She smiled at that. Smiled really, and wide, and unexpectedly.

He wasn't trying to save her. And she wasn't trying to become anyone else for him. But when they were together, she felt a little less jagged.

The next time they met, it rained again. Thomas brought an umbrella big enough for two. She teased him for being posh. He told her she swore like a pirate and walked like she was always expecting a fight.

"I don't," she said.

He gave her a sideways look. "You do. It's badass."

She didn't know how to respond, so she shoved his arm lightly and rolled her eyes.

They went to the cinema, then sat outside watching the clouds roll in. He let her talk about music, and she let him talk about his dog. It wasn't anything extraordinary. But it was nice.

As she lay on her mattress that night, her earbuds in, she let herself imagine a life that didn't feel so temporary. A future with her name on the lease. A room with curtains she chose herself. A bookshelf with stories she had written.

She scribbled a line into her notebook before sleep pulled her under:

Sometimes, surviving becomes living, and you don't even notice the moment it happens.

Chapter Eighteen

Iced Coffee

They met the following Saturday after work. Emily still wore her merch hoodie and beat-up trainers, but she'd changed into jeans that weren't torn at the knees and brushed mascara over her lashes in the toilets at Wembley.

Thomas was already waiting for her outside the station, holding two iced coffees.

"Didn't know what you liked," he said, handing her one. "So I guessed. Hope it's not gross."

She sipped it. It wasn't bad. "Could've been worse," she said, giving him a side glance.

He grinned. "I'll take that as high praise."

They walked. Nowhere specific. Just around. He led them through the backstreets and then out to a row of shops where he bought her noodles from a little Thai place. Paid without asking, without hesitating. She hated how nice that felt.

They sat on a low brick wall eating noodles out of paper cartons, legs dangling.

"So," he said between bites. "What's your story?"

Emily shrugged. "I don't have one."

"Come on," he said, smiling. "Everyone's got something."

"I just… don't talk about it. That's all."

He didn't push. Just nodded. "Okay."

Instead, he told her bits about himself. He lived in a nice part of town. His dad worked in finance. His mum ran a wellness business from their home. More about his dog named Rupert and a cleaner who came twice a week. Emily couldn't decide if she hated him for that or just found it funny.

But Thomas wasn't smug. He didn't throw it in her face. He talked like someone who didn't fully realise how easy his life was—and maybe that made it easier to stomach.

They spent the rest of the evening walking and talking, window shopping, watching the sun go down between buildings. At one point, he gently touched her arm to steer her out of the way of a cyclist, and the warmth of his hand lingered long after.

When it got dark, he walked her to the bus stop.

"You gonna be alright getting home?" he asked.

She nodded. "Done it before."

He hesitated, then smiled again. "Cool. Well... this was fun."

"Yeah," she said. "It was."

And before she could overthink it, she leaned forward and kissed him. Just a light press of her lips on his cheek. Quick. Uncertain.

But it made him blush.

"See you next week?" he asked.

"Yeah," she said, stepping onto the bus. "See you."

As the bus pulled away, she watched him standing there through the smeared window, hands in his pockets, shoulders hunched slightly from the breeze.

She didn't know what this was or what it meant, but it felt nice.

It was a Wednesday when Thomas texted her:

"My parents are away. Want to come over?"

The message buzzed her cheap phone as she sat in the back of the staff breakroom, picking at a flapjack she'd stolen off the shared snack table. Her first instinct was to say no. Something about it made her chest tighten. But then she thought about his eyes, that awkward little smile, the way he held doors open like someone raised by women who expected manners.

She said yes.

His house was massive. Detached. Gated. The kind of place she used to walk past as a kid and wonder who lived inside. The kind of place with hallway rugs that cost more than a month's rent and kitchen counters you weren't sure you were allowed to touch.

Thomas opened the door still damp from a shower, wearing joggers and a clean white T-shirt that clung to his chest.

"Hey," he said. "You made it."

She stood awkwardly in the entrance, her body suddenly aware of every thread in her clothes, how her trainers squeaked on the tiles.

"Yeah," she said. "Took the long route."

He led her upstairs, past perfectly staged rooms, to a big double bedroom with floor-length windows and a duvet that looked like clouds. She tried not to stare too much. She didn't want to look like someone who'd never been anywhere like this before, even though she hadn't.

They sat on his bed, watching videos on his phone. Laughing. Eating crisps from a bowl he'd brought up. Her body gradually eased beside his. Close. But not too close.

Then, without a word, he leaned in and kissed her. This time, it was different—deeper, slower. She kissed him back, her hands shaking slightly as they moved to his shoulders, the feel of his skin beneath the cotton. His scent was clean, like soap and something faintly woodsy.

He paused. Looked at her.

"Is this okay?"

She nodded.

They undressed in soft, awkward silence. She turned her back when she pulled her top off. He didn't rush. Didn't push.

Thomas was warm. Careful. His hands traced her like he was trying to hold onto the memory of how she felt.

She didn't cry. But she did close her eyes tightly for a moment, the ceiling above her spinning slightly as he slowly pushed himself inside her. She felt a burning between her legs as he applied more pressure.

He looked deep into her eyes for a moment. They weren't the pools of blue she remembered. They were darker now. Glazed over. After a moment he continued. She felt a warm liquid between her thighs as the burning intensified.

At first, it had felt surreal to be wanted—properly wanted—by someone like Thomas. He was clean and polite and polished, everything her world wasn't. She thought maybe this was what safety looked like, what being cared for could feel like. But the illusion cracked quickly.

His kisses had changed. They weren't soft anymore. They were hard and impatient.

She tried to say his name, gently at first. Her voice faltered, tangled up in her throat. He wasn't listening. Her body tensed beneath his hands and she pulled back, just a little.

"Thomas… wait…"

He didn't stop.

Something in her stomach dropped, a coldness washing through her. Her limbs froze as if her voice was suddenly made of glass and any sound might shatter her completely. Her heart pounded in her chest—not with excitement like she'd imagined, but with rising panic.

She wanted to say *no*. She *meant* to say no. But all that came out was silence.

She tried again—firmer this time—but the words still felt too small, too quiet. Was this what it felt like to realise you weren't seen as a person anymore? Just a moment, a thing, an idea that someone else had made up about you?

His weight pressed heavier. Her thoughts scattered. She stared at the ceiling, its white paint slightly flaking in the corners. Her vision blurred. She bent her knees and tried to push herself out from under him with her feet. They dragged the bedsheet across the mattress but did nothing to aid her pursuit.

How had it come to this?

He was supposed to be different.

She thought of her mother, of her father, of all the moments she hadn't been protected, hadn't been heard. And now here she was again—trapped inside someone else's idea of what she was supposed to give.

Hot tears slipped from her eyes, slow and silent.

After, he lay beside her. Still, quiet. They didn't talk much. He stroked her arm with two fingers, drawing invisible lines.

Emily stared at the ceiling, naked and bare, her body feeling strange. Not broken. Not whole.

Thomas fell asleep beside her. She lay awake, watching the moonlight cast shadows on the wall.

She wondered if this was what it was supposed to feel like. If maybe it was close enough.

Chapter Nineteen

Blue Ticks

She stared at the screen for too long before pressing send.

Hey x

The kiss on the end felt stupid as soon as it left her thumb. But she didn't delete it.

No reply.

The message sat there all day, two small grey ticks beside it. The longer it stayed unread, the more it seemed to grow—like it was mocking her.

By the next morning, the ticks had turned blue.

Still nothing.

She sent another.

Are you okay?

Then, later that night, *Did I do something?*

Still silence.

She checked his Instagram. New post. He was out with friends, arm slung around someone she didn't recognise. Laughing. Teeth white and straight and clean like always.

Her stomach curled in on itself, twisting and turning, tightening with a heat that wasn't quite anger, wasn't quite shame.

She sat on her bed and stared at her hands. She picked at her cuticles until one bled.

That night at his house kept replaying in her mind, like a film she didn't want to watch but couldn't look away from. Over and over.

She'd said *okay*.

She remembered that clearly. Her voice had been small. Shaky. But she'd said it.

Hadn't she?

She couldn't remember when or why exactly she'd changed her mind. She just remembered lying there, cold and far away from herself, and realising she wanted it to stop. But it hadn't.

Could he tell?

Did he even care?

Was it *rape* if she'd said *okay* at first?

Was it her fault for not fighting harder?

That afternoon at work, she cornered Eve behind the merch stand. It was noisy, chaotic, but in that moment it felt like the whole world quieted around her.

"Have you spoken to Thomas?"

Eve blinked, caught off guard. "Yeah," she said, but it was cautious. Too casual.

Emily tried to smile. It didn't reach her eyes. "Is he okay?"

Eve shrugged, looking uncomfortable. "He's fine… he just…" She let the sentence trail off into nothing.

Emily didn't say anything else. She nodded once, walked back to her side of the stand and didn't speak again for the rest of the shift.

It rained that evening. Cold and light and miserable. She turned down the lift home Eve offered and walked instead, hands deep in her pockets, hair sticking to her cheeks.

When she got in, the flat was dark. Her mum and Cynthia were out somewhere, probably staying at someone's for the night. Emily didn't turn on the light. She walked to her room, shut the door, and collapsed onto the bed fully dressed.

She still had the hoodie on he'd said he liked—navy blue, too big for her small frame. It smelled like washing powder now instead of him.

That was a good thing. She thought.

She didn't cry until her head hit the pillow.

The tears came slow at first, just a few. But then her chest tightened. She curled inwards, clutching the edge of the hoodie to her chest like it could somehow fix her.

"You fucking idiot," she whispered to herself in the dark.

Over and over again.

"Fucking idiot."

Chapter twenty

Bruises

The days blurred into one.

She stopped checking her phone for replies that never came. Deleted the messages. Then the photos. Then the number.

She never ran into Thomas again.

Not once.
Not at work. Not in the park. Not anywhere.

It was like he'd vanished—but she knew he hadn't. She still saw the evidence of him online, in glimpses through mutual follows and tagged photos she tried not to look at. But she didn't see *him*, and that felt both like a relief and a betrayal.

She didn't speak to Eve again either. There was no big argument, no final conversation. Just distance. A silence that grew between them like a closed door.

Eventually, she applied for a new job. Nothing fancy. Weekend shifts at Asda stocking shelves. Early mornings, plastic crates, the hum of fluorescent lights overhead. Nobody cared about her past there. Nobody asked questions. They told her where the uniform was, handed her a name badge, and pointed to aisle seven.

She kept her head down and did what she was told. She liked it that way.

She learned to move quietly. Keep her eyes on the task. Smile politely, but never too much.

Sometimes she caught her reflection in the freezer doors and barely recognised herself. There were no bruises. No scars. Nothing visible. But something about her posture was different now—like she was always bracing for something that never came.

Nights were hardest.

The flat was quiet more often than not. Cynthia barely spoke. Her mum only existed in fragments—half-finished cups of tea, cold food left on the counter, the sound of her voice behind a closed bathroom door.

Emily didn't tell them what had happened.

She wasn't even sure how she'd begin.

Instead, she got used to the ache. The way it lived just beneath her ribs. Some mornings it was dull. Manageable. Other days it bloomed like a bruise when she least expected it.

She told herself it would fade.

That one day it would just be something she *used* to think about.

But for now, she got up, got dressed, went to work. She scanned barcodes, stacked tins, said "thanks" when customers said "cheers, love."

She didn't feel strong. She didn't feel brave.

But she kept going.

Chapter Twenty-One

Still Standing

By nineteen, Emily had grown into the kind of woman you see in magazines.

Not vain or attention-seeking. Just… striking.

She was petite and slim, but not frail, curved in the right places, with a tiny waist and long legs that moved with quiet confidence. Her hair had grown thick and glossy, falling in waves down to the small of her back. She kept it clean and simple, rarely tied back, often left to fall like a curtain around her shoulders. Her skin glowed in that effortless way youth gives you when you're surviving on toast, corner-shop meal deals, and vending machine coffee.

She knew she was pretty now. Not in a vain way. Just in that way where people stared a second too long when she passed. It used to make her uncomfortable. Sometimes it still did. But mostly, she ignored it.

At work, she wore black leggings and a fitted crop top, mostly hidden under her green Asda fleece, zipped halfway up. It wasn't glamorous, but she always looked put together—fresh makeup, neat hair, soft perfume. She liked feeling clean, controlled, and presentable. She felt safer that way.

The flat she shared was small and a bit tired, but it was quiet and cheap. Her room had a single bed, a wardrobe missing one handle, and a small mirror screwed to the back of the door. The heating worked half the time. There was mould around the windows. But it was hers.

Sara, her flatmate, had offered her the room after a night out. They weren't best friends at the time, but Sara had a way of making people feel comfortable without even trying. She was twenty-two, chubby, and unapologetic about it. Her curls were always piled on top of her head, and she was always halfway through some funny story or sarcastic remark. She worked at a bank and hated it. But she liked the salary and stability and coming home to a quiet place where she didn't have to be "on."

Sara's parents had paid the flat off for her when she was eighteen, so she only asked Emily to contribute to the bills and a bit of rent. "We're just surviving, innit?" she'd said when they'd moved in. "Let's make it a soft landing for each other."

They did.

Sara's boyfriend, Marcel, was around a lot. He was tall, soft-voiced, and dressed like someone in a music video—fitted jeans, designer trainers, aftershave that lingered in the hallway for hours. Emily didn't know what he did for work, and she didn't ask. But he drove a silver BMW, always had cash, and never made her feel weird for staying quiet.

Sometimes they'd all eat together—Chinese from the place downstairs or oven chips and chicken nuggets thrown onto plates with a shrug. They'd talk about shows, bad customers, the worst songs to hear in the shop. It was easy. Light. Like she could breathe without constantly checking the exits.

She didn't talk about her past. Not with them. Not with anyone, really.

She hadn't dated since Thomas.

Men flirted sometimes—at work, at the pub, when she was walking home. She smiled, nodded, said as little as possible. She watched her drinks closely. She stayed close to her friends. She always sent her location before she left. No more blind trust. No more slipping into someone else's hands.

Once, over a year ago, she'd seen Louise. They were both on opposite sides of a bus stop in Camden. Just a glimpse through the glass. Louise looked older, sharper. Their eyes met for a second, and then the moment passed. No one waved. No one moved.

She still saw her mother and Cynthia a few times a year. Usually for a tense tea in someone else's kitchen. Conversations stayed surface-level—work, the weather, who was renting where. Emily didn't share much. There was too much under the surface, and none of them had the tools to dig it up.

So she worked. She kept her space tidy. She watched Netflix with Sara. She took long baths and read trashy novels from the charity shop. She liked knowing what came next.

Her life wasn't exciting. But it was steady.

And steady was all she needed.

Chapter Twenty-Two

Ghosts in the Supermarket

It started like any other shift. A Thursday. Grey sky, drizzle streaking down the windows by the tills. Emily scanned groceries on autopilot—milk, crisps, instant noodles, bottled water. The usual.

Her fingers moved quickly, her mind elsewhere. She was thinking about the laundry she'd forgotten in the machine, the fact she hadn't messaged Sara back about dinner, how her feet already ached and it was barely noon.

"Just these," a voice said—low, familiar.

She looked up, and the world slowed for a second.

Daz.

He was older now. Not just in the way time moves across a face, but in the way someone carries themselves. His jaw was more defined, his shoulders broader. He still had that scruffy charm—dark hair a bit too long, hoodie under a jacket, hands in his pockets—but now there was something grounded in him. A steadiness.

"Daz?" she said before she could stop herself.

He blinked, then grinned. "Emily?"

There was a pause. Then they both laughed, awkward and warm.

"No way," he said, stepping forward slightly. "You work here?"

She nodded, smiling despite herself. "Full time. You?"

"Mechanic," he said. "Well—apprentice, but pretty much full-time now. Got lucky with a decent garage over in Brent. Pays alright. Dirty work though."

She scanned his two items—A redbull and a sandwich. "Figures," she said, and he laughed again.

"Still sharp," he said, his eyes crinkling. "You look... good, Em."

There was a gentleness in the way he said it. No edge. No hunger. Just genuine surprise, like he hadn't expected to bump into her but was glad he had.

"You too," she said, then handed him his bag.

They stood there for a second longer than necessary.

"You on a break soon?" he asked, almost shy. "You fancy a coffee?"

Emily hesitated. The noise of the shop pressed in around her—beeps, chatter, kids crying somewhere in the frozen aisle. She hadn't seen him in what—five years? Six?

And yet... there was something comforting about him. Familiar, but not in a way that pulled her backwards.

Like a version of the past she didn't have to be afraid of.

"I've got one in ten minutes," she said. "Costa?"

"I'll wait," he said.

—

They sat in the corner by the window, paper cups steaming between them. Rain tapped the glass. People bustled past, coats pulled tight, hoods up.

Daz talked easily. About the garage, the long hours, the old banger he was trying to restore. He still lived with his nan but was saving to move out. He didn't pretend his life was perfect, but there was pride in his voice. He'd done something with it. Stepped up.

"You disappeared," he said after a moment. Not accusing. Just curious.

"So did you," she replied.

"Fair enough," he said, sipping his coffee.

There was a beat of silence. Then he asked, gently, "You alright though? You happy?"

She wasn't sure how to answer that. So she shrugged. "Getting there."

He nodded. Like he understood exactly what that meant.

They talked for another fifteen minutes. Easy. Light. But underneath, something hummed—recognition, possibility.

When her break ended, she stood slowly.

"Thanks for the coffee," she said.

"Can I get your number?" he asked. "No pressure. Just… would be good to talk again."

She hesitated, then took his outstretched phone.

She typed it in and smiled.

"I'll text you."

And for once, she believed he actually would.

As she went back to her till, she felt safe, something she hadn't felt in a long time.

Chapter Twenty-Three

Shopping baskets

The shift dragged on after lunch. Emily tried to keep her focus—polite smiles, barcode beeps, bagging requests—but her mind drifted constantly. Back to Daz. To the softness in his voice. The steadiness in the way he looked at her. Like he saw all the years that had passed but wasn't scared of them.

It unsettled her, not in a bad way. More like a feeling she hadn't expected to return—warm, cautious, quietly hopeful.

When six o'clock finally came, she signed off her till and grabbed a wire basket. She wandered the aisles half in a daze, picking up little things without much thought: pasta, a jar of sauce, a punnet of tomatoes slightly bruised but still good. Comfort food. Something to cook slowly.

She was supposed to go out with Sara that night—some friend's birthday drinks at the pub. But she'd messaged her on her break to say she wasn't feeling it.

"Head's a bit scrambled," she'd said. And Sara, as always, had been kind about it.

"Don't worry babe. Chill tonight. I'll bring you back chips."

Now, basket in hand, she moved through the store at her own pace. Her feet still ached, but she didn't mind. She stopped to look at flowers by the entrance, their sharp sweet scent infiltrating her nostrils—cheap bunches of carnations and tulips under the dim lights. She didn't buy any, but she liked the idea of them.

Her phone buzzed once in her pocket, and her heart jumped.

Not a message. Just an email. Still—hope stirred, uninvited.

She thought about Daz again. The way he'd smiled. The fact he'd waited for her break like it meant something. The way he'd asked if she was happy—not as a throwaway, but like he genuinely cared.

And she realised something she hadn't said out loud in years.

She missed him.

Not just the old him. The one from when they were kids, all laughter and chaos and bad music on tinny speakers. She missed who he was now. The man he'd become. The version of him that had grown up just like she had, in different directions but maybe not so far apart after all.

She felt proud of him. That was it. Properly proud.

He could have fallen into the same traps as everyone else. Could have vanished into the kind of life that swallowed people whole. But he hadn't.

And that meant something.

She paid for her bits and walked out into the cool evening, fleece zipped up, breath misting slightly. It wasn't raining anymore, but the clouds were threatening it still.

The walk home wasn't far. Fifteen minutes, max. A little flat above a row of rundown shops. Two rooms, one tiny kitchen, a bathroom that always smelled faintly of bleach and cheap perfume.

Hers and Sara's.

She let herself in quietly, the hum of the fridge welcoming her back. The lights were off—Sara must've gone already. A pair of sparkly heels sat abandoned by the doormat, waiting for someone to stumble back into them.

Emily put the kettle on, unpacked her dinner slowly, deliberately. She played some soft music on her phone and swayed a little while slicing the tomatoes. Her mind still with Daz. His voice. His laugh.

Would he text?

She didn't know. But she kind of hoped he would.

Chapter Twenty-Four

The end of the beginning

The buzzing of her phone woke her before her alarm. Emily blinked through the early light seeping through the blinds and reached over, still half-asleep. The screen lit up with a single message. She squinted to read it:

Daz: *"Hey, I know it's early. Just wanted to say it was really good seeing you yesterday. Would love to do it again if you're up for it? x"

A smile bloomed across her face before she could even think. The kind of smile that lived somewhere between her chest and her throat, tight and warm. She typed back, quickly then hesitated, deleted, retyped:

Emily: *"Same here x I'd love that. What about tonight?"

His reply came within seconds: *"Tonight sounds perfect. I'll pick you up after work? x"

She was already on her feet.

The day passed in a blur. The supermarket was quiet for a Saturday morning, and she found herself watching the clock more than watching customers. Each beep of the scanner, each greeting, each "Have a nice day," brought her closer to 6 p.m.

"You're in a good mood," said Mandy, the middle-aged woman on the till next to hers.

Emily shrugged, trying to play it cool. "Just a good day, I guess."

Mandy grinned knowingly. "You seeing someone?"

Emily flushed. "Just an old friend."

Back at the flat, Emily burst through the door and called out, but Sara was out, just like she said she would be. The place was quiet. She showered, washed the workday off, and wrapped herself in the soft pink towel Sara had bought her for Christmas. Standing in front of the mirror, she looked at herself.

Her body had changed. Curves she once hated had become something she felt proud of. She looked older now, womanly. Still had the same wide eyes, the same slightly crooked smile. But the girl from the bench in the park felt a world away.

She curled her hair with Sara's curlers, taking her time, letting each section fall into glossy waves. Then came the dress—a slinky dark green number Sara had barely worn. It hugged her waist and shimmered in the light. She paired it with sheer tights and her chunky knee-high boots, laced all the way up. The jacket she threw over her shoulders wasn't warm, but it didn't matter. She felt good.

Her phone buzzed again.

Daz: *"I'm outside :)"

She grabbed her bag, gave herself one last glance in the mirror, and left.

He looked up from his car as she walked down the steps. A slow, stunned smile spread across his face.

"Wow," he said as she climbed in. "You look... amazing."

She smiled, cheeks warm. "Thanks. You scrub up alright yourself."

He did. He wore a black jumper under a denim jacket, sleeves pushed to his elbows, tattoos visible. His hair was shorter now, neater. His jawline stronger, his skin still pale with those scattered freckles she remembered.

They drove in comfortable silence for a few moments before she spoke.

"I'm glad you texted."

He glanced at her, smiling. "Me too. I was worried you wouldn't reply."

"I almost didn't," she admitted. "But I'm glad I did."

They went to a quiet bar tucked behind the high street. One of those low-lit places with candles on the tables and mismatched chairs. They found a table near the back, just the two of them.

Over drinks, they talked. About everything and nothing.

About the first night they met, about the park, about how far they'd both come since then. He told her about the garage, about how he started with nothing, just sweeping floors, and worked his way up.

She listened, admiring not just the man he'd become, but the effort it must have taken to become him.

"I kept thinking about you," he said at one point, eyes on the table. "Over the years. Wondered where you were, how you were doing. I'm glad you're okay."

She nodded. "I wasn't okay for a while. But I'm getting there."

He looked up, eyes meeting hers. There was something heavy between them. Understanding. History. A thousand unsaid things.

They stayed until last orders. The street outside was quiet as they walked back to his car. The city hummed in the distance, but here it was peaceful. Cold, but not unpleasantly so.

Emily hesitated as they reached her building.

"Sara's out tonight," she said, voice quiet. "You want to come up? Just for a bit?"

He looked at her for a moment, then nodded. "Yeah. I'd like that."

Inside, she flicked the lights on. The flat was small, the living room leading straight into the kitchen. Her room was at the end of the hall.

"Make yourself at home," she said, taking off her jacket. "Want a tea or something?"

"Tea sounds good."

She busied herself in the kitchen, filling the kettle, pulling down mugs. Her hands shook slightly. Not with fear. With nerves. Anticipation.

When she turned around, he was watching her from the sofa, smiling softly.

They sat together, tea untouched. Close, but not touching. Talking, laughing, comfortable. Then, quiet. She turned to him, her heart thudding.

"I missed you," she said.

He leaned in, slowly, giving her time to pull away. She didn't.

Their lips met gently at first, tentative, like a question. Then again, deeper this time, sure.

He held her face like she was something precious. She felt like maybe she was.

They stayed up for hours, curled on the sofa, talking about everything and nothing. He told her about his mum, how he'd been looking after her since her health declined. She told him about work, about Sara, about the quiet nights she spent writing in her notebook, things she never told anyone.

When she finally yawned, he offered to leave.

"You can stay," she said softly. "Just sleep. It's late."

He nodded. "Only if you're sure."

She was.

They climbed into her bed, fully dressed. She curled into his chest, like years ago on that hostel mattress. Only this time, the air didn't feel heavy with fear.

She fell asleep with his arm around her.

Chapter Twenty-Five

A Day

Emily woke first.

The light filtering in through the blinds was soft and pale, the kind that made everything feel gentler. She lay still for a moment, blinking at the ceiling, trying to place the feeling in her chest. It was quiet. Calm. No alarms, no shouting, no need to be anywhere but here. She turned her head slowly.

Daz was beside her, still fully clothed, his hoodie bunched under his head like a pillow. One arm was draped across his middle, the other close to her but not touching. His mouth was slightly open, and his hair had fallen messily over his forehead. He looked so different like this—peaceful and somehow younger.

She smiled to herself.

Careful not to wake him, Emily slipped out from under the throw blanket they'd ended up sharing. Her boots were still by the door, coat tossed over the back of a chair. She padded quietly into the bathroom, washed her face, brushed her hair and teeth, and changed into fresh leggings and a cropped jumper. The jumper was pale green, her favourite soft knit. She applied a little mascara and lip balm, just enough to feel ready.

By the time she emerged, Daz was sitting up, rubbing his face groggily.

"Morning," she said, softly.

He blinked at her, then grinned. "Didn't mean to fall asleep. Hope I didn't snore."

"You didn't," she said, amused. "You just... passed out. Guess we were both tired."

Daz stretched and stood, rolling his neck. "I feel weirdly good. Like, clear-headed."

She leaned against the doorframe. "Do you want some tea or...?"

"I was thinking," he said, pulling his hoodie down straight, "I could take you for breakfast? Proper food. My treat."

Emily blinked in surprise. "You don't have to—"

"I want to," he cut in, giving her a small smile. "Come on. It's Sunday. The sun's out. Might as well enjoy it."

She hesitated, then nodded. "Alright. Give me five minutes."

They ended up at a small café tucked off the high street—one of those places with old wooden tables and plants hanging from the ceiling. Emily ordered poached eggs and toast; Daz got a full English. They sat by the window, people-watching and sharing stories in between bites.

"I used to come here with my granddad," Daz said, sipping his coffee. "Every other Saturday after football."

Emily looked up. "You played football?"

"Used to. Back when I had knees that worked properly," he joked. "You?"

"Me? Nah. I was more the kid reading on the field while everyone else ran around. Books made more sense than people."

Daz grinned. "You always were clever. Even back then."

Her cheeks warmed at the compliment. She reached for her tea, trying to hide the smile tugging at her lips.

After breakfast, neither of them wanted to go home. The morning was bright, unseasonably warm for spring. They took the train to Hampstead Heath, wandered through the tall grass and meandering paths, Daz picking up a stick and joking that it was his "nature sword."

They sat on a hill overlooking the city skyline, not quite touching, but close enough to feel it.

"This is the happiest I've felt in a long time," Emily said without thinking.

Daz glanced at her. "Same."

She looked at the skyline, fingers fiddling with a blade of grass. "It's weird. I didn't think I'd ever feel comfortable around someone again. Not really."

He was quiet for a beat. Then: "You can. And you should."

She looked at him. He met her eyes.

"I don't know what you've been through," he said, "but I want you to know you can trust me. No pressure, no rush. Just... whatever this is, we'll figure it out."

Her throat tightened unexpectedly. She nodded, not trusting her voice.

They stayed out all afternoon. Walked, talked, shared silly observations and long stretches of silence that weren't awkward at all. At one point, Daz bought her a melting 99 ice cream, and they sat on a bench while she tried to keep it from dripping on her shoes.

"You always this messy?" he teased.

"Shut up," she said, flicking a napkin at him.

It was a simple day. But something about it lodged itself deep inside her. She hadn't realised how much she needed to feel safe. To laugh. To be seen.

When the sun began to dip low and the air cooled, they made their way back. On the walk to her flat, Daz kept his hands in his pockets, close enough that their arms brushed with each step.

Outside her door, he stopped.

"Thanks for today," she said.

"No, thank you," he replied. "I needed it more than I knew."

For a moment, neither of them moved. Then he smiled again, softer this time.

"I'll text you later, yeah?"

She nodded, heart fluttering. "I'd like that."

He walked away, hands still in his pockets, head dipped slightly against the wind.

Emily watched until he turned the corner. Then she slipped inside, heart warm and hopeful.

Chapter Twenty-Six

Apple Crumble

It had been a few weeks since Emily and Daz had reconnected, and things were… good. There was no other word for it. Steady. Safe. The kind of good that felt earned after years of instability. Emily hadn't told anyone—not even Sara—how happy it made her feel to just exist beside him, to walk side by side or sit in silence and not feel like she had to explain herself.

So when he asked, a little sheepishly, if she wanted to come back to his nan's for Sunday dinner, she said yes without hesitation. She could tell it meant something. This wasn't just a casual drop-in. It was the kind of invitation that came with a certain level of trust.

Daz lived in a quiet part of North London, just past the high street where corner shops turned into sleepy side roads lined with semi-detached houses and overgrown hedges. His nan's house was small, tired around the edges, but warm and cared for. The paint on the front door was chipped, but the brass handle gleamed, and there was a hanging basket blooming with bright pink petunias swaying gently in the breeze.

He opened the door for her with a grin and a low, nervous "You ready?"

She nodded, brushing imaginary dust from her jeans. "Let's do it."

Inside, the house smelled like roast chicken, rosemary, and fabric softener. A hallway lined with framed photos—black and white wedding portraits, school pictures, a faded certificate in a cheap gold frame—led to a narrow front room with mismatched armchairs and a telly humming softly in the background.

"Nan!" Daz called out. "She's here."

From the kitchen came a voice, sharp and clear. "Well, don't just stand there with the door open! Let her in properly!"

A moment later, His Nan appeared—a small, wiry woman in her seventies wearing a floral apron and sensible shoes. Her hair was swept up in a neat bun, and her sharp blue eyes missed nothing.

"So you're Emily," she said, looking her up and down with a grin that was more knowing than friendly.

Emily smiled nervously. "That's me. Thank you for having me."

Nan gave a firm nod. "We're not posh here, love. No need for all that. You like chicken?"

"I do."

"Good. Sit down then, I'll shout when it's ready. Daz—make her a tea or something, don't just stand there gawping."

Daz rolled his eyes but moved to the kettle. Emily took a seat on the edge of the sofa, still glancing around the room. It was lived in—cozy, cluttered, clean but not spotless. It felt like a real home. Somewhere with history.

They chatted lightly for a while—Daz's Nan introduced herself as Doreen. She popped in and out from the kitchen, occasionally quizzing Emily about work, about where she grew up, about whether she had a "proper winter coat." Emily answered as best she could, the nerves softening as the warmth of the house settled into her bones.

Then came the sound of a door creaking upstairs.

Daz glanced up, then at Emily. "Just so you know… my mum's here. She stays mostly in her room."

Emily's expression sobered. "Is she okay?"

He paused. "She's not been great for a while. Early dementia. Some days are alright. Others… not so much. I'll introduce you if she's calm."

There was something in his voice that made Emily reach for his hand, briefly. A silent "I get it."

They didn't say anything more about it until after dinner.

The meal was hearty and delicious. Doreen had clearly pulled out all the stops—roast potatoes, stuffing, green beans, thick gravy, and apple crumble for afters. Daz helped dish everything out, making jokes and trying to keep the mood light, and Emily let herself fall into the comfort of it all.

But halfway through dessert, the calm was disrupted.

There was a thud upstairs. Then another. Then a voice—sharp, confused, angry.

"Where's my bag? I want my bloody bag!"

Nan froze mid-bite. Daz immediately stood.

"Stay here," he murmured to Emily, then headed for the stairs.

Emily looked to Doreen, unsure whether to speak. The older woman simply sighed and picked up her fork again.

"She gets worse when she forgets what day it is. Thinks someone's stolen something. Usually it's just under the bed or in the wardrobe."

"Does… does she remember who Daz is?"

"Some days. Some she thinks he's his dad. Poor lad just takes it on the chin. We're all used to it now."

Emily swallowed hard, her appetite gone.

They sat in quiet for a few minutes until Daz came back down. His face was blank, tired. He didn't say anything, just resumed his seat and pushed his dessert around the bowl.

Emily reached under the table and squeezed his knee.

"Can I meet her?" she said quietly.

He looked up, surprised. "You don't have to."

"I know."

Upstairs, the room was dimly lit. His mum was lying on the bed, still muttering under her breath about a missing bag. Daz knocked softly and stepped in.

"Mum? This is Emily. She's a friend."

His mum sat up slowly. Her eyes darted to Emily, narrowed. "You stealin' from me?"

"No," Emily said gently, "just here to say hi."

There was a flicker of recognition. A pause. Then, oddly, a smile.

"You've got nice eyes," his mum said. "You remind me of someone."

Emily smiled. "Thank you."

"She's got your dad's eyes, don't she?" she said to Daz, before frowning again. "Or was it mine? I forget."

Daz just sat beside her, brushing her hair back from her forehead.

"Don't worry, Mum."

Emily stood quietly by the door, heart heavy.

They left a short while later. Outside, the sky was beginning to darken, the streetlights flickering on.

"Sorry," Daz muttered as they walked to the bus stop. "I didn't know it would be one of those days."

"You don't need to apologise for your life," Emily said softly.

He looked at her, eyes tired but grateful. "Most people don't really want to be around her."

"I'm not most people."

They stood in silence for a moment, side by side.

And when the bus pulled up, she turned to him and said, "Thank you for trusting me."

He didn't speak—just kissed the side of her head and watched her board, hands buried in his pockets.

Chapter Twenty-Seven

Pop stars

The whole week, Emily had been floating. It wasn't just the promise of a surprise date—it was the way Daz had said it, like he couldn't wait to show her something special, something just for her. She'd never had that before. Never had anyone plan something with excitement in their voice, just to see her smile.

"You'll love it," he'd said with a grin, refusing to give a single hint.

So she did what girls do when something matters. She planned. She browsed outfits online for days, eventually settling on a soft satin blouse in muted lilac, paired with high-waisted black jeans and a new pair of boots—sleek, slightly heeled, just dressy enough. She braided her hair the way Sara once did for a wedding, fishtail-style, pinned neatly over one shoulder. Light makeup. A hint of perfume.

He picked her up just after five, dressed in a fresh black bomber jacket and clean trainers, his cologne noticeable the moment he hugged her.

"Ready?" he asked.

She nodded, slipping into the cab beside him. "More than."

They laughed all the way through the ride. Music played low on the car radio as the city passed by in blur—grey blocks of flats, red buses groaning at traffic lights, neon shopfronts. Emily leaned into Daz's shoulder, smiling, heart light.

But when they turned a corner and she saw the stadium rise in the distance, her stomach dropped.

Wembley.

It was beautiful, lit golden in the setting sun, the arch slicing through the sky like a crown. But to Emily, it didn't look like a celebration.

It looked like a memory.

"Here we are," Daz said, paying the cabbie.

He stepped out and reached for her hand, but her fingers were stiff.

"You alright?" he asked, squinting against the light.

"Yeah," she lied. "Just… wow. It's big."

He grinned. "We've got tickets. Proper ones. Not standing. You'll love it."

They joined the crowd, the steady hum of excitement building as people streamed in from every direction—teenagers in band t-shirts, couples holding hands, friends clutching drinks and laughing. Music pulsed faintly from the stadium.

Emily tried to stay present, but each step pulled her back. It was like something was dragging along the floor behind her, chained to her ankles.

The queue.
The staff wristbands.
The way Thomas had smiled at her across the counter.
His voice. His lies.
The night it went wrong.

She turned her head—and there it was.

The Stand.

Still there. Different people working inside. Different uniforms now. But it was the same shape, the same position, tucked near the main entrance. Her chest tightened.

She couldn't breathe.

"Em?"

She blinked.

Daz had stopped, noticing the way she'd frozen.

"I just… I need a minute," she mumbled.

Without another word, she turned and walked fast—too fast—away from the stadium. Through the crowd. Ducking. Pushing. Past laughing girls and men selling fake T-shirts and children with glowing sticks. She slipped through a gate and kept walking until her legs gave out near the back of a shut-up food truck.

She dropped to the curb, chest heaving, head between her knees.

Panic. That old familiar spiral.

Not now. Not tonight.

"Emily!"

Daz's voice. Near. Then closer.

He crouched beside her, hand on her back.

"Hey. Breathe. Look at me."

She tried. Failed. Her ears rang.

"I'm here," he said, gently. "You're safe. You're okay."

She pressed her hands to her face, shaking. Her nails leaving marks behind in her soft cheeks. "I'm sorry—I just—I can't. That booth. I used to work there. That's where I met him."

"Who?"

"Thomas. – He didn't listen! I said No! I wanted him to stop!"

Silence. Understanding dawned across his face, and a mixture of anger and sorrow.

"Oh." His eyebrows were furrowed.

She wiped her eyes. "I haven't been back here since. I didn't even think about it until I saw it. I—I didn't want to ruin tonight."

"You didn't ruin anything."

"I did. I'm sorry." Emily was sobbing, trying to catch her breath.

He shook his head, firm. "Don't be. You were brave to come at all."

She sniffed, laughing weakly. "Not that brave."

"Brave enough," he said. "Let's get out of here, yeah?"

Back at her flat, he made her tea without asking. He found a clean mug, filled the kettle, added just the right amount of milk. She watched from the sofa, wrapped in her blanket, the braid in her hair starting to unravel.

He brought the tea over and set it in front of her.

"Here. No pressure to talk. Just… sit."

She nodded, grateful.

After a long pause, she whispered, "I thought I was past all that."

"You are," he said. "But healing's messy. Sometimes it loops back."

"I didn't want you to see me like that."

He looked at her softly. "I'd rather see you real than pretending."

She looked up at him, eyes glassy. "Thanks for not leaving."

He smiled. "I've spent enough of my life watching people leave. I'd rather stay."

He didn't stay the night. Just pulled her blanket up around her and kissed her forehead before heading for the door.

"Text me in the morning?" she asked.

"You don't even have to ask," he said.

And with that, he left.

The door clicked shut.

Emily sat in the quiet, tea cooling on the table, heart somehow heavier and lighter at once.

And in that stillness, she knew:

Something had begun.

Chapter Twenty-Eight

Home sweet home

Emily hadn't been back home in months.

It wasn't just the distance or her busy schedule—there was something heavy in the air of that house. Something stale and unspoken that clung to her skin every time she stepped through the front door.

But today felt like the right time.

Her mum had called earlier in the week, slurring slightly but sounding vaguely warm for once. "Come by, Em. Bring that fella of yours. I'll cook a roast."

It wasn't a request. It was the closest thing to an olive branch her mother could offer. And against her better judgment, Emily accepted.

"I don't want you to feel like you have to invite me" Daz had said when she asked him to come.

"I don't. I want to. I want you to meet... them. Just the once though."

Daz had nodded, but something in his expression had hesitated. She put it down to nerves.

They took the bus.

As it trundled through the streets of North London, Emily grew quiet. Her fingers drummed lightly on her knees. Daz noticed and took her hand.

"You alright?"

"Yeah," she said. "They're just.. a bit shit."

They arrived just after four. The door was open a crack, and the TV inside blared some reality show rerun. Emily knocked anyway before nudging it open and leading Daz up the stairs.

"Hello?"

From the kitchen, her mother's voice rang out. "In here!"

The hallway smelled the same—cheap air freshener and faint smoke. The wallpaper was peeling slightly now, and there was a faint scuff mark where the corner of a chair had once scraped the wall.

Daz lingered behind Emily as they walked into the kitchen.

Her mum was at the counter, a cigarette in one hand, wooden spoon in the other. A wine glass sat half-full beside a tray of potatoes.

"Emily!" she said, eyes lighting up, her voice half-raspy with drink. "And this must be your young man!"

Daz extended a hand. "Hi. I'm Daz."

Her mum didn't take his hand, just looked him up and down. "Hmm. You're not what I pictured. Taller."

Emily cleared her throat. "Mum."

"I'm joking. Sit down, both of you. Dinner's nearly done."

They walked down the long thin hallway and sat at the table in the living room. It was warm, but not cosy. Too bright. Too quiet beneath the TV noise.

Then Cynthia appeared, as if summoned.

She moved slowly, deliberately, standing in the doorway like a shadow. Her long black hair hung in damp strands, and her eyes were unreadable as she looked from Emily to Daz.

"Didn't know you were coming," she said.

"You were in the group chat," Emily replied gently.

"Must've missed it."

Daz nodded politely. "Hi."

Cynthia didn't respond. Just watched him.

The tension coiled, subtle but sharp. Emily felt it immediately.

Her sister walked to the table and sat down, eyes still on Daz. "So you're the new one?"

Emily narrowed her eyes. "He's not the 'new one', Cynthia."

"Right." Cynthia looked down at her chipped nail polish, then back up. "You two meet recently?"

"Little while ago," Daz answered, keeping his tone steady.

Cynthia's lips curved into a half-smile. "You seem familiar."

Emily's spine stiffened. "He lived near us when we were young. Used to hang about down the road."

Cynthia shrugged. "No.. its not that. Dunno. Probably nothing. Just a feeling."

Daz shifted slightly in his chair. Emily noticed. So did Cynthia.

Their mum clattered plates down in front of them—roast chicken, carrots, gravy that looked like it had come from a packet.

"Eat up," she said, already back with her wine glass in hand.

Dinner passed slowly.

Emily kept glancing between Daz and Cynthia, and the unease in her stomach built with every exchange. Her mum kept talking about nonsense—shows she was watching, people from down the road. But

Cynthia barely spoke. And when she did, it was laced with something Emily couldn't quite place.

Halfway through the meal, Cynthia leaned back and tilted her head.

"You know, I think I remember you now. You used to hang around that estate near the canal, yeah?"

Daz blinked. "A long time ago, maybe."

"You were mates with some older boys. Those dodgy ones."

"Cyn," Emily snapped. "That's enough."

Cynthia smiled thinly. "Just making conversation."

But the damage was done. Daz was quiet the rest of the meal. Emily could feel the tension rolling off him like heat. Her own nerves were jangling.

After dessert—shop-bought Bread and butter pudding, still cold in the middle—they made their excuses.

"Thanks for dinner," Daz said to her mum.

She waved him off, distracted by the TV.

Cynthia stood by the hallway mirror, arms folded.

As Emily grabbed her coat, she turned to her sister. "What was that?"

Cynthia didn't answer.

"You were weird the whole night."

"Was I?" Cynthia said, mock-surprised.

"We used to know all kinds of people when we were kids. We used to hang out."

Cynthia finally met her eyes. "No, not that. Something I remember. But maybe I'm wrong."

Emily held her gaze for a long second. Something was there. A flicker. Not recognition—something darker.

"You're being creepy."

Cynthia smiled, but there was no warmth in it. "You should ask him who he used to run with. Before he got 'respectable'."

Emily's stomach turned. "He's not a kid anymore. You don't know him."

"No. But maybe you don't either."

On the bus ride home, Emily was quiet. So was Daz.

She watched the lights flicker past the window, her thoughts spiraling.

She knew people changed. She believed Daz was good. She trusted him.

Didn't she?

"Hey," he said softly, breaking the silence. "I'm sorry about that. I didn't expect... all that."

"It's not you. It's her," Emily said quickly. "She's always like that."

He nodded. "Still. I should've said something sooner."

Emily looked at him, frowning. "Said what?"

He hesitated.

Then smiled, but it didn't reach his eyes. "Nothing serious. Just... I used to knock about with some rough people. Like rougher than the ones you did. Back when I was young. Long gone now."

Emily didn't push it.

Not yet.

But something had shifted.

Just enough to make her wonder.

CHAPTER Twenty-Nine

Suspicious minds

Emily hadn't thought much of Cynthia's words at the time. They'd been tangled in the usual awkward family atmosphere—strained wine-fuelled glances across the table, Mum's snide digs in between sips, and Cynthia's quiet, cryptic remarks that always seemed to linger just a little too long.

But now, days later, the memory clung to her like something sticky. It wasn't just what Cynthia had said—it was how she'd said it. That look. Like she knew something. Like she wanted Emily to know something, too.

She sat on the edge of the bed that afternoon, her laptop perched on her knees, a documentary full-screen but paused, blinking back at her, completely unmoving. Daz had texted her half an hour ago:

"You. Me. Dinner tonight?"

She had smiled, instinctively. Things with him had been better than good lately. He made her laugh. He listened, really listened. He noticed small things—how she took her coffee, the way her eyes flicked when she was trying not to cry, how she chewed the inside of her cheek when she was worried. There were moments, especially late at night when they were tangled together on her tiny sofa or walking side by side through Camden Market, when she felt... safe. A word she didn't often allow herself to think.

But the dreams had started creeping in a few nights ago.

She didn't remember the specifics—just flickers. A figure at the edge of her vision. A sensation of being chased. A flash of silver. Her heart pounding so loud it woke her.

She had dismissed them as stress. Old trauma lingering in new spaces. The kind of dreams that always bubbled up when her mind had too much time to think. But in the back of her thoughts, Cynthia's voice echoed:

"You really don't know everything about him, do you?"

Emily shook her head and closed the laptop. She wasn't going to go down a spiral over a vague comment from a sister she barely trusted. Still... when Daz came to pick her up later that evening, she found herself studying him in a new light. Not suspicious, exactly—just curious. Watching for something beneath the surface.

He looked the same as always. Baggy hoodie. Clean jeans. A cheeky grin that tilted to the right. When he leaned in to kiss her, she paused for just a second too long.

"You alright?" he asked.

"Yeah," she said quickly, forcing a smile. "Just thinking."

"You think too much," he said, brushing her hair behind her ear. "Come on. I'm starving."

Dinner was easy. Casual. They ordered too many sides and laughed at how bad Daz was at using chopsticks. She let herself enjoy it. Let herself forget. But halfway through dessert, as Daz wiped a smudge of chocolate from her lip with his thumb, the question pushed forward again—uninvited.

"Did you ever... get in trouble, when you were younger?" she asked lightly.

He raised an eyebrow. "What, like police trouble?"

"Yeah. Or... I don't know. Just anything."

He leaned back in his chair, stretching. "Why, you doing a background check on me now?" he joked, grinning.

She forced a laugh. "Just curious."

He paused, then shrugged. "Nothing major. Bit of dumb stuff, like most kids. Shoplifting once. Nearly got done for trespassing. That's about it."

She nodded slowly, sipping her drink. "Cynthia said something weird the other day. About you. I don't know what she meant."

His face tightened just slightly. "Cynthia talks a lot of shit, doesn't she?"

"Probably."

There was a long pause. The air felt thicker suddenly.

"She just said... that I don't know everything about you. I think she was trying to wind me up."

He looked down at his plate. "Sounds like her."

She studied him, but his face was unreadable now. A wall had gone up. She let the subject drop.

They walked home in silence for a while, the streets slick with rain. She slipped her hand into his and he squeezed it gently, pulling her close under his arm. The tension between them eased.

Back at the flat, something shifted.

Maybe it was the wine. Maybe it was the way he kissed her when they got in—slow, searching, like he needed her to understand something he couldn't say.

Maybe it was just time. But when he whispered, "Can I stay?" she didn't hesitate.

They didn't rush. It wasn't desperate or messy. It was careful. Intimate. There was something sacred in the way he held her naked body, how he asked before every new step, the way his warm lips gently grazed her soft nipples. She said yes. Every time. Her heart beat loud in her chest, but this time, not from fear.

For the first time in her life, it didn't feel like something was being taken. It felt like she was giving something on her terms.

Afterwards, they lay side by side in the glow of the streetlights sneaking through the blinds. He traced shapes on her bare shoulder. She rested her head against him, eyes half-closed.

"You alright?" he asked, voice soft.

"Yeah," she said. And for once, it was true.

She fell asleep like that, tucked beneath his arm, her hand over his heart.

The next morning, she woke up before him. Sunlight filtered through the window in thick gold lines, lighting up the dust in the air. She watched him sleep for a moment. His mouth was slightly open. His hand rested on his chest.

He looked... young. Like the Daz she used to know. But now older. Stronger. More worn.

She slipped out of bed and padded into the kitchen to make tea. The kettle growled, and she poured the water, watching it swirl. That dream flickered again—shadows. Running. Her breath caught in her throat.

She shook it off. Not now.

Daz appeared in the doorway a few minutes later, his hair messy, rubbing his eyes. He smiled when he saw her. "Morning, Em."

She handed him a mug and leaned against the counter. "Sleep alright?"

"With you next to me?" he said, grinning. "Best night's sleep I've had in years."

She rolled her eyes but smiled. "Charmer."

He stepped forward, wrapping his arms around her waist. "You know I mean it."

They stood like that for a while, just holding each other. It felt good. Solid.

So why was there a voice still whispering in the back of her mind:

You don't know everything.

Chapter Thirty

The Forgotten Friend

It started with a photo.

A week had passed since the night Emily had let her guard down—since she'd felt like she could trust someone for the first time in a long time. Maybe even love someone? Daz had stayed over again. Things had felt warm. Natural. Her walls were coming down.

But then Cynthia sent her a message out of the blue.

"Come round. Just you. I need to show you something."

She stared at the text. Cryptic again. Typical Cynthia.

She debated not going. But curiosity was a louder voice today than common sense. That, and the strange twisting in her gut that hadn't quite gone away since their last dinner together. There was something unfinished. Something brewing just beneath the surface.

She arrived at Mum's flat late afternoon. The curtains were drawn. The living room was quiet, save for the distant hum of the TV playing something she wasn't really watching.

"Tea?" Cynthia offered flatly, already walking to the kitchen.

Emily followed slowly. "What's this about?"

"You'll see," Cynthia replied, her tone unreadable.

They sat opposite each other, two mugs between them on the table. Cynthia stood and reached for a side drawer, pulled out an old shoebox, and placed it in Emily's lap.

"What's this?" Emily asked.

"Memories," Cynthia said softly. "From before."

Emily hesitated, then lifted the lid.

"I thought Dad burnt everything!?"

"Not everything. I managed to salvage what I could."

Inside were scattered photographs, old wristbands, and faded receipts from concerts and nights out. Emily smiled faintly as she picked up a picture of them at Louise's 13th birthday party—her hair in uneven pigtails, Cynthia pretending not to smile, Mum blurry in the background a bright smile pasted on her face.

Another photo. A group of boys and girls from school, all wearing some variety of 'Dappy hat' from when N-Dubz were big, standing outside a chip shop in the cold. One of them caught Emily's eye.

He looked familiar—shaggy dark hair, strong jaw, hoodie pulled over his head.

Daz.

But it wasn't just him. Next to him, in the background, stood another boy. One Emily didn't recognise straight away, until she read the note scribbled on the back in her own handwriting:

"Jamie C—always tagging along lol"

Jamie. That name flickered something deep in her brain. Like a spark too small to catch flame.

"Why are you showing me this?" she asked, holding up the photo.

"Do you remember Jamie?" Cynthia asked quietly.

"Barely. He was in the year below, right?"

Cynthia nodded. "He died. Years ago."

Emily frowned. "I think I heard about that... didn't he overdose or something?"

Cynthia's expression didn't change. "That's what some people said."

A pause.

Emily's fingers tightened slightly on the photo. "What do you mean?"

Cynthia took a long sip of her tea. Then, eyes never leaving Emily's, she said, "He didn't overdose. He was stabbed."

The air left Emily's lungs.

"I don't—"

"It happened near the park. They were older then. Months after you left Dad. I don't know all the details. I only know what people said at the time. I wasn't even sure it was real until I saw that photo again a few weeks ago. Started connecting dots."

Emily's heart was pounding. "What dots?"

"There was talk. Years ago. Someone said Jamie had been bragging about knowing some lads who found you sleeping in a park. That they'd even... tried something. We all knew Daz found out. He was mad. But then he just went quiet. And then he was gone."

Cynthia leaned forward. "I didn't think anything of it back then. But now, with Daz... the way he is. The way he acts. I don't know, Em. It doesn't feel right."

Emily stared down at the photograph again. Her hands were shaking.

"Why are you telling me this now?"

"Because you deserve to know who you're letting into your life. You don't need to restart the cycle.

God knows none of us do." Cynthia said. "I'm not saying he did it. But if he did…"

Emily didn't answer. She couldn't. Her throat had closed.

That night, she lay in bed next to Daz, watching the slow rise and fall of his chest. His face looked peaceful. Gentle. The boy who carried her bags. Who made her tea with too much sugar. Who knew when to make her laugh and when to just hold her hand. The man who was soft and patient.

But now, the questions were louder than ever.

She couldn't sleep.

The next day, when Daz left to meet a mate, she pulled out her laptop and typed into the search bar:

"Jamie C stabbed North London 2014."

The results came slowly. Mostly dead ends. Then a short local news article popped up from an old archived blog:

"Teen fatally stabbed near disused railway bridge in North London.
A 15-year-old boy was killed in a knife attack last night in an area near Finsbury Park. The victim, Jamie C—, was found at around 11:30 PM. Police are appealing for witnesses. No arrests have been made."

No arrests.

Emily stared at the article for a long time. The date matched. The location too.

Her hands were cold.

She clicked on the comments. Most were spam. But one stood out:

"He wasn't perfect but he didn't deserve that. Everyone knew he talked too much. Should've kept quiet."

She closed the laptop.

That night, Daz noticed something was off.

"You're quiet," he said, watching her from the kitchen as she stirred soup without really seeing it.

"Just tired," she said.

He didn't press. But his eyes followed her more than usual. Like he could sense something was shifting.

Later, curled on the sofa, he reached for her hand. She let him take it. Her body leaned into his. But her mind was somewhere else entirely.

Because for a moment, she wasn't sure if she was falling in love with someone safe or someone dangerous.

Chapter Thirty-One

Why now?

Emily hadn't heard from Louise since that day.

The day she'd run from their father's house, trembling and silent, the front door slamming behind her like the end of a chapter. Louise hadn't followed. She hadn't even called.

But Emily had tried. Texts. Emails. A voicemail once, that she immediately regretted. Even a letter. Weeks turned to months. Nothing.

So when a message appeared on her phone—an unfamiliar number and a simple line:

"It's Louise. Can we talk?"

Emily's hands froze. Her chest tightened. The voice of her younger self whispered, *don't trust it*. But her heart answered before her head could speak.

"Okay. When and where?"

They met at a café behind Camden High Street. It was overcast and muggy, and the air smelled like wet stone. Emily arrived early, already on edge, stirring her tea though she hadn't added sugar.

When Louise walked in, Emily's breath caught.

She looked older, her face sharpened by time. Same dark hair. Same steady eyes. But there was a coldness now. A hardness that hadn't been there before.

Louise offered a stiff smile and sat down opposite her.

"Hi," she said quietly.

Emily nodded. "Hi."

The silence was awkward, brittle.

"You look well," Emily offered.

Louise shrugged. "Don't lie. I look like fucking shit."

Emily gave a small smile, unsure what she was allowed to say. "I tried to reach you. A lot."

"I know."

"You never answered."

Louise looked down, a sour expression enveloped her already firm facial features as she ran her thumb along the rim of her coffee cup. "I heard you were seeing Daz."

Emily blinked. "That's why you reached out?"

"No. I mean... yes, partly. But not really. I guess I just... couldn't stay silent anymore."

There was a tension in her voice, an undercurrent of something deeper.

"I heard some things about him," she added. "Things from back when we were kids. After you'd left."

Emily stiffened.

"I don't want to get into that," she said quickly.

"You might not want to," Louise said, leaning in, "but maybe you need to."

Emily studied her face. "Why are you here, Louise?"

Louise looked at her then—really looked. Her eyes burned, sharp and shining.

"You wanna fucking talk? I'm angry. I've been angry for fucking years."

Emily blinked. "At me?"

"At all of you," Louise snapped. "You left. All of you left. Mum fucked off first. Then Cynthia. Even you fucking ran off. You all got to go. And I—" She slammed her hand on the table. "I was *left*."

Emily was stunned into silence.

"I didn't get a choice," Louise said, quieter now but still shaking. "You get that, right? I couldn't go. Someone had to stay. Someone had to deal with him. And that someone was fucking me."

"I didn't know," Emily whispered. "I thought... I thought you wanted to be there. You never said anything."

"Of course I didn't," Louise snapped. "Because if I'd let myself speak, I would've fallen apart. And someone had to hold it together. Dad... he needed someone. He was grieving. Lost. But that doesn't mean he wasn't awful. He was. He *is*. And I stayed."

Emily's throat tightened.

"And what did you do?" Louise said. "You ran to *her*. That bitch who drank herself through half our childhood. Who smashed plates and screamed and passed out on the sofa. You went back to her like she was some kind of saviour."

"She's going to get sober." Emily said softly.

"So what?" Louise snapped. "Does that erase everything she did? All the nights we cried ourselves to sleep? All the times she scared the shit out of us?"

"No," Emily whispered. "It doesn't."

Louise looked away, her voice cracking. "You all got to start over. Make your own lives. Escape that fucking hell. I didn't. I stayed in that house. I heard every hateful word. Took every slap. Cleaned up every mess. I lost years."

Emily's eyes burned. "I'm so sorry."

"I don't want your apology," Louise said. "I just want you to *see* it. You fucked off. And I couldn't. I never got a choice."

Emily reached across the table. Louise hesitated, then let her hand be taken.

"I didn't know how bad it got," Emily said, voice trembling. "I should've tried harder. Fought harder to take you with me."

Louise didn't answer, but the silence between them softened. Less jagged now—still painful, but shared.

After a long pause, Louise pulled her hand away and said quietly, "There's more. About Daz. About what happened after everyone found out you got attacked in the park. I don't know everything. But I know something bad happened. And I think... I think you deserve to know it."

Emily's breath caught.

But before she could ask anything more, Louise stood up and slung her coat over her arm.

"Another time," she said. "When you're ready to hear it."

Then she was gone.

And Emily was left staring at the door, heart pounding, trying to hold together the fragile threads of what remained.

Chapter Thirty-Two

A Bad Influence

Emily stared at the message on her phone.

Louise: *Just come see him.*

She read it three times before locking the screen and setting the phone down on the table. The silence in the kitchen seemed louder afterward.

She hadn't spoken to Louise since the night outside the café a couple of weeks ago —the night the dam broke. Louise had vanished again after that. Disappeared back into whatever life she was living on the edges of everything.

Emily had tried. A few texts again. Another voicemail. Louise never responded.

And now this.

She stared at the screen until the words blurred. Her chest ached, a knot of emotions she hadn't untangled yet—resentment, guilt, love, confusion.

She hadn't told her mum about the message. Or Cynthia. She couldn't. Not because she was afraid of what they'd say—but because she already knew. Cynthia would curl her lip in disgust and say Louise had picked her side. Their mum would fall into one of her black moods, bottle in hand, muttering about betrayal and lost daughters and women who always chose cruel men.

It was better not to drag up old hurt. Let them keep thinking Louise had faded into the background of their lives. Let sleeping ghosts lie.

Emily pressed her fingers into her eyes. God, this wasn't fair.

She tapped a reply before she could overthink it.

Emily: *Fine. One visit.*

She immediately regretted it.

It had taken years to build a world that didn't include her father. A world where his voice didn't echo in her head. A world where she didn't flinch at sharp noises or feel her spine go cold at a raised voice.

And now Louise wanted to open that door again.

She told Daz later that night, while they were doing the washing up.

"Louise wants me to visit Dad."

Daz, mid-rinse, turned to look at her. "What?"

She shrugged. "She says he's changed. That he's… broken now. Her words."

He looked at her like she'd said she was going to walk across the M25.

"You're not seriously considering it."

Emily dried a plate, focusing hard on the circular motion. "I said I'd go. Once."

Daz set the sponge down, eyes fixed on her. "Emily, why?"

"I don't know," she snapped, then sighed. "Because Louise asked me to. Not because I want to. God, I don't want to. But if she's reaching out, maybe she needs me. Maybe I need her."

Daz's voice was gentle. "You're not doing this for him, then?"

"No." She swallowed. "I don't care if he's changed. I don't need closure from him. I'm doing it for her."

There was a pause, and then Daz nodded slowly.

"Alright. But I want you to text me the second you get there. And when you leave. I mean it."

"I will," she said quietly.

The morning of the visit, Emily stood staring at her reflection for longer than usual. Her hand hovered over her makeup bag. In the end, she decided not to bother. There was no point hiding behind mascara.

She dressed plainly. No jewellery. Nothing too bright. She didn't want to bring colour into that house. It would look out of place.

The Uber ride was silent. Her chest tightened with every turn, every familiar street name. By the time they pulled onto the road she'd once called home, her hands were damp with sweat. The seatbelt pressed into her like a weight.

The house looked worse than she remembered. The front step was cracked, the Driveway an overgrown mess, and the front window smeared with grime.

Louise stood at the front door like a statue. Her face was unreadable.

Emily climbed out slowly, gripping her bag with white knuckles.

"You came," Louise said.

"I said I would."

Louise nodded but didn't smile. "Cool."

They walked to the door side by side, like strangers who knew too much.

Her dad opened the door before they could knock. Same figure. Same slouch. But the moment his eyes found Emily, something flickered—something feral and bitter and twisted.

"Well, look who it is," he sneered. "Didn't think you'd ever have the guts to come back."

Emily didn't flinch. "Just here for a visit."

"Visit," he repeated, like it was a filthy word. "That what your mother calls it when she screws every new bloke that walks through the pub door?"

"Don't," Emily warned sharply.

"Why not? We all know it's true. She was never worth the air she breathed. Poisoned every one of you against me."

Emily stepped inside, jaw clenched so tight it ached. The house smelled like mildew and something faintly metallic.

They walked into the living room. Everything was as it had been a decade ago. Same sagging furniture. Same stained wallpaper. Even the little clock was the same one he'd ripped off the wall and thrown once, narrowly missing her head.

Louise sat on the sofa beside her quietly, as if it were normal. Like this was a routine.

Her dad dropped into his armchair. "So. What are you, then? Social worker now? Therapist? Come to fix dear old Daddy?"

"I work in Asda," Emily said flatly.

"Oh, of course. That bitch couldn't afford to pay for some poxy degree no?"

"I'm not here to talk about mum."

"She made you all soft," he snapped. "You used to be a good girl. Now you're just another little slag in London, crying about trauma and safe spaces."

Emily glanced at Louise. Her sister was staring into the middle distance, jaw tight.

"I'm not here to talk about the past," Emily said. "I'm here because Louise asked me to be."

That hit a nerve.

He laughed—a cold, bitter bark. "Oh, she did, did she? What, now you lot get to just waltz back in when it suits you? After abandoning us? After leaving *her* to pick up the pieces?"

Louise flinched.

"Don't talk about her like that," Emily snapped.

"She *stayed*! Unlike the rest of you cowards!"

Emily stood. "I think we're done here."

"Of course you are," he snarled. "Can't handle anything real. Just like that other freak. What was it Cynthia turned into? A man? A freak show? Can't even make sense of what *that* one became."

Emily spun on him, fury in her veins. "Say her name again and I swear—"

He stood too fast, knocking his drink over. "Go on then! Hit me! You're just like her. Full of fire but nothing to back it up."

Louise stepped between them. "*Stop it!*"

Her dad's chest heaved, breath coming fast and heavy.

Emily stared at him, disgust and pity and rage churning in equal measure.

"I see you haven't changed at all."

She turned on her heel and walked out.

The air outside was cold and sharp. Emily braced herself on the garden wall, trying to catch her breath.

Footsteps followed.

"Sorry," Louise said quietly.

Emily didn't look at her.

"He can be like that sometimes. I thought—" She stopped.

"You thought he was different," Emily said bitterly. "He's not. He's just tired. And when he's not tired, he's hateful."

Louise sighed. "yeah."

They stood there for a long moment.

"You asked me to come," Emily said. "I came. Why?"

Louise's voice cracked. "I wanted you to suffer. For a moment. The way I have done for years."

Emily turned then. Louise's face was wet with tears she wasn't bothering to hide.

"You all got out," she whispered. "You had each other. Mum, Cynthia, you. But I was the one left behind. I had to stay. Someone had to take care of him. And I did. I gave up *everything* for him. And he still talks about me like I'm a traitor."

"You're not."

Louise laughed hollowly. "Doesn't matter. That house eats people. And I let it eat me."

Emily moved closer and, for the first time in years, pulled her sister into a hug.

"You didn't have a choice."

"I did," Louise sobbed. "But I was scared. And angry. And I hated you all for leaving me. And I hated myself for staying."

"I'm sorry," Emily whispered. "I didn't know. I didn't want to see."

Louise gripped her back.

"I'm so tired, Em. I don't even know how to live outside of that house anymore."

"You can," Emily said. "It's not too late."

Louise looked up, eyes red.

"I have been past saving for longer than you know."

Emily nodded.

--

Later, in bed with Daz, Emily told him everything. The house. Her dad's vicious eyes. The way he seemed possessed by his own mind.

"I don't forgive him," she said. "I probably never will. But I think... I don't know. I saw something. The end of something."

Daz wrapped his arms around her.

"I'm proud of you."

Emily smiled into his chest. But the ache inside her didn't fade.

There was more to come. She could feel it in her bones.

And somewhere, in the back of her mind, she could still hear Cynthia's warning:

"There's more about Daz. You need to know."

Chapter Thirty-Three

Breakdown

The flat was quiet except for the faint hum of the radiator struggling against the cold. Emily sat on the edge of the narrow sofa, her hands wrapped around a mug of lukewarm tea she barely remembered to make. Outside, the sky had darkened into a dull grey, a bruised evening promising rain, but Emily didn't care. The world beyond these four walls felt distant, muted, as if it belonged to someone else entirely.

She pressed her forehead against the cool ceramic of the mug and closed her eyes, willing the pounding in her chest to slow. But it only grew louder—like a trapped bird frantically beating its wings inside her ribcage. The memories she'd tried to bury since returning from that house, from seeing him again, refused to stay silent.

The walls of the flat felt like they were closing in, the air heavy and thick. Every breath was a battle, sharp and shallow, as if her lungs had forgotten how to fill properly. Her fingers trembled, sending ripples through the surface of the tea. She wanted to throw the mug across the room, to shatter something — anything — to feel some release from the tension squeezing her alive. But she didn't move.

Her mind kept replaying the night with Louise — the way her sister's eyes had looked, hard and desperate, like she was carrying a secret too heavy to bear alone. How she had insisted Emily visit their father again, saying he was "broken," that he was "just a ghost now." Emily had resisted, every instinct screaming not to go back, but Louise's words stuck in her mind like a stubborn thorn.

And then, the visit itself. The stale smell of damp wood and old cigarettes in that cramped, dark living room. The bitter cold seeping through cracked windows. Her father's voice — rough and bitter, coated with venom as he lashed out, dragging their mother's name through the dirt again and again.

Emily remembered the sharp sting behind her eyes as he sneered about Cynthia, twisting words until they sounded cruel and unrecognizable. His rage had exploded suddenly, loud and terrifying, knocking the fragile silence apart. She'd left before things got worse, heart pounding, legs unsteady as she slipped out into the chill night air.

Since then, everything had unraveled.

The dreams came back first — dark, fragmented nightmares that dragged her under. She saw flashes of shadowy figures chasing her, the glint of knives in the dark, the cold steel pressing against her skin. She woke gasping for air, tears streaming down her face, hands clutching at blankets that did nothing to hold the terror at bay.

During the day, the panic lingered, like a weight settled deep in her gut. She couldn't eat — the thought of food turned her stomach. She was tired all the time but couldn't sleep, her mind racing through worst-case scenarios and memories she wanted to forget.

She'd quit her job last week. The supermarket aisles, the constant noise of beeping scanners and chatter — it all became too much. The friendly faces of colleagues and customers felt like strangers watching her, waiting for her to break.

Daz noticed, of course. He tried to reach her, calling and texting, dropping by the flat with cups of tea and gentle smiles. But the Emily he knew — the one who laughed with him, who held his hand and smiled softly — was slipping further away every day.

Sometimes, when he sat beside her on the sofa, she'd feel a flicker of warmth, a brief spark of hope that maybe, just maybe, she could hold onto something steady again. But the darkness was always there, lurking just beneath the surface.

Last night, he'd tried to talk to her. She remembered the way his voice had softened when she finally looked up, eyes red-rimmed and haunted.

"Emily, whatever it is, I'm here," he said. "You don't have to carry this alone."

But how could she explain the raw, ragged ache inside? The gnawing fear that even this — Daz, the one person she'd trusted — might not be enough? That maybe, there was something else, something she was afraid to face?

Cynthia's warning echoed in her mind, sharp and unyielding. Images of Jamie, the young innocent boy infiltrated her mind. She hadn't asked for details. Part of her didn't want to know. But the seed of doubt had been planted, twisting around her heart like a vine.

She was terrified. Terrified that Daz wasn't who she thought he was, terrified that her world — already so fragile — might shatter completely.

The cold mug slipped from her fingers, shattering on the floor. She flinched at the sharp crash, heart jolting.

"I'm losing it," she whispered, voice barely audible. She pulled her knees up to her chest and wrapped her arms around them, rocking gently like a frightened child.

The past weeks felt like a war she was losing. Between the shadows in her mind and the silence from those she loved, Emily was drowning.

She wanted to scream, to cry out for help, but the words caught in her throat. All she could do was sit there, trapped in a storm of memories and fears, waiting for something — anything — to break through the darkness. But the darkness was here to stay.

Chapter Thirty-Four

Static

The world outside had shifted — spring was trying to wake up, birds tentatively chirping in the early mornings, and the light stretching its stay each evening — but Emily stayed in the dark.

Her bedroom had become a cocoon.

The blinds were always drawn. Dust had gathered along the windowsill, grey and soft, like the fog inside her chest. Her bedsheets smelled faintly of sweat and something stale. She hadn't changed them in over two weeks. Maybe three. Time didn't move the same anymore — it melted together, days dissolving into one another like sugar left too long in a mug of tea.

She hadn't showered in five days. She'd meant to. She'd stood in the bathroom doorway once, hand on the light switch, staring blankly at the folded towel on the radiator. But something stopped her. The energy it took to pull her clothes off, to face the mirror, to stand upright under the water — it felt impossible.

Instead, she slid back under the duvet, her body still wrapped in the oversized T-shirt she'd been sleeping in. Her scalp itched. Her stomach twisted with hunger, but not for anything that required effort. Cold cereal straight from the box. Half a packet of digestive biscuits. The crust from an old sandwich she'd left on the nightstand.

Her room was a mess — old mugs stacked on the bedside table, bin overflowing, clothes crumpled on the floor and half a jar of jam.

Sara had knocked on her door yesterday. Emily hadn't answered at first. She'd stayed still, listening to the knock, the pause, then the familiar voice muffled through the wood.

"Em, it's me. I'm… I'm just checking in. Can you let me know you're okay?"

A pause.

"I also need to talk to you about the rent. I hate to even bring it up, but you're over a week late now."

Emily had closed her eyes, guilt pressing like a stone against her chest. She didn't reply. Eventually, she heard Sara sigh and walk away.

Now, today, the flat was completely silent except for the occasional creak of pipes. Emily lay flat on her back, staring at the ceiling. The paint above her bed was chipped slightly — she could see the faint outline of a crack snaking toward the light fixture. She counted the bumps in the texture. Made patterns out of them. Anything to stay anchored.

Her phone buzzed on the nightstand. She ignored it.

Then it buzzed again.

Daz.

She already knew it was him without looking. He still came around, still brought food — takeout containers, bags of groceries she mostly didn't touch. He'd text every few hours with a mixture of concern and helplessness.

"Please just talk to me."

"I'm worried about you."

"I don't know what to do anymore."

Sometimes she answered. Sometimes she didn't. When she did, her replies were short. Blunt. Nothing like how they used to be.

She couldn't explain it — the dull, gnawing disconnection growing between them. It wasn't that she didn't care. She did. But even his voice, once her comfort, now felt like another obligation. Another thing she was failing at.

Her phone buzzed again. A long message this time. She blinked, then slowly reached for it.

Daz:
I miss you. I don't know what's happening anymore. I feel like you're slipping away and I don't know how to stop it. You don't have to explain anything, just tell me what you need. I'm here. But I'm scared, Em. Really scared.

Emily read the message twice before locking her phone and tossing it facedown on the floor.

She didn't cry. She hadn't cried in days. It was as if the sadness had dried up and left only numbness in its place.

Her stomach growled. She ignored it.

A knock came again — softer this time, more tentative. Sara.

"Emily?" she called, not quite pressing her voice above the threshold of politeness. "Can I come in?"

Emily didn't move.

The door opened anyway.

She braced for anger — for a lecture or pleading — but Sara's face just looked tired. She hovered in the doorway, arms crossed tightly over her jumper, trying not to look at the mess.

"I'm sorry," Emily whispered hoarsely, not quite meeting her eyes.

Sara stepped inside, inching closer. "You haven't been yourself for a while now."

Emily stayed quiet.

Sara glanced at the half-eaten food on the bedside table, the unwashed mugs. "I'm worried," she said softly. "And I get that you're going through something. But your rent's overdue. We have bills to pay."

"I'll get it," Emily murmured, though even she didn't believe the words.

"You've said that," Sara replied gently. "I'm not trying to pressure you, but you've stopped working, and… I don't know what your plan is."

There was no plan. There was just… this.

Sara didn't wait for an answer. She gave a faint, tired smile. "You don't have to talk now. Just… think about what you want, yeah? And maybe open a window."

She left, closing the door behind her. Emily lay still, shame burning hot beneath her skin.

She hated herself for letting things get this bad. Hated that Sara, of all people — kind, practical Sara — had to see her like this. And Daz… She didn't even know what they were anymore.

There were moments — brief flickers — when she thought about telling someone everything. About her dad. About what he said. About the way the air in that house had clung to her like poison. About Cynthia's voice in her head, echoing warning after warning. About Louise, and the guilt curling like a vine in her gut.

About how scared she was to learn what she already suspected about Daz.

But every time the thought rose, so did the fear. The fear of tipping over completely, of being swallowed by it all.

So she stayed in bed.

And then it hit her — not with force, but with a creeping, cold certainty.

This was her mother's room. Not literally, of course. But the scene. The silence. The stillness. The closed blinds. The smell. The way she hadn't really stepped outside in days, the way Sara had begun knocking instead of speaking. The way Daz had stopped trying to pull her out and started tiptoeing around her like she was made of glass.

Just like when they were kids and used to tiptoe around Mum.

Emily blinked. Her throat tightened.

She remembered standing in the hallway as a child, clutching her cereal bowl, watching the door to her parents' room like it was a portal to another world. Waiting for it to open. Waiting to see her mother walk out like a normal person, like other mums did. But most days, it never opened. Not until evening. Not unless someone else opened it.

And when it did, there'd be the darkness, the smell of wine and something gone off, the blanket dragged across the bed and into the corner.

Emily glanced down at her own blanket — how it had fallen off the bed, how the sheets were tangled, how her phone sat screen-down with unanswered messages.

She was her mother.

Or at least… she was closer than she ever meant to be.

Her heart pounded, slow and sick.

She turned away from the window, pulled the duvet over her head like she had as a child, and wished she could disappear. Not forever. Just long enough to not feel like this.

Time passed in long, shapeless stretches. She dozed off and woke up again. Ate a few crackers. Checked her phone. Left it alone.

By the time the sky began to darken, she still hadn't moved from the bed.

The flat filled with shadows, and Emily curled onto her side, pulling the duvet tighter around her.

She didn't want to be this way. But she didn't know how to stop.

Chapter Thirty-Five

Confession

Emily hadn't showered in days. Maybe a week. The mirror was too foggy to see herself clearly, and that felt like a mercy. But today… Today, something stirred.

It wasn't hope, more like an obligation. She had told Cynthia she would meet her. That had to mean something. She stood under the stream of water for longer than necessary, letting it scald her skin. The sensation grounded her—sharp, real, undeniable.

The flat was quiet. Sara had left for work hours ago. Emily wandered barefoot back to her room. Dishes piled from days of half-hearted attempts at meals glared at her like little failures. She took them to the kitchen and washed them slowly, the warm water almost comforting against her fingers. The clatter of plates and the rhythmic sound of the tap filled the silence. Normal sounds. Human sounds.

She dressed carefully—not for anyone else, but for herself. Clean black jeans. A soft cream jumper she hadn't worn in months. She braided her hair and wiped off the smudges around her eyes. Her reflection looked pale and drawn, but alive.

Meeting Cynthia felt like something between a test and torture. She was already seated when Emily arrived at the café—a quiet spot tucked off a side street near Kentish Town. Cynthia had always liked corners and back walls, places with views of exits. She hadn't changed much, but there was something hard in her eyes today.

"You look like shit" Cynthia said.

Emily sat across from her. "Trying."

They made small talk, for a while. The kind that brushes the surface of things without ever dipping beneath. Work. Weather. The odd comment about their mum. It was forced, but civil. The kind of strained truce that only sisters could manage.

She didn't say that she didn't have work anymore. That she hadn't been outside in nearly a week. Or that her arms ached from lack of movement, her skin pale and clammy from days under blankets. Cynthia didn't know about Louise. Or their dad. And Emily wasn't planning on telling her. Not yet.

But Emily could feel the shift. The moment where the conversation teetered from casual to loaded.

The café Cynthia picked was quiet, tucked between a dry cleaner and a boarded-up betting shop. The chairs wobbled. The lighting buzzed. It felt private, though. Hidden. That suited Emily just fine.

Cynthia leaned in. "You remember that lad we talked about a while ago? Jamie?"

Emily stiffened. "The one who died?"

"Yeah. The one from the photo."

Emily nodded. "I remember."

"His brother…" Cynthia's expression darkened. "He was in the park that night you got assaulted."

Emily's stomach tightened.

"People talk.." Cynthia shrugged.

"I told you there were rumours about who stabbed Jamie," Cynthia continued. "That people whispered Daz's name. You didn't say much then. And I wasn't sure either."

Emily swallowed but said nothing.

"But I did more digging," Cynthia said. Her voice dropped lower, almost conspiratorial. "Talked to a girl who knew him. Jamie had started talking. Not just about his brother. About what happened in the park. But about Daz. Laughing. Running his mouth about what Daz would or wouldn't do."

"Running his mouth," Emily echoed softly.

Cynthia nodded. "He was careless. He didn't think anything would happen to him. And Daz… he didn't forgive things like that."

Emily's throat felt raw. "You think Daz killed him because of me?"

Cynthia didn't flinch. "I don't think it, Em. I know it."

Emily blinked. "You said there were rumours—"

"There were. But now I've spoken to someone who was there. Not during the stabbing, but that night. Jamie got in Daz's face at a party. Said some things. Made a scene. Daz left. Jamie never made it home."

Silence stretched.

Cynthia looked directly at her. "You should ask him."

Emily stared at the table. "I don't want to know."

"You already know," Cynthia said gently. "You just don't want it confirmed."

The breath in Emily's lungs felt tight. Trapped.

"He protected me that night," she whispered.

"He may have..," Cynthia said. "But he also avenged you."

Emily closed her eyes. Images blurred in her mind. The park. The screams. Daz stepping in to help her. The way he'd held her afterward. The silence between them in the days that followed.

"He never told me," she said.

"Of course not. Because then you'd see him for what he really is."

"He couldn't have done that."

Cynthia's face softened, but her words were sharp. "He made himself look like safety. But he's just dangerous. Just like the rest of them."

Emily stood abruptly. Her chair scraped across the floor.

"I need to go."

Cynthia didn't stop her. Just nodded. "Ask him, Em. Before you lose yourself completely."

Outside, the air was cold and harsh. Emily's fingers shook as she fumbled for her keys. Every step home felt like it echoed. Like the ground had shifted beneath her feet.

She didn't know what Daz would say. She didn't know if she wanted to hear it.

But one thing was painfully clear: She needed the truth.

Chapter Thirty-Six

Weight

The kettle clicked off, but Emily didn't move. She stood in the kitchen, hands wrapped around a cold mug she hadn't filled, her thoughts louder than any noise the flat could make.

The windows were steamed slightly, a contrast to the chilled tension in the room. Rain tapped at the glass— soft but persistent, like a thought you couldn't quite shake. The same way her heart felt, thudding a little too hard, a little too off-beat, as though it was trying to speak for her, to beg her to stop thinking.

She'd actually managed to shower that morning. That had felt like something. She'd stood under the hot water for too long, letting it sting her skin as though punishment would bring clarity. She'd even put on some clean clothes and thrown away the moulding bowl of noodles by the side of her bed.

She was climbing. Slowly, awkwardly, but climbing out of the pit that had almost swallowed her. But now this.

Cynthia's voice replayed in her head on a loop. *"You already know," "You just don't want it confirmed."*

The words were more than a revelation. They were an indictment. A judgment. A hand around the neck of something she'd thought was pure.

The room was still.

She reached for her phone, unlocking it instinctively even though she wasn't sure what she was doing. Unread notifications. Missed calls. She tapped to open her texts and hovered over Daz's name.

Her thumb shook.

She put the phone down again. Her head spun. She braced herself on the countertop, eyes squeezed shut.

It had taken so much effort to get this far. To sit upright. To eat something with substance. To clean her hair. And now, everything in her body felt like it was threatening to curl back into itself. Every cell screamed for escape.

It can't be true.

But it was. She knew it in her gut. Maybe she had always known. Not in words. Not in facts. But in the way he had sometimes looked away when she talked about the past. In how angry he got when he thought about what had been done to her.

In the way his eyes seemed to change when she told him, trembling, that she'd gone back to the house. To her father.

That same stillness. That same simmering.

Emily walked back to the living room and sat down on the edge of the sofa, legs tucked beneath her. She picked at the thread on her sleeve. Her jumper was too big now, hanging awkwardly over her shrinking frame. She could feel the way her ribs pressed against her skin.

She hated how familiar that felt. The shape of her body like this. The hollowness of being.

She felt the panic start to swell, but she shut it down with a long breath. Not now. She'd come too far to go back to that.

Her fingers closed around her phone again.

Emily: *Can you come over? I need to talk to you.*

She stared at the message. No softness. She didn't want to make it easy for him.

She hit send.

The reply was instant.

Daz: *Course. Be there soon x*

The kiss at the end made her sick. How many times had she found comfort in his presence? In his hands? His smile? How many times had she called him safety?

What did that make her now?

What kind of person loves someone who's taken a life?

She stood up again and moved through the flat. She opened the windows slightly, letting in the cold spring air. She lit the candle on the windowsill—lavender and sandalwood, the one Sara always said made the flat feel like a spa. It didn't help now.

She walked back to her room and looked around. It was cleaner than it had been in weeks. But still, she saw the shadows. The echoes of who she'd been in her darkest days clung to the corners. The dust in the creases. The memories in the fabric of the duvet.

She sat back down in the living room, arms wrapped around her knees, and waited.

The knock at the door was light, familiar.

She didn't answer right away. Her heart galloped against her ribs. She didn't know what she would say. Didn't know how even to look him in the eye.

The knock came again.

She dragged herself up and opened the door slowly.

Daz stood there, in a hoodie and his worn jeans, the ones with the stain on the thigh. He smiled when he saw her, but it faded quickly.

"You okay?" he asked, stepping in.

She nodded but didn't speak.

He pulled her into a hug automatically, but she didn't return it.

He noticed.

"What's wrong?"

She walked to the sofa and sat. "Close the door."

The door closed behind him with a soft clunk that felt far too ordinary for what Emily was about to do.

Daz gave her that soft half-smile she used to feel in her chest.

"Smells better in here," he said, nodding toward the flickering lavender candle.

Emily didn't smile back.

She just sat, arms crossed, her whole body tense as if holding itself together through sheer will.

Daz noticed.

"You okay?" he asked, taking a cautious step forward. "You look… different."

She looked different because she'd spent an hour forcing herself to. Brushed hair. Clean clothes. Makeup that tried to hide the bruising fatigue under her eyes. All of it a mask. A costume. A shield.

"I need to talk to you," she said quietly.

He stilled. "Alright. What's going on?"

She stood again. She couldn't sit. Sitting would feel too human, too casual. Her heart was already thudding so loudly she thought it might break her ribs.

"You remember Jamie?" she asked.

Daz blinked. "Jamie… yeah. Why?"

Her eyes never left his face.

"Jamie, the boy a year below me. His brother—one of the men who grabbed me in the park that night years ago. You remember?"

He nodded slowly. "Yeah, I remember."

"He's dead."

Another nod. Cautious now.

"I know," he said, voice barely above a whisper.

She took a step forward, arms still crossed. "You killed him."

There. She said it. Threw it into the air between them like a lit match.

Daz didn't react. Not immediately. His jaw tightened. His eyes dropped to the floor, then rose again.

He didn't deny it.

"You were both kids," she said. "He ran his mouth. Laughed about what happened. And you snapped."

Silence.

She stepped even closer. "I want you to say it. I want to hear it."

His voice was hoarse when it came. "Yeah. I killed him."

The room went quiet. Even the street outside seemed to still. All Emily could hear was the buzz of electricity in the walls and the slow, awful crumbling of the image she had carried of him for so long.

"I thought I was doing the right thing," Daz said after a moment. "He was laughing, Em. Like it was nothing. Like *you* were nothing."

She winced.

He went on, voice cracking with every word. "I couldn't let it slide. Not after what they did. I had all that anger and guilt and nowhere to put it. I wasn't thinking straight. I just... I lost it."

Emily shook her head, eyes filling with tears she refused to let fall.

"You thought it was justice," she said bitterly. "But it wasn't. It was revenge. You didn't do it for me. You did it to make yourself feel powerful again. To erase your own helplessness."

His hands were clenched now. "You don't know what it felt like—seeing you like that. Hearing what they said. I needed to protect you."

"So you killed a boy."

"He wasn't innocent."

"Neither were you," she snapped.

They stared at each other, the air between them thick and bitter.

"You think what they did to me was unforgivable," she said, voice trembling. "But what you did... is the same. You took something. You ended someone's life. Maybe he deserved consequences, but not like that. Not from you. Not like that."

Daz's face fell. "I couldn't live with letting it go."

"And I can't live with what you did."

He froze. The words hit him like a punch to the chest.

"You don't mean that."

"I do." Her voice broke. "I *have* to. Because if I don't—if I keep letting people do awful things and then call it love—I'll never get out."

His eyes were glossy now. Red.

"We've been through everything," he said. "We got through the past. I've always been here."

"I know," she whispered. "And I loved you for it. But now I see who you really are. What you're capable of."

"Em—"

"No." Her voice was final. "I'm not saying it didn't come from pain. I'm not saying you're evil. But I can't be with someone who sees murder as a solution. Who makes choices like that and keeps them hidden from me."

"I did it for *you*—"

"Don't." Her tears were coming now, sliding hot down her cheeks. "Don't put that on me. That blood isn't mine to carry."

He looked like he'd been shot. Like she'd reached into his chest and pulled something out.

"I love you," he said desperately.

She nodded. "I know. I love you too. But love isn't enough."

There was nothing left to say.

Daz backed away slowly. Turned toward the door like a man underwater. Before he left, he looked back once more—eyes full of pain, lips parted like he might beg.

But he didn't.

The door shut.

Emily crumpled to the floor, hands shaking. Her sobs came in waves, crashing against her ribs like breakers on a jagged shore.

She had finally broken free of everything.

And it felt like dying.

Chapter Thirty-Seven

Pressure

The office was quiet. Not the uncomfortable kind of quiet that hovered in her family home or followed an argument—but a soft, padded kind of silence. Like the room itself was breathing slowly, calmly, waiting.

Emily sat curled in the armchair across from the therapist. Her hands were locked tightly together, fingers white at the knuckles. The chair was surprisingly deep—too deep, maybe. She felt small in it, like a child swallowed by cushions, knees tucked up slightly, one foot brushing the floor.

Outside the window, the trees were barely swaying. A cloudy sky pressed down on the street.

She had been here twice before, once a week, said nothing much either time. Polite nods. Safe comments. An old story about stress at work. A hint of her breakup. Nothing real.

But today… she had come with something different.

The therapist—a woman named Jo, gentle-voiced and patient-eyed—waited quietly, a notebook open on her lap, pen in hand but not moving.

Emily stared at the tissue in her hand. She hadn't cried yet. But she could feel the pressure behind her eyes, like something was gathering. Like a dam was about to split.

"I don't know where to start," she said finally.

Jo nodded. "Anywhere you want to. There's no wrong place."

Emily took a breath.

Then another.

Then—

"My mum left when I was thirteen," Emily said finally. Her voice was flat. Factual. Like reading a weather report. "She just didn't come back."

Jo nodded. Said nothing.

"She was drunk most of the time anyway. Always shouting. Throwing stuff. Calling us names. But it was better than nothing."

Another pause.

"Then it *was* nothing."

Jo still didn't interrupt. That, somehow, made it easier to keep going.

"My dad… he was barely around. When he was, we wished he wasn't. We raised ourselves. No one came to check on us. No one helped."

Her hands twisted the tissue in her lap until it shredded.

"One night he lit all my sister's things on fire. Cynthia. And then she disappeared the next morning."

It wouldn't stop now, it just kept coming.

"He chased me with a sharp tool. I think it was a weeder or something. I just kept running."

Jo finally spoke, her voice low and even. "That must've been terrifying."

Emily shrugged. But her shoulders trembled.

"It was worse after that. Because I knew anyone could disappear. And no one would stop them."

Another silence. A deep breath.

"Even Thomas."

Jo tilted her head slightly. "Thomas?"

Emily blinked quickly. Swallowed.

"He made me feel like I mattered. For a while. I let him in. I let him… I thought it meant something. But when it was over, he was just *gone*."

She wiped at her face. The tears had snuck up on her.

"I said yes. So it's not like he hurt me. But I didn't want it like that. Not really. I just didn't know how to say no. Not after everything."

Jo's voice was gentle. "Giving consent when you feel you have no choice, when you feel it's the only way to be loved... that's not true consent."

Emily stared down at her lap.

"I guess... I just keep losing people. Everyone I care about."

"That's a deep wound," Jo said softly. "To be left again and again. Especially when you're still a child. It teaches you that you're not worth staying for. That love means vanishing."

Emily nodded, tears now steady.

"I'm tired," she whispered. "I'm so tired of being left. Of pretending it doesn't matter. Of carrying all this like it's normal."

"It's not normal," Jo said. "But you've survived it. That's not weakness. That's strength."

Emily didn't feel strong. She felt empty.

But maybe this was the beginning.

Maybe saying it—putting it into the air—was how you started to let it go.

She didn't know what came next. Healing, maybe. Or at least a little less hiding.

But for the first time, she'd told the truth.

And someone had stayed to hear it.

Chapter Thirty-Eight

Decline

The house was quiet.

Daz sat in the living room, one shoe off, one still laced up, staring at the blank screen of the TV like it might flicker to life and tell him what to do. The bottle in his hand was half-empty. Not his first of the night. Probably not his last.

It was 3 a.m. He hadn't slept. Again.

The silence used to mean peace. When he'd stay at Emily's, silence meant she was in the shower, or curled up in bed reading, or humming to herself in the kitchen while burning toast. Now, the silence sounded like the end of something. Like absence.

He rubbed his face with both hands, rough stubble scraping his palms.

"Fuck."

The word barely left his lips. It fell into the stillness and dissolved.

His phone buzzed once on the coffee table. He didn't pick it up. Probably someone asking if he was coming into work. Or Sara. Or his mates seeing if he was about.

He didn't want to go out.

He wanted Emily.

And she wasn't coming back.

He had seen it in her face that night—when she asked him straight, no tears, no softness. Just that quiet devastation in her eyes.

"Did you kill Jamie?"

He hadn't even answered at first. Didn't need to. The truth was already there between them, thick as smoke.

And when he finally said *yes*, her face shattered.

She'd disappeared from his life with the calm of someone drowning. Silent. Inevitable.

He slammed the bottle onto the table too hard. It wobbled, tipped, then spilled amber liquid across the glass surface. He didn't move to clean it. Just stared at the spreading mess like it had betrayed him.

How had it come to this?

He had done it *for* her. Jamie, that little prick, running his mouth about what happened. Smirking like it was a joke. Like Emily hadn't been broken for weeks after. Like it was some story to pass around.

Daz's jaw clenched.

He remembered the rage. The blinding white heat of it. The way Jamie had laughed. How small he looked once the fear kicked in.

He hadn't meant to kill him. Not at first.

But once it started… there was no turning back.

And now? Now he was the monster. The same kind of person who'd hurt her.

She was right. She had every right to end things.

But it didn't stop the ache. The emptiness. The *grief*.

He stood abruptly and kicked the overturned chair hard enough to crack the leg. His breath came fast now, erratic. His chest tight. He paced the room like a caged animal.

His vision blurred.

He picked up the hoodie she'd worn last time she came over. Held it close to his face. Inhaled.

It wrecked him.

She had been his whole world. The one thing he had ever done right. The one thing he protected—fiercely, always.

But now, she was healing. Without him.

He should have been happy about that.

Instead, it made him feel like a corpse.

He dropped onto the couch again, hoodie in hand. A tear slipped down his cheek, and he didn't bother to wipe it.

Maybe this was justice.

Maybe this was what it felt like to face who he was finally.

Not a protector.

Not a hero.

Just another broken boy who grew into a dangerous man.

He thought of his mum—how she used to cry in the bathroom with the door locked, bruises blooming on her arms. He had sworn he'd never be like the men who caused that. Sworn he'd be better.

But here he was.

Staring down the barrel of everything he promised never to become.

He took another swig from the bottle and let the burn remind him he was still here. Still breathing. Still broken.

The house was the same, cared for by his nan—a stark contrast to himself, greasy and smelling of smoke, sweat, and regret.

He hadn't eaten a proper meal in days. His Nan had offered him home-cooked meals, but he'd declined each time. His voicemail was full. His work had stopped calling after the third no-show.

He didn't care.

Without her, none of it meant anything.

The front door rattled once—probably wind—and for half a second, his heart leapt. He looked up, desperate, like a man waiting for a miracle.

But no one came.

Of course they didn't.

He was alone now, and he couldn't help but think it was what he deserved.

Chapter Thirty-Nine

History

Daz used to believe pain was just part of life.

He grew up in a house where the walls felt too thin for all the noise. The kind of place where Sunday dinners could turn to screaming matches before dessert. Where his mum would lock herself in the bathroom and turn on the taps to drown out her crying. Where laughter, when it came, was either too loud or too brief—an interruption rather than a presence.

His earliest memory was of hiding in the airing cupboard, the warm towels around him muffling the sounds of his dad throwing something heavy in the kitchen. Plates, probably. Or a chair. He remembered the sound of his mum's voice, high and cracking, begging. Not arguing. Not fighting back. Just begging.

"Please don't—"

Crash.

He was maybe four or five. And even then, he knew to stay hidden until it went quiet.

When his dad left—stormed out one night and never came back—it wasn't the relief people imagined. It was emptier than that. Like someone had vacuumed the whole house and left nothing but tension in the air. His mum didn't speak for days. Then she cried. Then she drank. Then she cried again.

By nine, Daz had started cleaning up after her. Making toast for dinner when she forgot to cook. Making excuses when she didn't show up to parents' evenings. Helping her into bed when she slurred her words and told him she loved him more than anything in the world, even if he didn't always believe it.

She had good days. Funny days, even. Sometimes they danced around the living room to old music, or watched cheesy soaps and took the piss out of the characters. He clung to those days like rope.

But mostly, it was him and the silence. Him and the fear.

By the time he hit secondary school, he already knew how to lie without blinking. Teachers praised his politeness, his quietness. He flew under the radar. Didn't bring attention to himself. Never brought friends home.

It was around then he started feeling the heat behind his ribs. A burning he couldn't explain. It showed up in stupid ways—punching the wall when he failed a test. Storming out of a classroom when someone made a joke about his clothes smelling like damp. He hated the way it felt, but also how alive it made him. Like he wasn't invisible anymore.

At sixteen, he met Chloe. She had chipped nail polish and a laugh that made everything feel okay. She called him sweet, which made him feel both proud and embarrassed. She didn't ask about his home. She just held his hand and kissed him behind the science block and talked about leaving London someday. About seeing the sea.

He didn't believe it, not really. But he liked how certain she was.

It happened outside a corner shop.

Some older lad—Connor —started with words. Called Chloe names. Grabbed at her arm.

"Just ignore him," she said, brushing it off.

But Daz couldn't.

Something surged in him. Like a switch flipped.

He stepped in front of her.

"Back off."

Connor laughed. Said something crude.

Then Daz snapped.

He didn't remember the first punch. Just the feeling of his fist connecting. The sting in his knuckles. The sound of Connor hitting the pavement. Chloe screaming his name. People shouting. Someone pulling him back.

He'd broken Connors' nose. Maybe his cheekbone. Blood everywhere. Daz had a busted lip and hands that wouldn't stop shaking.

He threw up in the alley ten minutes later.

Couldn't sleep that night. Every time he closed his eyes, he saw Chloe's face. Shocked. Scared. Not of Connor.

Of him.

She didn't answer his messages after that.

He told himself he'd done the right thing. Protected her. Done what no one ever did for his mum.

But the guilt didn't go away. Not then. Not ever.

It lingered. Twisting around his heart like barbed wire.

Still, part of him held onto that moment. Because for once, he hadn't been helpless. For once, he'd *done something*.

That belief—the one that violence could be righteous—stuck with him longer than it should have. It felt like justice in the moment.

But it always ended the same way.

With silence.

And shame.

And someone else walking away.

Chapter Forty

Crossings

Daz wasn't supposed to be there that night. He hadn't planned on anything. Just walking. Restless. That kind of pacing, that kind of silence, when your brain won't turn off and the streetlight feels like your only company. He'd spent the better part of that week crashing on someone else's sofa, drifting through familiar estates and dimly lit corners of North London like a shadow people forgot. But when he saw her — Emily — running from her father's house like the whole building was on fire, everything stilled.

He didn't call her name. He didn't make a sound. Just followed, careful as a ghost. Watched her duck into the alleyways and swerve around corners. Her shoulders were heaving. She thought she was alone when she finally stopped at a bench.

And then they came. Four lads, not much older than him, one of them already loud with the stink of beer. The kind of swagger Daz recognised. False confidence. Cheap cologne and worse ideas.

One of them said something about warming her up.

Emily straightened up, tried to push past. Another grabbed her wrist.

Daz saw red. Not the blinding kind. The cold kind. Sharp. Focused. He moved.

"Let her go."

The lads turned. Saw him. He wasn't big, but he looked unafraid. That mattered.

"Or what?" one of them sneered.

Daz didn't speak. He just pulled the knife from his jacket. Not waving it, not threatening. Just showing it. Like a fact.

"Jesus, man, relax. We were just messin'."

They backed off. Fast. One called him a freak. Another spat near his feet. But they left. Daz waited until their footsteps disappeared into the city hum.

Emily hadn't moved.

"Are you alright?"

She nodded, then shook her head, eyes wide and vacant. Shock.

He stepped closer. "Come on. You're not stayin' out here."

The hostel was shit. Thin walls, thicker smells. But it was warm. And the receptionist knew Daz. Gave him a room without question.

Emily sat on the bed, her arms wrapped around her knees. He handed her a bottle of water from the vending machine. She took it but didn't drink.

He didn't ask what had happened with her dad. Didn't need to.

He sat beside her, not touching. Just being.

"Stay?" she said.

He nodded. Kicked off his trainers and lay back, fully clothed. She followed, curling up next to him, her head resting on his chest. His heart thundered. Not because of lust. But because she trusted him.

They didn't speak. Not really. She sniffled once. He breathed slow and even.

When he woke in the grey dawn, she was sitting up, staring at the wall. They didn't say much. Just exchanged a glance, something tired and soft. She left. He let her.

Months passed. They slipped back into old rhythms. Friends, mostly. Or that's what she thought. That's what he let her believe. Because it was easier. Because the minute he admitted it, he would lose something.

Jamie had always been around the edges. Younger. Slicker. Richer. One of those kids whose mum packed carrot sticks and gave them therapy when their cat died. But he liked the look of Emily. Always had.

And Daz had seen it.

The way Jamie watched her in group conversations. The extra beat he let his eyes linger when she laughed. The way he tried to insert himself next to her at every house party or park gathering. Emily never saw it. Or maybe she did and pretended not to.

Jamie was harmless, Daz told himself. Annoying. But not a threat.

Until the party.

It was a flat in Archway. Someone's older brother was gone for the weekend. Daz didn't want to go, but he did. Too much time alone and the walls started breathing.

He saw Jamie near the kitchen, drink in hand, arms wide, voice too loud, holding court with a couple of other lads. They were laughing. Not with him. At him. The way they always did when someone tried too hard.

"I swear down," Jamie was saying. "They said she was on her knees. Begging. Said she was moaning. If it weren't for that freak, whatshisname — the psycho with the knife — she'd have taken all four of 'em."

Daz stopped breathing.

"Fucking joke, man," Jamie laughed. "She looked like she loved it. Probably still thinks about it."

Someone made a face. "You serious? That girl's messed up."

Jamie shrugged. "Doesn't matter. I'd still do her."

Daz didn't remember putting down his drink. Didn't remember moving through the bodies or out the front door. The cold outside bit his skin. He waited. Leaned against the wall of the corner shop across the road. Lit a cigarette with shaking hands.

Twenty minutes later, Jamie stumbled out, alone.

The walk to the canal was silent.

Daz followed at a distance, boots soft on the wet pavement. Jamie had his phone out. Didn't look back once. When he cut across the footbridge by the warehouses, Daz knew it would happen there.

It was quiet. No cameras. No people.

Jamie leaned on the railing, scrolling.

"Oi."

He turned. Squinted. "Daz? What the fuck do you want?"

Daz said nothing.

Jamie chuckled. Nervous now. "You been followin' me? Jesus. What is it with you, man? You got some obsession?"

Daz walked closer.

"She told them to leave her alone," he said.

Jamie frowned. "What?"

"Emily. That night. You laughed about it. Said she wanted it."

Jamie straightened up. "Mate, it was a joke. You can't seriously be this pressed over banter. Come on. Grow up."

"You said she begged."

"I didn't touch her! It wasn't even me! I wasn't there, alright? I just heard stories. Jesus, are you actually mental?"

Daz reached into his jacket.

Jamie backed up, tripped against the rail.

"Woah, woah! You gonna stab me for what? For words? You're a fucking psycho. She doesn't even like you. She talks to me more than she talks to you."

Daz's hand closed around the knife.

"You don't get to talk about her."

Jamie's face changed. Not scared. Not yet. But close.

"You think this makes you the hero? You think this makes you a good man?"

Daz lunged.

It wasn't graceful. It wasn't clean. The first stab caught Jamie in the ribs. He screamed. The second went lower. Panic. Struggle. Jamie clawed at him, blood already soaking through his hoodie.

Daz pinned him. Held him against the railing as he drove the knife in again.

"She trusted me," he said, voice shaking.

Jamie tried to speak. Blood bubbled from his mouth. His body sagged.

It was done.

Daz stumbled back. Dropped the knife into the water. His hands were shaking. His breath came fast. He wanted to vomit, but couldn't.

He walked. Didn't run.

Back in his flat, the silence screamed. He scrubbed his hands until they were raw. Looked at himself in the mirror.

He saw the boy who had held Emily that night. The boy who hadn't wanted to scare her. Who had stayed because she asked him to. Who hadn't crossed a line.

He told himself Jamie crossed the line.

He told himself he was still a good man.

Emily had been the last piece. The last fragile thing worth saving.

And Daz had tried. God, he had tried.

But even good men break.

And when they do, they bleed justice.

Chapter Forty-One

Lost

Daz stood at the bottom of the concrete steps, staring up at Emily's flat like it was a fortress. The air had bite to it, damp from earlier rain, and the sky was low and grey. The windows were closed. Curtains drawn. No sign of her.

He swallowed, hands in his jacket pockets. His fingers were numb. Or maybe it was just everything else that felt frozen.

He climbed the steps slowly, trying not to think about the last time he stood there. When he still had her.

The knock echoed too loud on the door. Once. Then again.

Footsteps approached on the other side. And then—Sara. She opened it a crack and stepped into the doorway, pulling the door shut behind her.

Her expression was hard. Not angry, exactly—just… protective.

"She doesn't want to see you," she said.

Daz's mouth opened, but nothing came out at first.

"Please," he finally managed. "I just want to talk to her."

"I know," Sara said. "But it's not happening. She's… she's doing better, Daz. You need to let her have that."

"Better?" His voice caught.

"She was a mess, yeah. For a while." Daz looked past her shoulder instinctively, toward the silent door.

"She's not that person anymore," Sara went on. "She's getting stronger. She's sleeping. Seeing people again. Talking to someone professionally. She even came out with me, once or twice."

He blinked. The burn behind his eyes started to rise.

"I just need to explain."

"No," Sara said sharply.

The word hit him like a brick to the ribs.

"I know you probably didn't mean to hurt her," Sara said, a little softer. "But you did. And if you care about her at all, you'll walk away. Because she's healing. And you… you bring too much with you."

He opened his mouth again. Nothing came out.

"She's doing well," Sara repeated. "And I'm not letting you take that from her."

He stared at her for a long second. Then he nodded, just once. Numb. She shut the door without another word.

He didn't walk back down the stairs. Not right away. He stood there for a long time, just listening. But there was nothing. No footsteps. No voice. Just silence.

The kind that comes after someone's really gone.

The street lights flickered on by the time he reached his Nans. He padded up the stairs. He needed to see her. Not Emily. His mum.

She was in bed, of course. She rarely left it these days. The TV buzzed from the room, tuned to static again.

He knocked softly on her door.

"Mum?"

She didn't look up right away. Then she turned her head, slow and foggy-eyed.

"Darren?" she said.

"Yeah. It's me."

She blinked. He couldn't tell if she recognised him. But she didn't scream or ask who he was, so that was something.

He sat at the edge of the bed. The sheets were tangled, her robe loose around her shoulders. She looked like a bird, hollow-boned and delicate.

"I lost her," he said after a long pause. "Emily."

She blinked again.

"She's not coming back. I know that now."

Her fingers tugged at the edge of the blanket, but her eyes didn't leave his face.

"I did something," he went on. "Something I thought would make it right. But it just ruined everything."

She stared, unblinking. Then, somehow, her hand reached for his. She gripped it tightly.

"I hurt someone, Mum."

The silence sucked the air from the room.

"A boy. Younger than me. A kid really. I thought I was making the world right again. After what they did to her. But I didn't fix anything. I just broke more."

She was quiet for a long time. Then her voice came, strange and clear.

"You were always trying to carry too much."

He stared at her.

"I should've helped you," she murmured. "I should've known."

"You didn't do anything wrong," he whispered.

"You think that makes it better?" she asked, voice trembling. "You think knowing you're broken explains what you did?"

Tears blurred his vision.

"I just wanted her to feel safe again."

"You don't get to give someone peace by handing them someone else's blood."

He closed his eyes. Her voice sounded different. Sharp. Like herself again, for a moment. That rare clarity that surfaced like a gasp of air.

Then she softened. Her hand squeezed his.

"You were just a boy," she said. "And you didn't learn anything except how to survive. But it's not enough anymore. You want to change? Stop surviving. Start *living*."

He let her hold him. Let her rock him the way she did when he was little. His face pressed to her chest. Her thin arms around his shoulders. It was the most real thing he'd felt in days.

But it didn't last.

She stiffened.

Her hands jerked away.

"Who are you?" she snapped. "What are you doing in my room?"

"It's me, Mum. It's Daz."

"Get out!" she cried, wild and frantic. "Get away from me!"

She slapped at him, pushing with trembling arms. He rose quickly, not resisting.

"I'm going—"

"Don't touch me! I said *get out!*"

He backed into the hallway, the door slamming behind him.

In the corridor, he leaned against the wall. His knees weak. His hands shaking.

One moment of warmth.

Then the world took it back.

Just like Emily.

Chapter Forty-Two

From Afar

Daz didn't go back to Emily's flat again. He told himself that was over. He heard Sara's words every time he thought about it—"She's healing"—and something about that lodged deep in his chest like a shard of glass. She was healing. Without him. Because of it. Maybe even despite him.

He didn't deserve to be part of her new world. He knew that now.

But it didn't mean he could forget her.

Not really.

The days passed in a blur of aimless movement. He stopped answering calls. Cut the lads off. Didn't drink as much, not because he didn't want to—because it dulled his focus. And now, that's all he had left. Watching. Waiting. Looking out for her in the shadows like a ghost.

He told himself it was love. Something selfless. A form of protection, even. If he couldn't stand beside her, he could still make sure no one else hurt her. Not like before. Not ever again.

It started with a morning walk.

The first time, he didn't even realise what he was doing. He was just out. Hood up. Hands in pockets. Rain misting down, clinging to his eyelashes. And then he saw her. Stepping out of the building, dressed smartly—black trousers, a navy blouse tucked in at the waist, her curls tied back into something neat and sensible.

She looked… different.

There was light in her. She walked with a kind of quiet intent, a focus he hadn't seen in months. Not since before it all broke open. She even smiled to herself, just a flicker, but it was real.

He stepped back instinctively into the alleyway between buildings and watched her walk. She headed toward the main road, where the buses ran. Her bag slung over one shoulder, a small umbrella folded in her other hand. He stayed on the opposite side of the street. Far enough. Hidden in the crowds. She didn't notice him.

But just before she reached the stop, she paused.

Looked around.

Not like she'd forgotten something.

More like something had brushed her skin—an invisible touch on the back of her neck. She turned in a slow arc, her eyes scanning the street.

Daz froze.

She stared directly across the road. Past him. Through him.

Then, after a few seconds, she shook her head and turned back.

The bus came. She got on.

He stayed where he was, heart thudding.

It became a routine after that.

He told himself he needed to make sure she was okay. That this was closure, not obsession.

She was trying for something new, he could tell. A different job, probably. She came out most mornings dressed like that. Smart. Sharp. She wore lipstick now. And boots with a little heel. She moved like she belonged somewhere again.

He followed her a few times. Always at a distance. Through the streets, to unfamiliar buildings. Office blocks. Community centres. Once, a retail park on the edge of town. She walked into a big glass-fronted building with a confident nod to the receptionist. Sat straight in the waiting area. Her foot tapped the floor lightly—nerves, he could tell—but she smiled when someone came out to greet her.

He felt something break in him, watching that.

Pride. Pain.

It was hard to tell the difference anymore.

She kept looking over her shoulder, though. Not always. But sometimes. Especially when she walked home. She'd turn suddenly, frowning. Slow down, like she was listening. Once she even crossed the street early, avoiding a dark patch of pavement.

She *knew*.

Not about him. Not specifically. But her body knew something wasn't right. That someone was there.

And still, he came back the next day.

Daz told himself this wasn't dangerous. He wasn't a threat. He didn't want to speak to her. Didn't want to touch her. Just… be near. Know she was safe. That she was making it.

But late at night, that voice inside grew quieter. Doubt crept in like rising water.

Was this love?

Or was this another kind of control?

He remembered what she'd said. That he was no different from the ones who hurt her. That revenge wasn't the same as protection.

He'd tried to make it right.

But even now, in the silence of his empty bedroom, the echoes remained. Her voice. Her sobs. Her silence after the truth landed between them.

He hadn't expected to lose her forever.

Not really.

It was Thursday when she finally saw him.

He was careful. Always was. But he'd lingered too long across the road from the café where she sometimes stopped. She was sitting at the window, nursing a coffee and flicking through papers in a folder. Her brow furrowed with concentration, a pen tucked behind her ear.

He leaned against the brick wall across the street, pretending to scroll his phone.

Then she looked up.

Right at him.

No pause this time.

Her eyes locked on his.

His blood turned cold.

For a moment, neither moved. Her face went blank. No surprise. No fear. Just a quiet knowing.

Then, she slowly placed the cup down and stood.

He ducked away immediately, slipping into the side alley.

Didn't run.

Didn't need to.

She wouldn't follow him.

And she didn't.

That night, Daz sat in his mum's old chair, staring at the patterned wallpaper.

His whole body ached with the weight of being unwelcome. Unneeded.

She was living.

She'd spotted him, and she hadn't called out. Hadn't rushed to him. She'd just watched. Calm. Measured. Like she already knew he was there.

He curled his fingers into his palm until the skin went white.

He told himself again and again that this wasn't about control. That he was just watching from afar. Just looking out.

But maybe Emily had been right all along.

Maybe *this*—this need to hover near her, to be close without being known—maybe it was just another kind of taking. Another violation.

He hadn't touched her. But he hadn't let her go, either.

Chapter Forty-Three

Unsaid

The kettle growled, and Andrea fumbled with the mugs, her hands trembling ever so slightly as she carried them to the living room and set them down on the table. Emily stood awkwardly near the doorframe, hands in her coat pockets, eyes scanning the room. The flat was smaller than she remembered it being. Or maybe it had just seemed larger when her mother filled it with storms.

It was cleaner now. Neat, even. Sunlight poured in through freshly wiped windows, softening the room's edges. There were framed pictures on the wall—none from their family, but photographs of hills and lakes, postcards from cities Andrea had never visited. A woman trying to build peace out of stillness.

"Sit down," Andrea said gently, motioning to the small round table.

Emily hesitated, then nodded. She slipped off her coat and hung it over the back of a chair. Andrea poured tea, added sugar the way she remembered Emily liked it, and slid a mug over to her.

They sat in silence for a long moment, with just the clink of teaspoons and the whistle of traffic outside.

"Thanks for inviting me," Emily said eventually.

Andrea nodded. "Thank you for coming."

Another silence.

Emily stared into her tea. "So, what made you decide to try to stop drinking?"

Andrea flinched slightly at the directness. But she didn't avoid the question. Not this time.

"I can't do it anymore. The blackouts, the shame, the mornings I couldn't remember what I'd said or done. I woke up one day and just... knew I was done being someone else's nightmare."

Emily's eyes flicked to her, cautious. "Was that who you were?"

Andrea's voice cracked. "Yes."

Emily looked down. Her fingers traced the rim of the mug.

Andrea went on. "I've started going to meetings. AA. Got a sponsor. It's slow work, but... I haven't had a drink in a while now."

"That's good," Emily said, and to her own surprise, she meant it.

Andrea reached across the table, but didn't touch her. "I know I've got a long way to go, Em. I know I can't fix what I broke. But I want to understand it. If you'll let me."

Emily took a breath. She didn't know if she could. But she was here, wasn't she?

"Why did you leave? That night."

Andrea looked away, her eyes wet. She pulled a tissue from her sleeve, dabbed at her face.

"It wasn't just that night. It was years, Emily. Years of rot and damage and pretending."

She exhaled shakily.

"Your father... he wasn't always distant. Not in the beginning. He was a good Dad. He could be charming. Gentle. But after each pregnancy, he drifted. He was losing pieces of his mind it seemed. The meds help for a little. But when Louise was born, something in him snapped. He wouldn't help or talk, and if I pushed too hard, he'd break things. Doors. Plates. Me."

Emily's stomach twisted. Her fingers clenched around the mug.

"I stayed," Andrea continued. "Because I thought I had to. Because I had no money, no options, and then, three girls who needed me. And I thought... if I just kept the house nice, kept him happy, he'd stop. He'd get better. But it never stopped."

Andrea finally looked at her.

"You girls. You saw things you never should have. Heard things I should've shielded you from. But I was drowning. And the more I drowned, the more I drank."

Emily didn't interrupt.

"And then... then I started to think you hated me. That I was the villain. He was good at twisting it to look that way. Even when I wasn't drinking, the house felt cold. You were angry all the time. Louise locked herself in her room or went out with her friends. Cynthia barely spoke. I started to believe that nothing I did mattered anymore. That I'd already lost you."

She wiped at her eyes again.

"So I left. Not because I didn't love you. But because I thought you'd be better off without me."

Emily swallowed hard. Her voice came low.

"We weren't. You left us with him."

Andrea nodded slowly, as though she already knew. "I know. I know that now."

Emily stood abruptly, pushing the chair back. She paced toward the counter, arms folded tightly across her chest.

"You abandoned us. You abandoned *me*. I was thirteen, Mum. Thirteen! And suddenly, I was cooking dinners, cleaning up smashed bottles, and holding Louise while she screamed in her sleep. And you were *gone*."

Andrea stood, too. She didn't try to come closer.

"I thought about you every single day. But the guilt... it eats you alive, Emily. I convinced myself I couldn't come back because I didn't deserve to."

Emily turned sharply. Her eyes were wet.

"And Louise? Do you think she deserved that? Do you even know where she is now?"

Andrea's face broke. She sank back into her chair like her legs had given way.

"No. I've tried to get in touch with her. I asked around. Checked her old social media. Nothing. She's angry. She doesn't want me anymore."

Emily leaned against the counter, breathing hard. A tear slipped down her cheek.

"You still have two daughters. You still have *me*."

Andrea looked up, her expression devastated and hopeful all at once.

"Do I?"

Emily didn't answer right away. She returned to the table slowly, sitting down again. She stared at her tea.

"I don't know."

Andrea nodded. She didn't argue.

They sat in silence again. This time, it felt less like a wall and more like a bridge slowly forming.

After a while, Andrea said, "I keep a box of letters. Stuff I wrote but never sent. To you, to Louise, even to your dad."

Emily raised an eyebrow.

"You wrote to him?"

"Not kind letters. Just things I needed to say to let go. To stop feeling like a failure for staying."

Emily looked at her mother's face, really looked. The years had etched themselves deep, but there was something softer now. Not weak. Just... tired. Human.

"Can I read them?"

Andrea hesitated, then nodded. "I'll get them."

She disappeared into the bedroom, and Emily sat with the tea cooling in her hands. The flat felt different now. Like the demons were being slowly exorcised.

When Andrea returned, she held a shoebox wrapped in a scarf and carefully set it down between them.

Emily opened the lid.

Dozens of pages. Old envelopes. Scrawled dates. Apologies. Memories. Pleas.

She picked one up and began to read.

The space between them wasn't full of shouting or silence for the first time in years.

It was full of something like possibility.

Chapter Forty-Four

Watchful Silence

Daz learned to be careful. Quieter in his watching. Less obvious. He moved with shadows and stayed behind glass, pillars, parked vans. His footsteps memorised her routine better than she probably had.

Months had passed since she last laid eyes on him. Not since that brief encounter outside the café, when she'd looked up and seen him across the street. He'd vanished before she could stand, retreating like a ghost into a back alley, never to be caught again.

He didn't let it happen twice.

She was getting stronger. He saw it in the way she walked, her chin up, her eyes scanning the world like she had a place in it again. And now, she was posting on social media. Carefully curated squares of her new life, but enough for him to track her without leaving his flat.

It had started slow—photos of coffee, books, sunrises from her balcony.

Then came the job announcement.

"New beginnings 💼✨ Wish me luck!"

She stood in front of a slick, mirrored building in a navy coat and pointed heels that gave her bum a nice shape. Her curls framed her face in soft waves, and her smile looked effortless. Almost proud.

Daz stared at the photo until the screen dimmed.

Insurance. A big firm. Fancy. He could see it when he followed her there. Wide glass doors that whooshed open like something from the future. Men and women in tailored clothes laughing in the foyer. She didn't look out of place among them. She looked like she belonged.

He stood across the street the first few days, pretending to smoke, watching her arrive just before nine. She tapped her access badge, sipped her takeaway coffee, waved to reception. Sometimes she wore lipstick. Sometimes she wore glasses. She always looked good.

It hurt in a way that didn't have a name. A slow kind of ache, like watching a stranger wear someone else's smile.

But still, he followed.

She'd leave work late some days, around seven. He'd watch her duck into the corner shop for oat milk and microwave meals, then catch the bus or train, depending on the time. She'd started wearing headphones again, something she used to avoid.

That unnerved him.

She wasn't being careful anymore.

Didn't she know what kind of world she lived in?

That was what he told himself, anyway. That he wasn't doing this for him. That it wasn't obsession—it was protection. He wasn't watching her life pass without him. He was guarding the perimeter.

She'd never know how close she'd come to danger.

He'd make sure of it.

It was a Friday when he saw her with the man.

He wasn't tall, but he had that polished, charming look—checked shirt, neat beard, leather laptop bag. They met outside a small bar tucked between a closed deli and a second-hand bookstore. Up-market kind of place. Emily was laughing when she arrived. She kissed the man on the cheek.

Daz stopped across the road, out of sight behind a parked Uber. His fists clenched inside his jacket pockets.

They got drinks. Sat close at the window. She leaned in when she talked, her fingers twirling the edge of her glass. The man nodded at all the right moments. He made her laugh again.

It was a date.

It *had* to be.

Something cold settled into Daz's chest. Not rage—not yet—but something that buzzed under the surface, dangerous and sad. She hadn't even known this man a year ago. He didn't know what she'd been through. He hadn't held her when she cried so hard she couldn't breathe. He hadn't cleaned the blood from her knees after that night in the park. He hadn't kept her safe.

But she was smiling at him like she might let him try.

Daz left before they came out. He didn't want to see what came next.

The thought of Emily kept the other parts of his life out of his mind.

His mum was dying.

It had started slowly—hard to even remember when. But now there was nothing to be done. Nothing left of the woman who raised him. Just a corpse wearing her face. He was told to make memories while he could.

Now, the memories were all gone.

Her mind had become a maze of flickering lights, sometimes bright, sometimes lost in darkness. She didn't know who he was half the time. Called him "that man" or "Billy," her brother who'd died thirty years ago. Once she screamed at him and locked herself in the bathroom because she thought he'd come to rob her.

He tried to look after her, to help. But it got worse quickly.

Then came the hospital stay. Then the hospice.

"She's not in pain," the nurse had said gently. "But it won't be long."

Daz sat by her bed, watching her chest rise and fall like a fragile wave. Her skin was thinner now, translucent like paper. Her hands trembled even in sleep. He tried talking to her, telling her stories from their old flat, childhood birthdays, neighbours she used to complain about.

Sometimes her eyes opened, and for a moment she looked at him like she *knew* him.

But those moments passed quickly.

Now, the only thing that kept him upright was Emily.

She didn't know, of course. He couldn't tell her. She didn't want anything from him anymore. Not love. Not grief. Not anything.

But watching her gave him purpose.

He told himself it was the last thing he had to give.

On Tuesday evening, he followed her home from work.

She wore her hair up, with small gold earrings glinting when the streetlights caught them. She stopped at a café, bought a takeaway soup, and sat on a bench to eat while scrolling her phone.

The sky above her was streaked with pink. A warm breeze played with the edge of her scarf.

She didn't look around that night.

Didn't feel him near.

He wondered what she was reading. Whether she still listened to sad music when she walked. Whether she missed him, even a little, in the quiet hours of the night.

Then he reminded himself none of that mattered.

He had made his choices.

She had made hers.

And somewhere, deep beneath all the layers of anger and loss, he was glad she was okay. He could see it in her posture, her smile, the way she tossed her empty soup container in the bin and walked away like she had somewhere to be.

He'd stay behind. He always would.

He'd keep watch.

Keep her safe.

Chapter Forty-Five

Loss

For the first time in what felt like years—maybe ever—Emily felt light.

She had a morning routine now. The good kind. Wake up with the sun, toast with almond butter, the perfect bus that arrived at 8:17 if she timed it right. She dressed in silky blouses and wide-legged trousers that made her feel like someone who could be trusted to manage money and meetings.

She worked on the twelfth floor of a sleek glass building with coffee machines that hissed like dragons and floor-to-ceiling windows that flooded the space with light. The people were surprisingly warm. No one called her "sweetheart" in a demeaning tone or asked invasive questions. They shared recipes. They held open doors. She had friends.

And she was good at what she did.

She liked the order of it—the clear numbers, the timelines, the way everything made sense if you worked through it carefully. There was something comforting in the logic of spreadsheets, in the clean tick of boxes, in problem-solving that didn't involve feelings.

Outside of work, things weren't perfect, but they were steady.

She was still seeing Alex. They weren't serious—God, no—but she liked the way he didn't try to fix her. They went for drinks after work every couple of weeks, sometimes dinner. Once, he brought her a book he thought she'd like. He was kind and grounded and had this calm way about him that made her feel less... jagged.

He didn't push. Didn't pry. And he never reminded her of Daz.

That helped.

Sara was her favourite part of the week. They had grown into something more than flatmates now. They were friends. Real ones. They cooked together, watched trashy TV with face masks on, and even threw a tiny Christmas party in their flat with fairy lights and mulled wine.

Sometimes they talked about the past.

More often, they didn't.

Her mum had been sober for two months.

Emily tried not to get her hopes up. But she had shown up to coffee dates. Texted her just to say "good morning." Even sent her a card on her birthday with the words **"I'm proud of you"** scrawled across the bottom.

It wasn't everything. But it was a start.

It was a Sunday when she saw the post.

She was curled on the sofa with a blanket and a cinnamon bun, scrolling through Facebook while Sara hoovered in the next room. A photo popped up in her feed: Daz's nan—Maureen, she remembered—

posting a black and white image of Daz's mum in her twenties. Big hair, bigger smile. The caption read:

"Rest in peace, my beautiful girl. You were always too bright for this world. The funeral will be held on Friday, 11am, St. Luke's Chapel. All welcome to say goodbye."

Emily froze.

Her thumb hovered over the screen.

There was no mention of Daz. No photo of him. Just the woman she'd met briefly, once or twice— scattered memories of her sitting in a chair with a mug of tea, kind, glazed eyes.

Daz's mum was dead.

A wave of something washed over her. It wasn't grief, not exactly. But it was sadness. For the loss. For the boy who had clung so tightly to his mother's fading mind. For the man who had lost himself somewhere in trying to protect her.

She hadn't thought about him much lately. Not in detail. Not consciously.

Sometimes, she thought she saw him across the street. Or felt someone watching. But the therapist said that was normal after trauma. Sometimes the past echoed like that.

Still, she hadn't tried to find him.

And he hadn't tried to reach her again.

She liked to think they'd made peace that way—by letting go.

But now this.

She put her phone down. Pulled the blanket tighter around her.

Sara came in, dragging the hoover behind her. "Want a cuppa?"

"Yeah. Please."

The decision wasn't instant.

Emily sat with it for a few days. She didn't talk about it. She didn't post anything online. She didn't even look at the comments under the photo.

She wasn't going for him. That much she knew.

She didn't want know if she wanted to see him. Didn't want the past to crack open just as she'd finally sealed it shut.

But still, something in her said: *go*.

Maybe because grief deserves witnesses. Maybe because she remembered how gentle his mother had been, even in confusion. Maybe because she was finally strong enough to look into the past and not fall apart.

Whatever the reason, on Friday morning, she pulled on a long black coat, tied her curls back, and took the bus to St. Luke's Chapel.

She didn't text him. Didn't comment on the post.

She was just there, quiet at the back.

To pay her respects.

Nothing more.

Chapter Forty-Six

Passing Ships

The funeral car was silent except for the engine's hum and the faint clicking of his nan's rosary beads. Daz sat in the backseat, eyes locked on the hearse in front of them, his shoulders squared, his hands trembling in his lap. He didn't cry. Not now. Not yet. There was something about watching his mum's coffin glide down the street in front of him that turned everything inside him to concrete. Heavy. Cold. Still.

His nan sat beside him, her weathered hand clutching a handkerchief with little blue flowers on the corners. She stared out of the window, unmoving, lips pressed thin in a line that had taken decades to form. She hadn't said much since the hospital. Just occasional bursts of emotion: anger, grief, quiet weeping in the middle of the night. Daz had heard her.

He hadn't slept since Tuesday.

The funeral was held in St. Luke's Chapel, a small, faded church nestled between two housing estates. Old bricks, crooked headstones, and a crooked priest with clouded eyes who called his mum "a woman of resilience." He didn't mention the dementia. Didn't mention the years Daz spent spoon-feeding her and calming her screams when she forgot where she was. But maybe that was for the best.

Daz sat in the front row. His back straight. His jaw tight. There were about twenty people. Mostly old friends, a few neighbours, and women from his nan's knitting group. None of them really knew his mum the way she used to be. He was the only one who remembered her laughing while she danced to Tina Turner in the kitchen, or the way she'd trace circles on his back to help him sleep.

He hadn't expected Emily to come. He hadn't even dared to imagine it.

It wasn't until after the service that he saw her.

He was standing outside the church under the crooked wooden cross, trying to light a cigarette that had snapped in his coat pocket. The wind kept whipping the flame out. He was already angry before he saw her.

And then there she was.

She stepped out of the chapel among the others, her coat long and black, curls tied back in a loose bun. She didn't look like someone mourning. She looked... radiant. Healthy. Strong.

His first instinct was to duck away. To disappear before she noticed. But something stronger pulled him forward.

He approached slowly, weaving through the trickle of mourners. She was standing near the old stone wall, looking down at her phone, eyes soft.

"Emily," he said.

She turned.

Her face didn't change. No smile, no frown. Just a stillness that made him feel like he wasn't real.

"Hi," she said.

He scratched at the back of his neck, suddenly unsure of where to look. "Didn't expect to see you here."

"I saw the post your nan made," she said. "I thought I should come. Pay my respects."

He nodded, swallowed hard. "Thanks. That means something."

They stood in silence for a moment. The wind carried the scent of damp grass and old incense. He looked at her again, really looked.

"You look well," he said.

She gave a half-smile. "I've been trying."

He nodded again. Too much nodding. Too many words unspoken. He looked down at his boots.

"I thought I saw you," she said. "A while ago. Maybe a month back. Outside my work."

He froze. Just a fraction of a second, but she caught it.

He shrugged. "Nah. Must've been someone else. I've been... busy."

She didn't push. Just stared at him like she was trying to solve a puzzle.

"You haven't reached out," she said softly. "Not once."

His throat felt tight. "I figured... I didn't have the right. After everything."

"You could've said something. A message. Anything."

He looked up, eyes sharp but tired. "What would I have said? I ruined everything. You were getting better. I didn't want to drag you back into it."

"You didn't ruin everything," she said. "But you did make choices I can't carry."

He nodded again, this time slower. "I know."

More silence. The kind that builds pressure in your chest.

"I still think about you," he admitted.

She didn't reply right away. Just looked at him with something like pity.

"You were the only person who made me feel safe for a long time," she said. "But safety and love aren't the same thing."

He flinched, but nodded.

She looked toward the horizon. "I hope you find peace, Daz. Really. I do."

"You too," he said quietly. "You deserve it."

And then she turned, her heels crunching on gravel as she walked away.

He didn't follow.

Didn't call out.

Just stood there, a man in black, in the shadow of a church, watching the one person he had ever truly loved disappear down the path.

It wasn't hard to let her go, knowing he would be seeing her again soon.

Chapter Forty-Seven

A Plan

The winter had set in properly now. Sharp winds licked the corners of buildings, the skies stayed grey for days, and the trees stood like bare skeletons along the roads. Daz sat in the rusted Vauxhall he hadn't bothered to clean in weeks, condensation blooming on the inside of the windows. His breath fogged up the windscreen as he watched Emily across the street, from a shadowed spot beside a hedge that was overgrown.

She hadn't seen him. Not once. Or maybe she had. Maybe that one time at the funeral, when she tilted her head slightly and said, "I thought I saw you last month," was her way of telling him: I know. I've always known.

He told himself it didn't matter. He wasn't there to hurt her. Just to make sure no one else did.

He watched as she walked up the front steps of that house—her old home. The place where, once upon a time, they had found each other. The door opened, and Louise stood there. They exchanged a few words, and Emily went inside.

Daz leaned his head back against the seat and closed his eyes. His mum had only been gone three weeks. The grief was a constant stone in his stomach, cold and heavy, but oddly empty. There had been no great release when she passed. No moment of peace. Just silence. Like she'd taken all the softness of his life with her.

She'd been slipping for months, her mind fragmenting until she barely knew him. One night, she'd clutched his hand and whispered, "You always protected her, even when I didn't understand."

That was the last real thing she ever said to him.

And now, Emily was the only thing left that made sense. Even from afar.

Forty minutes passed.

Emily reappeared. Her shoulders were hunched, her coat only half-zipped, and her face—even from a distance—was pale, crumpled. She wiped her cheeks as she came down the path.

Daz sat up, muscles coiling tight in his chest.

They'd hurt her again. That was what this was.

He didn't need to be inside to know what happened. He knew the house. He knew the people in it. Her dad had always been the source of rot in that place. Louise—maybe she tried, maybe she didn't. But Emily had come out looking like a broken child.

And Daz couldn't take that. Not again.

As she turned the corner and disappeared, Daz started the car. The engine coughed but eventually gave in. He drove slowly, not after her, not today. Today was for thinking.

His knuckles tightened around the wheel.

He thought about how easy it would be. How quickly he could end the pain. Not Emily's—his. If the world had shown him anything, it was that nothing good stayed for long. His mum, Emily, even the version of himself he liked, the boy who just wanted to make someone feel safe. That boy was long gone.

But there were still ways to make things right.

He pulled into a car park at the edge of the estate down the road and killed the engine. Sat in the quiet. The only sound was the ticking of the engine cooling and the distant barking of a dog.

He took out his phone. Opened Facebook. Searched Emily's name. Her profile picture was bright—a photo of her in a yellow dress at some fancy party. Her smile, real and warm. Her eyes held no fear. That was good. That was what he wanted.

He scrolled down. No mention of today. No sign of tears or sadness. She was good at hiding things. Always had been. He was the only one who could see beneath it. He knew her like that.

He dropped the phone into the passenger seat.

Maybe it was time to remind her who really had her back.

No.

No, not like that.

He wasn't going to chase her. He wasn't going to beg. But he could still keep her safe. That was what he had to do.

Protect her. From them.

He reached into the glovebox, where a folded piece of paper had lived for months. On it something illegible in his mum's scratchy handwriting from their last lucid conversation. He grabbed a pen from the middle console.

He opened the paper now. Just looked at the page in front of him.

Could he? Could he really drag up Emily's past like that? Would she thank him? Would she even speak to him again?

He let the paper fall back.

No. That wasn't the plan. The plan wasn't about talking to her. It was about removing the threat. Making sure that house never made her cry again.

He thought of Louise.

She should have protected Emily too.

Maybe she tried. Maybe she failed.

Didn't matter.

He had a plan.

He repositioned himself and began scribbling frantically on the paper.

He would watch. Wait. And when the time was right, he would make sure her dad couldn't touch her again.

It didn't have to be violence. Not straight away. He could find out things. Gather what he needed. He had time.

He leaned his head back, eyes fixed on the ceiling of the car.

"I'll fix this," he whispered.

Chapter Forty-Eight

The Predator

Daz's mind burned with the image of Emily leaving her father's house in tears. It looped in his head like a scratched record. That broken look in her eyes, the way her shoulders slumped, how she wiped at her face like she was trying to erase whatever had just happened inside. It haunted him.

She'd tried. Again. And whatever was left of her relationship with her father had shattered a second time. Maybe a final time.

Daz couldn't let it go. Couldn't sit with it. Couldn't unsee the agony she carried with her like a second skin. It clawed at his ribs, gnawed at his stomach. That man was still walking free, still poisoning the world with his bile. Still hurting people. Hurting her.

So Daz shifted focus.

If he couldn't be in Emily's life, he'd dedicate himself to removing what poisoned it.

He started watching her father.

It wasn't hard. He hung around the area sometimes, half for nostalgia, half because he knew Emily had been there recently. The old man was a creature of habit. Same ratty overalls. Same scowl. Same haunts. The local pub. The off-license. The betting shop. It was like he had a set route carved into the pavement, trodden down by years of bad living.

And then there were the women.

Daz had noticed it first outside the corner shop. Emily's dad talking too close to a young mum holding a toddler. Something off in his posture, the sneer disguised as a smile. The way she shifted her weight back, inching away. Daz had seen it before — the fake charm that turned sour if you didn't play along.

He didn't like it. Not one bit.

Another day, he followed him into a greasy spoons and sat two booths back, pretending to scroll through his phone. The man berated a young waitress for being slow. Called her a "stupid little girl." Slapped a tenner on the table like it was a favour, not payment.

Daz kept watching.

One weekday afternoon, he spotted them together — Emily's dad and Louise — in the middle of the frozen foods aisle at the local supermarket. It was the first time he'd seen her up close since he was young. Louise was pushing the trolley, tense, her face pale and tight. Their dad was speaking low but harshly. Daz couldn't hear it, but he knew that tone. The kind that cut deep without needing to raise volume.

Louise paused at the milk section, and their dad reached over and slapped something into the trolley with force. She flinched. Not much. Just enough for Daz to see.

He didn't think. He moved.

He pushed his trolley — empty save for a bottle of Coke and some crisps — straight down the aisle, and just before passing, deliberately turned to the right and 'accidentally' bumped shoulders.

"Sorry, mate," Daz said, feigning a friendly tone.

Emily's dad looked up, eyes sharp and sour. "Watch where you're going."

His voice was rough, worn down by years of whiskey and anger.

"No problem," Daz said, but his eyes locked on his. He smiled faintly.

The man squinted at him, sizing him up, clearly not recognising him. Louise glanced up, her eyes flicking between the two men. She didn't say anything.

Daz walked away slowly, heart pounding, anger simmering.

He didn't think the old man even realised how much danger he was in. Didn't realise who he had just met.

Later that night, Daz sat alone in the cold dark of his flat, staring at the ceiling. His mum's funeral had been some time ago now. The grief had hit in strange waves — sharp then dull then nothing. But seeing Emily's father? It brought the pain back in full colour.

The man didn't deserve to live.

He imagined it sometimes — the things he could do. Quick and clean. Or long and loud. Make him vanish, like he never existed.

But not yet.

He needed to watch longer. Learn his movements. His patterns. He wasn't going to make the same mistake he had with Jamie. That had been rage — hot and sudden. This would be different.

This would be justice.

For Emily.

For the pain she'd buried for too long.

Daz had made up his mind.

Emily's father wouldn't hurt her anymore. Not with words. Not with looks. Not with the ghost of his presence.

He would remove the threat.

Quietly. Carefully.

Permanently.

Chapter Forty-Nine

The Countdown

Daz sat hunched at the kitchen table, the glow of his laptop the only light in the dark, damp room. The fridge let out an occasional groan, like even it was tired of existing here. Wallpaper reflecting the blue glow of the screen behind him. He scratched at his jaw, eyes bloodshot, fixated on the screen.

He'd zoomed in on a map to Emily's dad's house , memorising every turn, every route in and out. It wasn't the first time he'd studied it. The area was familiar to him now. He'd been there enough times to know who smoked out the front of their house and which house had a dog that never shut up. He knew what time the bin men came. Knew the sound the gate made if it wasn't closed properly. Knew the rhythm of the street.

He flipped the page in his notebook. The cover was torn, water-stained. Inside, scribbled timings, names, thoughts, sketches. A detailed log of her father's routines. When he left the house. When he returned. Who he was with. What he bought. How often he shouted.

Emily didn't know. She couldn't know.

She had a life now—a new life. He'd seen it. Watched it form like glass blowing into shape. That fancy insurance job she was proud of, that soft-looking man she saw every few weeks, that shared laughter with colleagues at a cocktail bar, the Instagram pictures with filters and smiles and hashtags. She looked alive again. Rebuilt.

And yet, beneath that, Daz knew what lingered. The rot never left. Her father was still in her life. He saw it. That recent visit where she emerged in tears. The haunted look on her face, like she'd gone back in time. It gutted him. Made his fists clench involuntarily. That man still had the power to unravel her.

He couldn't let it happen again.

It wasn't about revenge.

He scribbled a date. Tomorrow. Louise had a late shift, he'd confirmed that much. Emily was away—a weekend trip to Brighton. A train selfie, posted just that morning. The timing was perfect. It was clean.

He leaned back in his chair, stretching until his spine cracked. He felt the weight of the crowbar beneath the table. Just bought. Still in plastic wrap. Just in case.

He didn't want to use it.

But he might have to.

He closed the laptop. Rubbed his eyes. It was past midnight.

Emily was smiling at her phone. She was curled into the small chair on the train heading for a weekend away with some girlfriends from work. On the screen she inspected the photo she'd just posted of them all huddled together to fit into the small frame, big grins, cheeks squashed into each others. A message from Alex popped up.

"You're probably the most organised person I've ever met. Remind me again when my mum's birthday is?"

She laughed softly, typing a reply with a grin.

"Third of September. You're welcome. Also: get her flowers."

Alex had been a slow burn. Sweet, gentle, grounded. No big declarations, no red flags. Just presence. Coffee dates, walks in the park, the occasional sleepover where nothing bad happened and she woke up still feeling safe. That was rare. That was gold.

She was okay now. Not perfect, but okay. Sara said she was doing amazing. Her therapist agreed. Her mum—now over two months sober and counting—was trying. It wasn't perfect, but it was better. Her new job gave her structure. Colleagues made her laugh. Louise was still difficult to manage, but at least they talked every now and again. At least there were boundaries.

Still, when she got a message from Louise later that afternoon, her stomach dropped.

"Dad's been off lately. Said he saw someone hanging around again. Seemed paranoid. You haven't noticed anything weird, have you?"

Emily stared at the screen.

She replied:

"No. I haven't seen anything. Maybe he's just trying to wind you up."

But something inside her stirred.

The next morning, Daz woke up before dawn.

He stood in front of the cracked mirror, inspecting his own face like it was a stranger's. Pale. Sunken. Tired. His mother's face flashed across his memory. The way she'd looked at him in her last lucid moment: loving, proud, scared. Then gone.

He grabbed the gym bag he'd packed the night before. Change of clothes. Gloves. The crowbar. A burner phone already set to wipe after use if he needed it. A bottle of water.

He texted his nan:

"Won't be home tonight. Love you."

He left through the back door.

The car was waiting. A beat-up Vauxhall, plates changed, windows tinted just enough. He'd parked it a few streets away from the house, out of view. No paper trail. No digital footprints. He wasn't an idiot.

He sat in the driver's seat, heart thudding like a drum. He wasn't nervous. Just wired. He felt sharp. Purposeful. He watched the clock on the dashboard count down. 6:43 a.m. Louise would leave in twenty minutes.

He sipped water and waited.

Emily and her friends were walking along the beach, the wind pulling at their hair. She was wrapped in a chunky cardigan, laughing as a wave licked at their boots.

"This place is freezing," she said.

"It's the North Sea," Sam smirked. "What did you expect? Spain?"

She shoved her playfully. The other girls laughed.

"Thank you for bringing me here," she said softly.

"Anytime. You deserve a little peace."

She looked out to the grey water. In the distance, a dog chased gulls. For a moment, the world felt vast and safe. She didn't know what was brewing back in London. Didn't know what was circling. But something in her bones ached.

Chapter Fifty

Dead end

It began as a quiet night in late September. The air was dry, heavy with the dying heat of summer, but the streets were silent, except for the occasional hum of traffic in the distance. A streetlamp buzzed above

Daz's head as he crouched low behind the hedges across from Emily's childhood home. He had been there for nearly an hour, unmoving, watching the familiar windows glow with warm yellow light.

Inside, he knew, Emily's dad was alone. Louise had left ten minutes ago, storming out in a flurry of raised voices and slammed doors. Daz had heard it all. He had followed them earlier in the week—watched the old man bark at her in the supermarket, eyes cold, voice loud enough for strangers to glance over. Now, it was time. Daz's heartbeat was calm. His hands, gloved and steady, didn't shake.

Then, bag on shoulder, hood up, gloves on, he walked to the house.

He approached the door quietly. No lights on outside, no neighbours nearby. He'd chosen the day carefully—no football on TV, no community events, no nosy postmen. Just a man in his house. A man who had hurt Emily.

He didn't knock. He used the key he had stolen weeks ago, the one from Louise's coat pocket when she left it slung over a café chair. It clicked smoothly in the lock.

The living room smelled as he'd always imagined. Grease, and the faint acidic stench of whisky soaked into the curtains. Emily's dad—Mike—was in his armchair, the television flickering before him. He didn't notice Daz at first. Not until the floorboard creaked.

"What the fuck—" Mike twisted around, squinting through dim light. "Who the hell are you?"

Daz didn't speak. He shut the door behind him and locked it.

Mike rose. "You can't just—"

Daz moved forward fast, shoving him backward into the chair. "Sit down."

Mike growled. "You got a bloody death wish, mate?"

He was older now. Slower. No match for Daz, who'd been working out, training, waiting. His muscles were tense but ready.

"Do you know who I am?" Daz asked quietly. "Think about it."

Mike scanned his face. The silence stretched.

Daz stepped closer. "I know everything. What you did to her. To Emily."

Mike's expression didn't change. A shrug, almost amused. "You don't know shit."

"I know enough."

Mike rose again, slow this time, his face twisting into something darker. "She's a liar. All of them. Always were. Girls like her want attention, so they twist things—"

Daz punched him. A single blow to the jaw that knocked Mike sideways into the wall. A vase shattered. The TV kept playing.

"You don't get to talk about her," Daz said.

Mike laughed, wiping blood from his mouth. "What, you her knight in shining armour now? You think coming in here and hurting me makes you a hero? You're just as sick."

He lunged. Surprising. Stronger than he looked. The two of them crashed into the table, glass flying, wood splintering. Daz wrestled free, landing a brutal elbow to Mike's ribs. A wheeze of pain followed. Mike grabbed for something—a bottle, maybe—but Daz was faster.

He pulled the crowbar from his bag. The same one he'd meticulously selected and packed in his kit. Cold. Clean. Ready.

Mike paused. Stared at it.

Daz didn't give him time to plead.

It happened quickly. Four, maybe five deep blows. Chest. Side. Stomach. Head. Mike collapsed in a heap, gasping like a fish on dry land. Blood poured out of him, soaking the carpet, the edge of the broken table.

Daz stepped back, panting. His arms trembled now. The weapon dropped from his hand and clattered to the floor.

There was no glory in it. No triumph. Just silence, apart from the TV and Mike's spluttering. Fading breaths.

Daz stared at the body.

"You deserved worse," he whispered.

Then he turned.

The cleanup was clinical. He knew what to do. He had bleach in the bag. Gloves. Extra clothes. Bin bags. He scrubbed where he could, careful not to overdo it—he needed it to look messy, not staged. He wiped the door handle. Flushed the gloves. Wrapped the Crowbar in cloth and stuffed it in a manhole two miles away.

His car, parked five streets away, was wiped down, his license plate swapped. He drove for hours, finally stopping in a layby near a petrol station on the A11, engine off, hoodie pulled low.

He didn't cry. He didn't think.

He replayed the moment, over and over. Not the killing. Emily's face. Her voice, soft and strong. The way she used to look at him like he was the only solid thing in a broken world.

That world was behind him now.

He told himself: *I did it for her. He was going to hurt her again. He would've ruined her. I had to.*

And then, in a whisper only he could hear:

"I'm still protecting her."

He closed his eyes.

And slept like the dead.

Chapter Fifty-One

The Weekend Breaks

The sea breeze danced through the open window of the Airbnb, lifting the light curtains rhythmically. Emily stood barefoot by the windowsill, sipping her coffee and watching the waves ripple under the soft morning sun. Brighton had been good to her. Three full days of laughter, bottomless brunches, overpriced cocktails, and walking along the pebbled beach barefoot like they were teenagers again.

Behind her, the chaos of checkout hummed through the apartment.

"Em, where's the bloody dry shampoo?" Mia called from the bathroom.

"Check the front pocket of my bag!" Emily shouted back.

She grinned to herself and sipped the last of her lukewarm coffee. Her phone vibrated against the table, the screen lighting up with a message from Sara.

Sara: "Hey… are you still in Brighton? Just saw something on a local Facebook group. Looked like your old street. Bit grim."

Emily frowned and picked up her phone.

Emily: "Still here, heading back this afternoon. What kind of grim?"

Sara sent a screenshot. A blurry photo of police cars lining a familiar street. Her street. And above it, the caption:

"BREAKING: Body found at Northfield Avenue home early this morning. Circumstances unclear. More to follow."

Emily's stomach dropped.

She quickly typed:

"That looks like my old house."
"Do they say who?"

Sara responded a minute later.

Sara: "Not yet. But I'm sure that's your Dad's place. Do you recognise the van in the drive?"

Emily's fingers hovered over her screen. The thought came fast and cold. She hadn't seen her father in weeks, not since the last disastrous visit. She thought about Louise. Had she been home? Was she okay?

Emily: "I'll message Louise."

Her fingers trembled slightly as she typed the text.

"Hey… I saw something on the local Facebook page. Are you okay? Is Dad okay? What's happened?"

No response.

She stared at the screen, waiting for the ellipsis to appear. Nothing.

The others were still bustling around her, half-dressed and laughing as they scrambled to pack. It felt strange—jarring—that the world was still moving at normal speed while hers had tilted.

"You alright?" Sam asked, suddenly beside her. "You look like you've seen a ghost."

Emily blinked. "Yeah. Just—there's something going on back home. I don't know yet. Facebook post. Police on my old street."

Sam's face softened. "You wanna skip brunch? Go back early?"

Emily shook her head. "No. I can't do anything from here. Might as well eat. I'll message my sister again later."

Sam didn't push.

The café was as busy as ever, the smell of coffee and syrup sweet in the air. The girls ordered their usual over-indulgent spread, and for a while, Emily managed to forget the gnawing worry in her stomach. She laughed at Char's story about falling asleep in a bathtub and cheered when Paige managed to sweet-talk their waiter into free muffins.

But her phone stayed face-up on the table the whole time.

No reply.

By the time they were back on the train, the tension had crept higher into her chest. She stared out the window, watching green fields blur past, and scrolled through the Facebook group for any updates. Still nothing concrete. Just comments.

"I live two doors down. Loads of coppers."

"Heard someone say they found him inside, but no one's confirming anything."

"Hope it's not who I think it is…"

Her phone buzzed.

Louise.

Emily sat up straight, her heart suddenly pounding.

Louise: "It's true. Don't know what to do. Will message you later."

That was it. No details. No explanation. Just confirmation.

It's true.

Her breath left her slowly. She leaned back in her seat, her hand still clutched around her phone. It felt heavy now, like it carried the weight of something she couldn't understand yet.

It was real. He was dead.

Back at the flat, the silence felt too loud. Sara wasn't home yet. She was alone. Emily dropped her bags by the door and stood in the middle of her living room, not knowing what to do. Her jacket still smelled like sea air. There was glitter in her hair. Less than twelve hours ago, she'd been drinking cocktails on a rooftop bar.

And now her father was dead.

She hadn't cried. Not yet.

She didn't know if she was going to.

She curled up on the sofa and pulled a throw blanket over herself, flicking the TV on for noise but not watching it. Her thoughts spiralled.

It felt wrong to feel so numb. But maybe that was the part of her that had grieved already—grieved the version of her dad that never existed, grieved the fantasy of a relationship they never had.

She thought of Louise again. Poor Louise. Always the one still trying, hoping and still coming back.

Emily opened their chat again and typed.

"I'm here if you want to talk. I'm so sorry."

No reply.

She didn't push.

Eventually, she drifted off to the background noise of a cooking show, still wrapped in her coat, the flickering light of the TV casting shadows on the wall.

Chapter Fifty-Two

Blanket Fairies

The flat was quiet, dim morning light creeping through the blinds and stretching long across the carpet. Emily stirred, half-curled on the sofa, the faint sound of birdsong leaking in through the double glazing. Her neck ached from the awkward position, and her mouth was dry. As she slowly blinked awake, the blanket draped over her shoulders shifted slightly.

She didn't remember putting it there.

The TV was off now. Her phone was still resting on the chair next to her, and she reached for it groggily, rubbing her eyes. Notifications blinked up at her. A message from Sara, sent late last night:

"Didn't want to wake you. Just got in. You looked shattered. Blanket fairy strikes again x"

Emily smiled faintly, but the comfort was short-lived. Reality caught up quickly.

Her father. Dead.

She sat up properly, clutching the blanket around her. Her fingers moved automatically to open the news app. Local section. There it was, second headline down:

"Murder Investigation Launched After Body Found in Northfield Avenue Home"

The words felt surreal. Cold and clinical. She clicked the article.

"Police have launched a murder investigation following the discovery of a man's body at a property on Northfield Avenue in North London yesterday morning. Emergency services were called to the scene just after 7 a.m. The victim, who has not yet been formally identified by authorities but is believed to be in his fifties, was pronounced dead at the scene."

"The Metropolitan Police confirmed that the death is being treated as suspicious and a post-mortem is scheduled. No arrests have been made, and the police are urging anyone with information or who may have seen anything suspicious in the area to come forward."

Emily dropped the phone into her lap and stared at the wall.

Murder.

Her chest tightened. She felt the air being sucked from the room.

Not a heart attack. Not an accident. Not natural causes.

Someone killed him.

She stood up too fast, legs shaky, pacing the room. "Murder…" she whispered to herself. Her father was a lot of things, but he wasn't the type to get himself involved in something like this. Was he?

She thought of Louise again. Had she seen it? Had she heard it? Was she there?

The nausea crept up slowly. Emily clutched the arm of the sofa to steady herself.

It didn't make sense. Burglaries could go wrong, sure. But that house had almost nothing in it worth taking. Had he gotten into a fight? Someone from the pub? Someone from his past?

And then, without invitation, another thought crept in. Dark. Unwelcome.

Daz.

The air in the room seemed to drop in temperature.

No. That was a long time ago.

But still, she remembered. That strange numb look in his eyes when she first learned what he'd done. The first time he confessed that he had taken a life. How it hadn't felt like something he'd wanted to talk about, just something he accepted.

"It was him or me," he had said.

She'd believed him. She *had* believed him. And maybe that was still true. But still…

He'd done it before.

There were the times she thought she saw someone behind her in the street, the feeling of being watched in the office car park, the moment outside his mother's funeral when they locked eyes and she felt… wrong. Unsettled.

Had that been her paranoia?

Was he really still around?

Emily moved to the window and looked out at the street below. Everything looked the same. A jogger passed with headphones in. A mum pushed a buggy. A delivery driver double-parked and ran up a stairwell with a parcel.

Normal.

But in her head, alarms were starting to ring.

She went back to the sofa and pulled her phone up again, scrolling through her messages. She read Louise's again.

"It's true. Don't know what to do. Will message you later."

So vague. So flat.

She typed a reply.

"Was it a break-in? Do they know what happened? Are you okay? Please let me know."

She hesitated before hitting send. She didn't want to push. But she needed to know.

Daz hadn't reached out. Not even a like on one of her photos in months. Not since the funeral. Not since he said he was letting her go.

She stared at the old message thread they once shared.

Nothing.

No red flags. No reason to think he would do something like this.

But people didn't just *kill* other people.

Except when they did.

She thought about the way her dad had looked at her that day. The last day she saw him. Cruel. Cold. He'd barely let her speak. Barely let her exist. She left crying, again. Same cycle. Over and over.

And now that cycle was over for good.

Her hands trembled. She pushed the thought of Daz down. He had moved on. She had moved on. He was out of her life. She didn't need to dig up old ghosts.

Still, the nausea remained.

Sara padded into the room from the kitchen, wearing a dressing gown and holding two mugs. Her hair was a mess of curls piled high, and her eyes were still puffy from sleep.

"Morning," she said softly, passing a mug to Emily. "You were like ASLEEP asleep"

Emily took the mug gratefully. "Thanks for the blanket."

Sara sat beside her, curling her legs underneath herself. "Thought about you this morning when I scrolled. You okay? I mean, I know that's a dumb question but…"

Emily shook her head. "No. I don't know. It doesn't feel real. They confirmed it was murder. Police don't have anyone yet."

Sara's eyes widened. "God, Em. I'm so sorry. That's awful."

Emily nodded slowly, gripping the mug. "He wasn't perfect. You know? Not like normal Dad's I guess"

Sara reached over and squeezed her knee. "Anything you need, I'm here."

Emily forced a small smile. "Thanks."

But she didn't say what was really going through her mind. That tiny, poisoned thought that had crept in and refused to leave.

Daz.

Could he have been watching again? Could he have seen her go there that day? Could he have followed?

She shook her head sharply.

No. That was ridiculous. There was no proof. No reason.

People don't just kill people.

Except sometimes… they do.

And sometimes, they think they're protecting you when they do it.

Chapter Fifty-Three

Unanswered Questions

The office buzzed with muted chatter and the rhythmic tapping of keyboards, but Emily sat in a bubble of silence, her gaze anchored to the corner of her screen where a blank email draft waited. It was supposed to be a follow-up to a high-profile client.

Something about adjusted policies and projected coverage plans. But the words refused to form.

She clicked the tab over to Facebook instead, thumb hovering on the refresh icon for the local news group page she had now checked at least six times that morning. Still nothing. No updates. No developments. Just the same statement from the police: *"A man in his late fifties was found dead in a residential property on the outskirts of North London. Police are treating it as a suspicious death and are urging witnesses to come forward."*

Her father.

She hadn't said the word aloud, not even to herself. It sat heavy in her gut like a stone. Not grief. Not sorrow. Just... a weight. Something ugly and unresolved. And underneath that, the slow burn of something else—fear?

She'd messaged Louise again the night before. Just two words: *"Please respond."* But nothing came back. The read notification taunted her.

She looked up from her screen as her colleague Megan walked past with two coffees, chatting to someone about Friday's rooftop party. Emily smiled briefly, but it didn't reach her eyes. She turned back to her screen and clicked open the work email, forcing herself to type two sentences before the buzz of her phone derailed her again.

It was a message from one of the old neighbours—Mrs. O'Sullivan. She was well-known in the street for knowing *everything*.

"Police were at the house all day yesterday. Still no answers. But people say they're looking for someone. No signs of a break-in. Bit strange, isn't it?"

Emily's mouth went dry. She read the message twice. *No signs of a break-in.* So not a robbery gone wrong, then. Not a random act.

Her heart beat harder. She leaned back in her chair and stared at the office ceiling, suddenly aware of the taste of bile in her mouth. Someone *wanted* him dead.

Her therapist's voice echoed in her mind: *"When you're overwhelmed by the unknown, anchor yourself in what you do know."*

What did she know?

Her father was dead. It was being treated as murder. Louise wasn't talking. And Daz—

No.

She shook her head as if she could physically shake the thought away. That wasn't fair. That was paranoia. Just because he *had* killed before... that didn't mean—

But hadn't he said it himself? *"I'd do anything to protect you."*

She shut her laptop a little too quickly and stood, grabbing her coat. "I'm heading out for lunch," she told Megan, who blinked at her sudden appearance.

Outside, the wind slapped her cheeks as if trying to snap her out of her spiralling thoughts. She walked with no destination, hands in her coat pockets, weaving through crowded pavements and half-heard conversations. Everything felt louder and sharper— the screech of tires, the barking of a dog, the high-pitched laughter from a schoolyard across the street.

What if he did it?

The question slipped into her mind like a whispered secret.

What if he didn't?

Even worse, she realised, was the uncertainty. The not knowing. Because either answer meant her world would tilt again, and she didn't know how many more times she could survive that.

She kept the therapy appointment. She hadn't been in weeks, not since before Brighton. But today she sat on the couch, hands fidgeting in her lap.

"I feel like I'm watching the news about someone else's life," she said softly. "Like, I know it's real. I know it's *him*. But I feel... nothing."

Her therapist nodded, encouraging. "That's not uncommon. Especially if the relationship was traumatic or complicated."

"It was more than complicated," Emily admitted. "After all her put me through. And now he's dead and I don't feel relief or grief, I just feel... out of sync."

"Your emotional response doesn't have to follow a script. There is no 'right' way to feel."

Emily nodded, but her thoughts were elsewhere. Floating like dust motes in the beam of sunlight pouring through the office window. *Daz.*

She hadn't said his name. Couldn't bring herself to.

"I keep thinking about the past," she said instead. "People who used to be in my life. How much power they had over me. And how even now, when I've done all this work, tried to build something stable... one thing can knock it all down again."

The therapist leaned forward. "Do you feel like it's all going to fall apart?"

Emily was quiet. Then: "Yes."

That night, she sat on the sofa with Sara, a bottle of wine between them, the telly playing something neither of them were really watching.

"You're quiet," Sara said gently.

Emily offered a small shrug. "Just thinking."

"About him?"

A nod.

"You know... it's okay to not be sad."

"I know. It's not that." Emily turned her wine glass in her hand. "It's the *not knowing* that's eating me. No suspect. No leads. Just silence. And I don't know what that means. I don't know if I'm being paranoid or—"

She stopped herself.

"Or?"

Emily met Sara's eyes, her voice a whisper. "Or.. Never mind. I'm just being silly."

Sara didn't press. Just placed her hand gently over Emily's.

The next morning, Emily scrolled through the usual feeds over coffee. Still nothing concrete. No new updates. No arrests.

She checked Louise's messages. Nothing. Not even a read receipt. Emily typed another message, then deleted it. What could she even say?

Her work inbox pinged with a new meeting invite. She took a long sip of coffee, trying to shake the lingering dread from her body.

But it clung to her, like smoke.

The thought had rooted itself.

If it was him... would I even want to know?

Chapter Fifty-Four

Anxiety

Daz sat in his car outside a twenty-four-hour garage, a half-drunk bottle of cheap cola sweating in the cupholder. The engine was off, windows cracked. Midnight air drifted in, thick with damp and petrol fumes. He hadn't been home in days. Not that he really had a home anymore. His mum was gone. Her room was being cleared out by his nan. His job had let him go weeks ago after too many no-shows. His bank balance had dipped into red.

But all of that was a distant hum beneath the louder, more frantic noise inside his own skull.

They know.

No, they don't.

You were careful.

You left no prints.

But what about the neighbour? What if they saw something? A shape? A car? What about CCTV? What about her?

Emily.

He thought of her face at the funeral—soft, concerned. Like she really cared. But he'd seen her since then. Laughed with her friends. Smiling in the street. Lips painted in a soft pink. A handbag swinging at her side. She looked radiant. And safe.

Because of him.

He'd taken away the threat. The disease at the centre of it all. Her dad would never hurt her again. He wouldn't twist her face into that tight, broken expression Daz had seen when she came out of that house crying. No more controlling words. No more undercurrents of fear.

But now, the silence since the murder was louder than any scream. He knew how these things went. The news would break it open soon enough. More articles. More digging. He'd read the first headline—**"Man Found Dead in Family Home – Police Appeal for Information"**—and his stomach had turned to ice. But nothing more had come. No names. No suspects.

Still… it was only a matter of time.

He scratched his knuckles until the skin went raw. He stared down at his hands like they were strangers.

Those hands had held that weapon.

Those hands had brought it down with power.

And now, they trembled.

Sleep came in fractured, jagged pieces. When he closed his eyes, he saw the aftermath. The blood. The stillness. The silence that followed a man's final breath. Daz would wake in cold sweats in the backseat of his car, unsure for a moment where he was, who he was, or what he'd done.

Then it would come back to him.

And he'd drive. Nowhere in particular. Sometimes past Emily's workplace. Past her favourite lunch spot. He knew her habits by now. She always ordered an oat latte, no syrup. She always smiled at the same doorman. Her hair was longer now. She'd styled it slightly differently.

Sometimes he saw her and didn't follow. Just watched from a distance.

Sometimes he couldn't help himself.

He had to be sure she was still okay. That she was safe.

That this had been worth it.

One afternoon, he parked across the road from her building and watched as she stepped outside with a colleague. A man, maybe mid-thirties, neat hair, blue shirt. He made her laugh. The kind of laugh that lit up her whole face. Her eyes crinkled and her shoulders relaxed. She reached out and touched the man's arm lightly.

Daz felt something heavy thud in his chest.

It was fine. She deserved this life. A soft life. Kind people.

But the ache didn't go away.

And with it came the whisper: *She doesn't even know what you've done for her.*

He punched the steering wheel. The horn blared. Someone on the pavement jumped and glared.

He drove off.

In the darker moments, he thought about confessing. Walking into a station. Just laying it all out. But then what? A life inside? Stripped down to nothing. No more watching over her. No more freedom. And would they even believe it was justice?

Or would he just become what he feared most—another monster?

He thought about his mum. She'd understood for a second, that day he told her. In one of her rare lucid flashes, she had looked at him and cupped his face like he was six years old again. Told him he'd always been good. Always trying to protect. But the moment had vanished, swallowed by confusion, and she'd screamed until he'd fled the room.

He couldn't go back.

He couldn't go forward either.

At night, he drove past the house where it happened. It had been boarded up now. Police tape long gone, but the shadows still clung to the bricks. A memory carved into the foundations. He didn't stop. Just circled the block. Once. Twice. Then left.

He thought of Louise. Of how she must be coping. He hadn't followed her. Didn't need to. She wasn't the one haunted. She hadn't carried the wound the same way Emily had. She hadn't become the girl curled up in his hoodie, shaking on his couch, asking him not to let anyone in.

Emily was the centre of it. The reason he did it. The reason he couldn't regret it.

Not really.

Still, the paranoia grew.

A siren in the distance made his pulse jump. The knock of a car door. The echo of footsteps. Every sound became a threat. Every face a potential witness. He changed the plates on his car. Took side streets. Avoided petrol stations with cameras. He was constantly scanning. Constantly ready to run.

But he stayed. Always nearby. Like a ghost orbiting Emily's life. Close enough to touch, but never daring to cross the line again.

He knew it was twisted. Wrong. But in his mind, it made sense. He was protecting her. Still doing what he always had. Even if she never knew.

Even if she'd hate him for it.

One night, he parked a few streets from her flat and walked the block slowly. A hoodie pulled over his head, hands buried in his pockets. He didn't go near her building. Just enough to feel close. To confirm she was safe.

Lights on.

Curtains drawn.

Inside, laughter. Music. He could faintly hear it through an open window.

She was okay.

He turned away.

As he walked back to his car, he caught his reflection in a dark shop window.

Hollow eyes. Gaunt face. A man unraveling.

And for the first time in a while, he didn't recognise himself.

Back in the driver's seat, he rested his head on the steering wheel.

This can't go on.

But it has to.

He didn't know how to stop. Or if he even wanted to.

And all the while, the ticking clock in his head reminded him:

They could knock at any moment.

They could take everything.

But for now, he still had this—watching her, unseen. Making sure she was safe in the only way he knew how.

It wasn't love anymore.

It was something else.

Something darker.

Something permanent.

Chapter Fifty-Five

Questions

It was late afternoon when Emily's phone buzzed. She was sitting by the window of her flat, curled up with a hot cup of tea, scrolling half-heartedly through social media. Her mind had been elsewhere for days. The news still hadn't said much more about her father's death. A few vague updates online. Police still looking for information. The odd post in a Facebook group about sirens and flashing lights. But nothing solid. Nothing that helped it make sense.

So when her phone vibrated with a number she didn't recognise, she nearly ignored it.

Then something tugged at her.

She answered.

"Hello?"

"Is this Emily?" a calm female voice asked.

Emily sat up straighter. "Yes... who's this?"

"Detective Sergeant Willow Morgan. I'm with Westbridge CID. I was hoping you might have time to talk to us—just an informal chat. Regarding your father."

Emily's heart skipped. For a moment, she couldn't speak. Then, "Am I in trouble?"

"No, absolutely not. You're not under suspicion or anything of the sort. We're just speaking with family and acquaintances to piece together more information. There's no pressure—if now's not a good time, we can arrange something else."

Emily swallowed. "No, it's... it's okay. I can come in."

The station was more clinical than she had expected. Grey walls. Brown plastic chairs. The smell of stale coffee. Emily sat in a small interview room, a glass of water in front of her, hands folded tightly in her lap.

Detective Morgan was kind but precise. Mid-40s, her presence steady and practical, like she'd spoken to a thousand grieving relatives in her time. She wasn't harsh, but she didn't coddle either. Another officer, a younger man named Freddie, sat in the corner with a notebook. They weren't recording. Just notes, they said. Routine.

"We understand you hadn't been in contact with your father much recently," Morgan began.

Emily nodded. "Not really. We weren't close."

"When was the last time you saw him?"

"A good few weeks ago now. I visited the house. Louise was there. I thought maybe... I don't know. I wanted to reconnect. It didn't go well."

Morgan nodded, scribbling something down. "Can you tell us more about that?"

Emily took a deep breath. "He wasn't... he was always difficult. Controlling. When we were kids, it was his way or nothing. After I moved out, I tried to put some distance between us. Louise stayed. I never understood why. But when I went back recently, he was just the same. Cold. Dismissive. He barely looked at me. Louise didn't say much either. She looked tired. Scared, even. I only stayed for about forty minutes. Then I left."

"You haven't spoken to your sister since?"

Emily shook her head. "I've tried. Messaged. Called. Nothing. She just sent one message back after I asked if what I read online was true. She said: 'It's true.' That was it."

Morgan exchanged a glance with the other officer. "Had your father ever mentioned having any enemies? Anyone who might have wished him harm?"

Emily gave a short, humourless laugh. "Plenty of people disliked him. He was arrogant, dismissive, thought he was better than everyone. He rubbed people the wrong way all the time. But no, not that I know of. Not enough to... you know."

"And had you noticed anything unusual in the weeks before his death? Messages, behaviour, anything that seemed off?"

Emily paused. Should she mention the strange feeling she'd had that someone had been watching her that day? No. It felt silly now. Like paranoia. She shook her head. "Nothing like that."

"And you're sure?" Morgan asked gently.

Emily nodded. "Yes."

There was one name she hadn't said. Daz. But why would she? She hadn't seen him in ages. Not properly. The last real moment had been at his mother's funeral. A brief exchange. A goodbye. And then he disappeared again. There was no reason to think he had anything to do with this. Even if her brain tried to make connections, they were flimsy. She wouldn't drag his name into this mess unless she had something real.

Morgan seemed satisfied. She closed her notebook. "Thank you, Emily. I know this isn't easy. We're just trying to understand what happened. If anything else comes to you, anything at all, you can call me directly."

Emily took the card she offered. "Thanks."

She walked home in a daze. It wasn't a long journey, but it felt like miles. When she got back to the flat, she found it empty. Sara must still be at work. The place was quiet.

Emily kicked off her shoes and sat on the edge of the sofa. The police hadn't told her much. Just that they were working on leads. That it was too early to say anything definite. But the word hung in the air now, unavoidable and sharp: **murder**.

She hadn't cried. Not for her father. Not yet. She knew she probably wouldn't ever.

Instead, she sat there, staring at nothing, letting the silence wrap around her like a blanket she hadn't asked for. Everything was uncertain. Her sister no longer communicating with her. Her father dead. A killer out there, unnamed. She wasn't in trouble—but something told her this was far from over.

Still, she'd done her part. Answered their questions. Told them what little she knew.

Chapter Fifty-Six

A Glimpse

Emily tilted her head back and let the cool fizz of her prosecco sit on her tongue before swallowing. The bar was warm, filled with a low hum of Friday evening laughter and the clinking of glasses. She liked this place—marble countertops, velvet seating, the soft brass lighting that made everyone look a little more glamorous than they actually were. She liked how it made her feel normal. Safe.

Alex leaned over the table slightly, brushing a thumb across her knuckles in that gentle way he always did before he said something more thoughtful. "You seem happier tonight," he said, eyes crinkling at the corners.

"I feel it," she replied, surprising even herself with the truth of it. "Not all the time, but… most days now."

"That's good. You've been through more than most. You deserve the calm."

Emily looked down into her glass. Calm. It was a word she'd come to revere, as if peace were a rare delicacy she was only just learning how to savour without guilt.

She nodded slowly, grateful, but her thoughts wandered. "My mum's acting weird, though. Like… floaty. Absent. She says she's fine but I don't know. And Cynthia's been distant. Even more than usual. I don't know if they're just processing it all in their own ways, or if there's something else…"

Alex reached for a chip from the shared plate between them. "Maybe they're just giving you space."

"Maybe." Emily didn't believe that.

The conversation drifted to lighter things—his work, her annoying new colleague who thought sarcasm was a personality trait—but something unsettled in her chest. She couldn't name it. She'd been good at pushing those instincts down lately. At ignoring the hum in her gut that said *look again.*

But then she did.

She glanced toward the bar, letting her eyes skim past the crowd of people queuing for drinks. Her gaze snagged, stopped.

And there he was.

Daz.

Standing at the far end, half-shadowed by a pillar. Still, eyes locked on hers.

Emily froze. Her blood stopped moving. Her body buzzed with a strange heat that started in her spine and crawled up her neck.

It wasn't a mistake.

He didn't look away quickly, didn't pretend he was looking past her. He was watching her. *Waiting*. His face was pale. His eyes sunken. He looked thinner, drawn. But it was him.

"Emily?" Alex said, following her line of sight. "What is it?"

She blinked. Her body jolted as if it had forgotten how to be hers. When she looked again, Daz was gone. She stood up abruptly, heart pounding.

"I have to go."

"What? Wait, Emily—"

"I'm sorry. I just—I have to go."

She didn't explain. She couldn't.

She weaved her way out of the bar, pushing through the crowd. The night air slapped her in the face, brisk and damp with the early signs of rain. The street was busy but not enough to lose him in.

She scanned. Left. Right.

He couldn't have gone far.

Her chest burned. What the hell was he doing? Watching her like that? After all this time? After the funeral and the silence and the murder she still couldn't fully process?

Why now?

Emily started walking fast in the direction she thought he might've gone. The alley beside the bar. The side street that curved down toward the bus stop. She didn't know what she was expecting—to catch him, to scream at him, to demand answers he would never give?

But she couldn't do nothing.

Not again.

The city lights flickered across wet pavements, painting the ground in glistening oranges and reds.

She turned a corner. No sign of him. Her breath came faster. Was she being stupid? Chasing shadows?

She stopped. Her hands trembled.

A group of girls walked past, laughing loudly, and she blinked again. Her thoughts were whirring too fast. What if he *had* something to do with what happened to her dad? What if the police were missing something? What if her gut had been right all along?

And more than anything else—

Why the hell was he watching her again now?

Her phone buzzed in her bag. She pulled it out.

Alex: *Are you okay? What's going on?*

She stared at the message, then shoved the phone back in without replying.

This wasn't something Alex could understand. This wasn't a normal ex-boyfriend situation. Daz had never just been an ex. He was a trauma wound. A living scar. He had saved her. Loved her. Broken her. Changed her. And now he was back. Watching.

Was it grief? Obsession? Guilt?

She didn't know.

Back at the flat, Sara was out. Emily sat curled on the sofa, hands gripping a lukewarm mug of tea she'd forgotten she made. The light from the TV cast soft shadows across the room, but she wasn't watching it.

Her mind kept replaying that moment. Daz. Eyes on hers. Not shocked to see her—almost like he expected to.

And then gone.

Like he was never there.

But he was there. She wasn't making it up. This wasn't paranoia or stress or unresolved trauma. He was real. He was near.

And that scared her more than anything.

She picked up her phone again, stared at it. Part of her wanted to message him, to scream at him. Another part—the quieter, wiser part—knew that would be a mistake.

Instead, she opened Facebook and typed his name in the search bar.

Nothing new.

No posts. No tags. Just the same old profile photo. Him and his mum, taken long before her illness. Before everything crumbled.

She closed the app.

It was late now. She stood, locking the windows and the front door, checking the peephole out of habit.

Nothing. Just the quiet hallway and soft hum of someone else's TV playing somewhere down the hall.

Still, she couldn't shake the feeling that someone was nearby.

The next morning, Emily sat in the therapist's office, her leg bouncing uncontrollably.

"I saw him," she said after a pause. "Daz."

The therapist looked up from her notes. "That's the first time in a while, isn't it?"

Emily nodded. "Since the funeral. But this time he didn't speak to me. He was just... watching. And then he ran."

"How did it make you feel?"

Emily laughed lightly, bitter. "Like I'm prey. Like I'm being followed. And what scares me is... I think I've felt that before. Without seeing him. I think he's been doing this longer than I've known."

Her therapist paused. "Do you believe he would harm you?"

"No." She said it too quickly. Too instinctively.

Then: "I don't know."

They let that hang for a moment. Emily's hands twisted in her lap.

"I'm not scared of him, not like that," she added. "But I am scared of *why* he's here. Why now. I thought we'd closed that chapter."

"Sometimes people reappear when they haven't fully let go. And sometimes... they reappear when *we* haven't."

Emily looked away. That hit too close to home.

That night, Emily lay awake in bed, staring at the ceiling. The city buzzed beyond her window, but her flat was still. Peaceful.

But her thoughts weren't.

She kept seeing his face. That look. Not anger. Not sadness. Something else. Something unreadable.

What did he want?

What was he planning?

And then, the unthinkable—

What if he thinks he's protecting me? Again?

That was the Daz she had known. The boy who stood up for her. The one who retaliated when no one else would. The one who crossed a line so far he couldn't return.

And now her father was dead.

Her stomach twisted.

"No," she whispered to herself in the dark. "No. He wouldn't..."

But she didn't believe that anymore. Not fully.

She pulled the covers over her and tried to steady her breathing.

Outside, a car drove slowly past. A pause. Then gone.

She didn't check the window.

She didn't want to know.

Chapter Fifty-Seven

The Watcher

Daz hadn't meant to follow her again that night. Not at first.

It started with a scroll. Just a mindless scroll on his burner Facebook profile—no friends, no posts, no name anyone would recognise. He just used it to lurk. And then he saw it: a photo. Someone had tagged the bar in Shoreditch. One of those trendy places with neon signs and cocktails in jam jars. And there she was, blurry, holding a glass of prosecco, laughing.

Emily.

She looked the same. Hair longer, face softer. The kind of softness that came with time, and maybe peace. She was smiling.

He should have clicked off.

He didn't.

He found the bar on Google Maps. Checked the street view. Looked up the train times. Told himself he was just going to look. That was all.

But now he was here.

Hidden by a pillar, heart pounding harder than it had during any of the mess that came before. Harder than when he stood over the body, blood on his hands. Harder than when he dropped the crowbar into the darkness and dragged the cover back over it, hands trembling. Because this—*her* —was the real danger.

Emily.

Laughing.

With someone else.

A guy with good hair and clean shoes and teeth too white to be anything but polished. Daz had seen him before. They'd been dating casually for a while now. She looked... happy. And that stung. Not because he thought she owed him anything. Not anymore. But because it confirmed what he'd been trying to bury:

She moved on.

He watched longer than he should have. Couldn't help it. She tilted her head back when she laughed. She always did that. Her hand on the guy's forearm. Easy, casual. Not forced. Not afraid.

Not like before.

He felt a weird swell in his chest. A mix of pride and sorrow. She looked good. She was okay.

That should have been enough.

But then she saw him.

Her eyes locked with his. It was like being struck by lightning. He hadn't felt it in years. His breath caught. His chest tightened.

She stood.

He panicked.

He ran.

Not far. Just around the corner. Behind a parked van. Then further still, to the busier street. It was second nature now. Disappear. Blend in. Ghost mode.

He didn't stop until he was back in his car three boroughs over, parked outside a 24-hour Tesco, hands shaking.

What the fuck was he doing?

He watched her. Like he always did. Like some creep. Like he was one of *them*. But it didn't feel like that to him. It never had. He wasn't following her to hurt her. He was watching to make sure no one else did.

That's what he told himself.

That was the justification he clung to.

But tonight had changed things. She'd seen him. That wasn't part of the plan. And she'd recognised him, too. Her eyes had widened. Her mouth had parted like she was going to speak.

He didn't want to know what she might have said.

Now she'd be thinking. Remembering. Putting pieces together.

What if she figured it out?

His mind raced. He had tried so hard to be careful. No digital trail. No camera exposure. In and out of the house quickly. Gloves. Clean shoes. Cleaned off. Burned the clothes. Deleted everything.

But what if that didn't matter?

What if she *knew*?

Daz sat in the car, head resting on the wheel. His stomach churned. He hadn't eaten since yesterday, but he couldn't face food. All he could think about was her face. That split-second of connection.

What would she do?

Tell someone?

The police?

He didn't think she would. Not yet. She was loyal. Still soft in that way. But he also knew she was smart. And if she started digging... it wouldn't take long.

He lit a cigarette with shaking fingers, even though he hated the taste. It was something to do. Something to numb the noise.

And the noise was *loud*.

You murdered a man.

You looked his daughter in the eye and ran.

He tried to remind himself why. Why he'd done it. Why it *had* to be done. Her dad wasn't just a bad man. He was poison. Filth. He hurt people and wore a smile to cover the stench. The world was better without him.

He'd done her a favour. She just didn't know it yet.

But the truth didn't sit clean. It never had.

Not even that night, when the rage had consumed him. When the image of Emily's face, bruised and trembling at fifteen, flashed into his skull and wouldn't leave.

He hadn't planned it. He just wanted to scare him. Confront him. Make him admit it. Make him *see*. But it escalated. Like it always did. Words turned to shouting. Shouting turned to shoving. The old bastard grabbed a bottle. Swung. Missed.

Daz didn't.

And when it was done, when the red faded and the silence settled, he knew there was no turning back.

So he covered his tracks. Like he always did.

Only this time, there was a witness.

Not to the act. But now, maybe to the consequences.

Emily.

He flicked the cigarette out the window and leaned back. The ache in his head pulsed behind his eyes. He was tired. So tired.

But he couldn't stop.

He had to see her again. Just once more. Make sure she was okay. Make sure she wasn't going to ruin everything.

Maybe talk to her. Explain.

No. He couldn't. That would be selfish. Dangerous. Reckless.

But still...

He grabbed his burner phone. Opened the Facebook app again. No new posts. No updates. Just the same photos.

Her smile.

He exhaled slowly.

Maybe it was time to leave.

But then he remembered the look in her eyes.

And he knew he wouldn't.

Not yet.

Chapter Fifty-Eight

Uncovered

Emily sat in her office, staring at the blinking cursor on her screen. The numbers blurred together in her spreadsheet, refusing to make any sense. Her phone buzzed with a notification, and she flinched. It had been days since she'd seen Daz watching her from across the street. The image haunted her, lingering like smoke. But since then—nothing. Not a message. Not a shadow. Just silence.

She picked up her phone, hoping for something—anything—that might give her clarity. A missed call, a message, a new headline.

And then she saw it.

Local Police Recover Item Believed to Be Weapon in Recent Homicide Investigation

Her heart dropped.

She tapped the article. A Crowbar had been discovered in a manhole on the outskirts of town. The police were "actively pursuing forensic analysis" and appealing to the public for any information. They didn't name her father. They didn't name suspects. But she knew exactly what they meant.

Her chest tightened. She swallowed hard and pushed her phone face down on the desk. Her mind raced, questions circling like vultures. Could it be? Was that the weapon? The final piece of the puzzle?

She barely registered the suited man saunter up behind her. Her colleague, Jordan.

"Hey, Emily, just wanted to remind you we've got the team meeting in fifteen minutes."

She nodded automatically. "Right. Thanks."

He gave her a quick smile and left. She waited for him to return to his desk, then leaned back in her chair, exhaling slowly. She couldn't shake the sense that everything was accelerating. That the walls were closing in—not around her, but around Daz.

And yet, she still hadn't told anyone.

She hadn't mentioned the way he looked at her from across the street. The haunted, desperate intensity in his eyes. She hadn't mentioned how she was sure—absolutely sure—it hadn't been the first time he'd watched her unnoticed.

She hadn't told Alex, though he would've listened. He'd probably try to fix it somehow, to make her feel safe. But Daz wasn't a man who could be fixed by someone else. He had made his choice. And yet, she still couldn't bring herself to stop looking for him.

Later that night, Emily sat on the edge of her bed with her laptop, scrolling through old social media posts, neighbourhood groups, even forums where people speculated on local crime. The Crowbar discovery had become a subject of intense debate.

Why ditch it in there unless you were hiding something?

I live near that area. It's not somewhere you just happen to stumble on.

They're closing in. Whoever it is should just hand themselves in.

Emily closed the tab and ran her hands through her hair.

Sara came to her bedroom door, peeking in. "You alright, babe?"

"Yeah. Just reading."

"You're always reading lately."

"I know." She hesitated. "Sar, do you think people can change?"

Sara tilted her head. "Change how?"

"Like... do something terrible. And still be good. Or... redeemable? I know its stupid.."

Sara came in and sat beside her. "People are complicated, mate. And I think we all have the capacity for good and bad. But love doesn't mean you excuse everything. Sometimes, the most loving thing is walking away."

Emily didn't respond. She just leaned into her friends shoulder and let the warmth of the moment settle her spinning mind.

Days passed. Then a week. The news stayed quiet. Forensics hadn't released anything publicly. The murder weapon was still being "analysed."

Cynthia hadn't reached out. Louise was still silent. And Emily, despite herself, had begun to map her routes. She changed the times she left for work. Took new roads. Checked over her shoulder.

She wasn't scared—not exactly. She was waiting. She knew Daz would come back into her life. It was a gut feeling. A pull. Something unfinished lingering in the air.

One evening after work, she took the long way home, through the city centre. She stopped by a small café near the library, bought herself a tea, and sat near the window, watching the world pass.

And then, out of the corner of her eye, she thought she saw someone across the street.

A dark figure, half-shrouded by the bus stop. Watching.

She stood slowly, heart thudding.

But when she stepped out onto the pavement, the figure was gone. Swallowed by the crowd.

Emily exhaled shakily. She turned to go home.

She didn't notice the man who had watched her vanish into the back alley between two buildings. She didn't see the familiar silhouette slip into shadow.

Daz was always closer than she thought.

From his position between the bins, Daz stared at the spot where she had stood. Her expression had changed. She was more aware. She was sensing him. He'd gotten too close this time.

He knew she hadn't told the police about him. If she had, they'd have come by now. He still had time.

Time to make sure she was safe. Time to make sure this would never touch her.

He turned away and began walking the long way back to where he'd left his car. His mind raced with thoughts of loose ends. Evidence. Cameras. Witnesses. The weapon.

He tried to shove them away. He had done what he had to do.

But even now, Daz couldn't decide if that made him the hero—or the villain.

He reminded himself of the way Emily looked when she smiled. The way she had looked with that man—Alex. Happy. Confident. Strong.

She was alive. Free. And her father was dead.

Whatever came next, that part at least, was done.

Back at home, Emily paced the living room. Sara had gone to bed. The flat was quiet.

She pulled up her phone, scrolling again through Louise's profile. Still nothing. She opened her own inbox.

Her fingers hovered over Daz's name in her old message threads.

Still nothing.

She tapped out a message:

I know you're still around. If you're reading this... Can you just talk to me?

She stared at it. Then deleted it. Then typed it again.

And again, she deleted it.

She tossed her phone onto the couch and sat down heavily.

No answers. Just a growing sense that her world—finally rebuilt, finally stable—was about to shift again.

And when it did, she needed to be ready.

In the quiet shadows of a nearby car park, Daz sat in his battered car. The engine off. The lights dimmed.

Her flat's lights had just gone out.

He hadn't read the message she nearly sent. But he would have understood it.

He looked up at the stars, the sky silent above.

He wouldn't let the darkness touch her again.

Even if that meant disappearing into it himself.

Chapter Fifty-Nine

Routines

Emily had started walking a little differently these days. Not because she was scared—no, not anymore—but because she was aware. Every reflection in a window, every shadow on the pavement, every faint shift in her periphery caught her attention. She knew he was there. Somewhere. Watching her, always a few steps behind or a breath away. She didn't need confirmation. She just knew.

It had been a week since she'd seen him outside the cafe. A blur of a moment, one that had lodged itself into her chest like a shard of glass. That look in his eyes—guilty, desperate—it hadn't left her since. She knew Daz wasn't done. Not with her. Not with this.

She began her walk that Saturday afternoon like she had the last few—routine, almost practiced. Grey sky overhead, a mild wind flicking her coat as she turned down the street with the little corner shop. She always passed it. Not because she needed anything, but because he always seemed to be nearby.

Sure enough, today was no different.

She spotted him as she crossed the road, her gaze fixed ahead. But in the corner of her eye, she saw him—leaning against the brick wall of the shop, half-shielded by the old telephone box beside it. He looked rougher than usual. Tired. Beard unkempt. Clothes a little too loose, like he'd lost weight. His eyes weren't on her this time—they were down, scanning the ground like he'd lost something.

Emily slowed her pace by a fraction.

She pretended to check her phone. Her heart thundered. This was it. She had waited for this.

Out of nowhere, the corner shop door banged open. A man in his fifties—stocky, irritated, apron tied carelessly around his waist—stepped out and gestured sharply.

"Oi! You again? You've been hanging around for over an hour. People are asking questions. You've got to move on, mate."

Emily watched out of the corner of her eye. Daz straightened but didn't flinch.

"I'm not doing anything. Just leave it, yeah?"

"You can't loiter out here. This ain't a shelter."

"I said leave it," Daz snapped.

Emily made her move.

Her steps were silent on the pavement as she crossed the road. The wind tossed a few strands of hair across her eyes, and she tucked them behind her ear as she approached.

"Daz."

He turned.

The change in his face was immediate. A raw flicker of recognition, then fear, then something harder to place—longing, maybe. Guilt. Pain. He opened his mouth, closed it again.

The man from the shop narrowed his eyes.

"You know this twat?" he asked Emily.

She nodded. "Yeah. I've got it from here."

The shopkeeper hesitated, then grunted and retreated inside.

Daz stood there, stunned.

Emily took a slow step closer. "You're not very good at hiding."

"I wasn't hiding," he murmured. "Just standing here."

"Same thing, Daz."

He looked away, down the street, like he might bolt. But he didn't.

She crossed her arms. "Why?"

He rubbed a hand down his face. "I just wanna make sure you're safe."

Emily exhaled sharply. "From what?"

He didn't answer.

"From what, Daz?"

His jaw clenched. "You know."

She stared at him. Her voice dropped. "Did you do it?"

A silence stretched between them, long and tense. Then:

"You know I did."

Emily's stomach twisted. She didn't need the confirmation—but hearing it, finally hearing it, cracked something inside her.

He took a half-step toward her, but she held up a hand.

"No. Stay there."

He froze.

"I saw the news," she said. "The weapon. The police… they're still looking."

"I was careful," he said quietly. "I didn't leave anything."

Her voice was tight. "And what? That makes it okay?"

"No," he said. "But I did it for you."

Emily shook her head, fighting the ache rising in her chest. "You don't get to say that. You don't get to follow me around like a stray and claim it was for me."

Daz looked like he might cry, but no tears came. "He hurt you. He ruined you. He ruined everything."

"No Daz. That was you." she said.

A pause.

Daz looked at the pavement. "I just… I needed to make it right."

Emily's voice cracked. "You didn't."

Silence settled again. She took a shaky breath.

"You can't follow me anymore. This ends here."

He nodded slowly.

"I mean it, Daz. If I see you again… if I even feel like you're close."

Another nod.

"You need to go. Get help for fuck's sake. Or turn yourself in. I don't care what you do. But stay away from me."

He looked at her for a long time. "I can't lose you."

"You already did."

Emily turned and walked away.

He didn't follow.

She didn't look back.

Chapter Sixty

Truth

Emily couldn't stop shaking. Even hours later, her hands trembled with the shock of it—of *him*. She stood in the middle of her bedroom, jacket still on, bag dropped to the floor beside her feet, like she hadn't quite managed to re-enter the real world.

Daz had said it out loud.

"You know I did."

He hadn't shouted it. He hadn't cried. He'd said it like he was giving her the weather report. Like he was letting her in on something he'd been carrying too long. And in that moment, her breath had caught in her throat.

She hadn't screamed. She hadn't called the police. She'd just stood there—while the man she once loved told her he killed her father.

Now, in the silence of her home, her thoughts were screaming.

She walked into the kitchen on autopilot, opened the cupboard, closed it again. She didn't know what she was looking for. Her body moved for distraction, but her mind kept replaying it.

He had been outside the shop when she approached. Arguing with the shopkeeper, telling the man to back off. Then she'd said his name. Just his name. And he had turned.

Like he'd been waiting for it.

Like he'd known this was coming.

They hadn't spoken in years. Not properly. Not since his mother's funeral. Not since the quiet end of a long, messy chapter in their lives. And yet when he looked at her—really looked at her—it was like no time had passed. Like something unfinished had snapped back into place.

She'd asked him the question she never thought she'd ask.

"Did you do it?"

He didn't even try to deny it. He just looked at her, eyes shadowed and tired, and nodded. A single, solemn nod that landed like a bomb.

"You know I did."

That had been the part that made her stagger back.

She had known.

Now, back in the quiet of her home, Emily gripped the edge of the kitchen counter and tried to breathe through the nausea rolling in her stomach. Her head was spinning, but beneath the chaos of thoughts, one thing was clear: she knew the truth.

He had murdered her father.

And she had no idea what to do about it.

She sat on the sofa, arms wrapped tightly around herself. The TV was on, volume low, some sitcom playing that she couldn't pay attention to. The laughter track felt grotesque. Wrong.

Her phone buzzed. A message from Alex.

"You home? Was a bit worried the other night x"

She didn't respond. She couldn't. What could she say?

Hi, yeah, sorry about that, just ran into my ex who confessed to killing my dad.

The thought was surreal. It didn't feel real. It felt like she was playing a part in someone else's nightmare.

And yet every part of her ached with the reality of it.

Her father—abusive, distant, controlling. But still *her father*. She hadn't loved him. No. But she hadn't wished him dead. Not like that at least.

And Daz—broken, loyal, obsessive. He had taken that decision into his own hands. Like it was his right. Like she needed avenging. Again. Like she was a victim.

Maybe she had been. But this... this wasn't justice.

This was murder.

Her stomach clenched. She ran to the bathroom and vomited. Cold sweat broke across her forehead as she sank to the floor, shaking.

She could hear his voice in her head:

"I was careful," he said quietly. *"I didn't leave anything."*

He had spoken like he was freeing her from something. Like she should thank him.

She rinsed her mouth and stumbled back to the sofa. Curled up beneath a blanket, she stared at the wall. The silence pressed in from all sides.

She didn't tell Sara.

She didn't call Louise.

She didn't message Cynthia, who had already retreated into silence weeks ago.

She told no one.

Because she didn't know what kind of person she was if she *didn't* report him.

But she also didn't know who she'd become if she *did*.

Her therapist had told her once that trauma doesn't just make you afraid—it makes you confused. It makes you question your instincts, your memories, your morals. And now here she was, questioning everything.

She paced the living room, heart racing. Every instinct screamed: *call the police.* Do the right thing. Put an end to it.

But another voice—quiet, persistent—asked: *What will happen to him?*

She had seen the look in Daz's eyes. He wasn't gloating. He wasn't proud. He looked tired. Wrecked. Guilty.

He had done it. And he wasn't running.

But he wasn't asking for forgiveness, either.

She grabbed her phone, stared at it. Her fingers hovered over the number 9.

She didn't press it.

Instead, she opened her notes app. She typed:

"He said he killed my father. I believe him. I don't know what to do."

She read it over and over. Then deleted it.

That night, sleep didn't come. Every creak in the house made her jump. Every shadow outside the window made her pulse spike.

She sat by the window at 3AM, watching the street. Part of her hoped to see him again. Part of her prayed she never would.

The sky lightened slowly. The world began to stir.

And Emily sat in the stillness, knowing she had crossed a threshold. Nothing would ever be the same.

Her father was gone.

Daz had taken him.

And now the question wasn't just *what do I do?*

It was *who am I now?*

She didn't have the answer.

But she knew she couldn't carry the truth forever, and very soon, she would have to choose.

Chapter Sixty-One

The edge

Emily sat at the edge of her bed, her knees tucked close to her chest, arms wrapped tightly around them. A familiar scene by now. The faint hum of traffic from outside filtered through the cracked window, the world carrying on as if everything was fine. But inside her room, time had slowed. The weight of what she knew sat heavily on her chest, pressing against her ribs, each breath more difficult than the last.

She had barely slept. The image of Daz—broken, yet still somehow defiant—played on a loop in her mind. His words echoed louder than any traffic, louder than any logic or instinct.

"I did it for you."

Her mind was frozen in that moment. Part of her already knew. Maybe she always had, deep down, just like she had known what her father was truly capable of. But to hear Daz say it—calmly, with conviction—had cracked something inside her. The world had already spun too many times out of her control. And now, just when she had begun to reclaim it, he had dragged her back to the chaos.

She stood now, padding barefoot to the kitchen, pouring a glass of orange juice with shaking hands. The decision was there, looming, pressing. She couldn't un-know what she knew. And she couldn't ignore what it meant.

She had told no one. Not Sara, not Alex, not her therapist. She had carried it for a day and a half like a stone in her stomach, trying to pretend life could continue as normal. She went to work. She smiled. She replied to messages. But underneath, the clock was ticking.

She sat back down, glass cradled in her hands a faint orange still tinting her lips. She thought about Daz. About the boy she once loved so fiercely. The boy who had carried her through darkness, who made her laugh, who knew every corner of her pain without needing words. But also the boy who had killed a man once before. And now, again.

Even if her father was a monster, even if he had hurt her in ways that should never be forgiven, it didn't make it okay. It didn't make it right. She couldn't let herself believe that.

She had battled through too much to justify that kind of violence now.

She pulled out her phone. Her thumb hovered over his name in her contacts, but she didn't press it. Not this time. Her chest tightened. She wanted to say goodbye. To end it cleanly. She had questions. She had things to say. But no conversation could fix this. No closure would ever be enough.

She deleted the number.

Instead, she scrolled to the number the police had left on a card after her last conversation with them. The lead detective. Detective Walker.

Her fingers trembled slightly as she tapped it. It rang three times before a calm, female voice answered.

"Detective Walker."

"Hi. It's Emily Keane. I need to talk to you again. It's important."

There was a pause. "Of course, Emily. When are you available?"

Emily swallowed. "Today. As soon as possible."

"Come down to the station. I'll be here all afternoon. We can talk in private."

Emily exhaled, as though she'd been holding her breath for days. "Thank you."

After hanging up, she sat still for a long time, letting the silence settle around her. Then she rose, slowly but deliberately, and walked to her wardrobe. She chose simple clothes: jeans, a plain navy jumper. No makeup. Hair tied back. She didn't want to be anything but herself.

When she stepped outside, the sky was bright but cold. A breeze kissed her cheeks, and she closed her eyes for a moment, letting it ground her. This was her choice. Her path.

She stopped for coffee on the way, holding the cup tight as though it could anchor her. She stared out the window of the café for a few minutes, watching people pass. A world full of people living ordinary lives. She longed for that ordinariness, even as she knew she never truly had it.

As she walked through the automatic doors of the station, the buzz of nerves returned. The building was stark, quiet, professional. A woman at the desk directed her to the same small room as before. Within minutes, Detective Walker entered, holding a notepad and a steady, unreadable expression.

Emily cleared her throat. "What I'm about to tell you... I haven't told anyone else. Not yet."

Walker nodded, pulling out her chair. "Take your time."

And so, she spoke. She told her everything. About Daz. About the conversation they had. The words he used. The way he looked. The years of history between them. She spoke with quiet intensity, her voice only breaking when she described her fear. Not of him hurting her—she never believed he would. But of what it meant to be complicit. Of knowing and doing nothing.

Detective Walker didn't interrupt. When Emily finished, there was a long pause.

"Thank you," she said finally. "You did the right thing coming in. This helps us. And it helps you."

Emily nodded. She felt lighter, but the ache remained.

"Will I be in trouble? For not saying anything sooner?"

Walker shook her head. "Not if you cooperate now. And you are. We'll need a formal statement. And we may ask you to testify, if it comes to that."

Emily looked down at her hands. "Okay."

The rest of the meeting passed in a blur. Paperwork. Dates. She tried her best to answer the questions. By the time she stepped out of the station, the sun had dipped lower, and the sky was streaked with purple and grey.

She stood there on the pavement for a while, arms wrapped around herself. Cold, uncertain, but resolute.

She had made her choice.

She walked home in silence, her phone buzzing with messages she didn't read. Alex had messaged. Sara too. But she needed space. Needed to breathe.

Back in the flat, she stood by the window, looking out at the world below. People walking dogs. Children on scooters. A couple laughing on a bench. Life, continuing.

She pressed her palm to the glass.

"Bye," she whispered. "Sorry."

And she turned away.

Chapter Sixty-Two

Duffel bags

Daz had always imagined the moment Emily might confront him. A part of him even longed for it, a fantasy where she might understand, might forgive. But the way she'd looked at him the other night—equal parts horror and heartbreak—told him everything he needed to know. There was no going back.

She knew.

He hadn't meant to admit it. But the words had tumbled out. Raw and ugly and true. He'd killed her father. And once the truth had been spoken, there was no pulling it back into the shadows.

Since then, he'd watched her. Not out of obsession this time—but desperation. He followed her movements over the next day and a half like a man counting down the final beats of a ticking clock.

She was quiet. Thoughtful. Her face gave nothing away, but Daz had learned to read her in ways others hadn't. There was determination there. He saw it in the way she walked—no longer weighed down, but purposeful. She wasn't floundering. She wasn't doubting. She had made a decision.

And he knew what it was.

That morning, he watched from a bench across the street as she stepped into a coffee shop. Her hair was tied back, and she wore no makeup. Comfortable, confident, calm. It reminded him of another version of her—a version before the pain and the darkness. A version he had tried to protect. Maybe had even tried to possess.

She sat by the window, fingers wrapped around the warmth of a drink she barely sipped. She stared out the window. Not at him. Past him. Through him. And then she stood.

His heart pounded. His legs felt like concrete, locked into place.

He watched as she turned the corner. He knew where she was going. The police station wasn't far.

Daz stood and followed, staying a good distance behind, careful not to be seen. He watched her walk with that same deliberate pace, each step hammering another nail into the coffin of the life he could have had. He felt it in his chest. Pressure. Pain. Panic.

When she disappeared into the building, he knew.

It was over.

The silence inside him broke like glass. His thoughts, usually sharp and disciplined, scattered. He walked for hours, avoiding cameras, taking back streets and alleyways. At one point, he ducked into an old disused garage to sit in the dark and think.

He had no illusions. He'd killed a man. Emily's father. A man who'd deserved justice—but not like that. Not without consequence. And now it was coming.

He texted his nan:

"Don't worry about me. I'm safe. Don't try to call. I love you."

Then he powered off his phone, removed the battery, and threw it into a storm drain near the industrial estate. His backup burner had already been destroyed earlier that week. He knew this day might come. He had prepared.

He made his way to the lock-up he'd rented under a fake name months ago. Inside, a duffle bag waited—cash, clothes, a passport with a terrible photo and an even worse alias. Everything a man needed to disappear.

His breathing was shallow now. Adrenaline dulled the edge of fear, but it didn't erase it.

He thought of Emily.

He pictured her smile. The real one. Not the polite, closed-lipped version she gave the world, but the one he used to see when they were younger—when she'd laugh at something stupid he said, her head thrown back, eyes sparkling. He'd clung to that image for years. It had been his reason for everything. His purpose.

But that version of Emily was gone now. And maybe it had been him who destroyed her. Maybe he'd taken something from her she could never reclaim.

He zipped up the duffle bag and slung it over his shoulder. He couldn't think like that. Not now.

He walked out of the lock-up, sealing the door behind him, knowing he'd never come back.

He was no longer Daz. He couldn't be.

He'd find a new name. A new place. A new way to exist. There was no redemption, only survival.

But as he made his way to the bus terminal, hood up, eyes lowered, every footstep heavy with finality, he felt it: the echo of what could have been. Of who he might have been if things had turned out differently.

He didn't look back.

Because Emily wasn't behind him anymore. She was ahead. In a new life. One that didn't need him in it.

And he finally understood: protecting her didn't mean being near her.

It meant leaving her alone.

Chapter Sixty-Three

The Hunt

Emily sat at the edge of the sofa. Her eyes were fixed on the television screen, but her mind was far away—flicking between memory, fear, and disbelief. The headlines rolled across the bottom of the screen in stark white letters:

"MANHUNT UNDERWAY – POLICE SEEKING DARREN 'DAZ' HENDERSON IN CONNECTION WITH MURDER."

It had been three days since she left the police station. Four since she knew, truly knew, that there was no turning back. And now... now Daz was missing. Gone. Disappeared into whatever plan he'd had waiting for this moment.

Her phone buzzed again. She didn't look at it. She already knew what it was—more messages from people she hadn't spoken to in years. People from her old school, old neighbours, vague acquaintances. Everyone had something to say. Everyone had seen the news.

"Isn't that the guy you used to hang around with?"
"Emily... you okay?"
"Wasn't he your... like, your fella'?"
"I always thought he was weird."
"Did you ask him to do it?"

She hadn't replied to a single one.

Even her mother had tried to call. Twice. Cynthia had messaged her, too—just one line:

"What the hell is going on?"

She hadn't answered them either. Not because she didn't want to. But because she couldn't. She didn't have the words for this. Didn't know how to explain how things had come to this point. Daz had been a presence in her life so loud, so furious, so constant— and now he was everywhere and nowhere at once.

The manhunt was already being shared across Facebook. Grainy pictures of Daz from years ago, a blurry CCTV image that might've been him walking through a petrol station forecourt in the early hours of the morning. "Do not approach," they said. "If you see him, call 999." The words felt so strange, so final.

Sara entered the room quietly, setting down a fresh cup of tea beside her before sitting beside her on the sofa.

"You haven't eaten today," Sara said gently. "You want me to make something?"

Emily shook her head. "No. I'm not hungry."

Sara didn't push. She just sat there, her presence warm and calm, like an anchor. That had been the pattern of the last few days—Sara stepping in where everyone else was shut out. Emily didn't even have to ask. She just knew.

"I thought I'd feel something," Emily murmured finally. "Like… relief. Or safety. But all I feel is sick."

Sara reached out, wrapping an arm around her. "It's trauma, Em. Your body's still in survival mode. You've been through something massive. It's going to take time."

Emily swallowed. "He admitted it. To me. He didn't even try to lie. He said it like it was obvious. Like he was doing me a favour."

Silence hung between them.

"I keep thinking about how he watched me," she continued. "All those months. And I didn't even realise. I didn't feel it, or maybe I did and I ignored it. He was just there. I was living my life and he was… there."

Sara's grip tightened. "It's not your fault. You didn't do anything wrong. You were trying to move forward."

"But I brought him into my life. I let him into our home. I trusted him when no one else did."

Sara didn't answer. There was nothing to say to that.

Outside, the late evening light was beginning to fade. Emily's phone buzzed again. She finally glanced down at it—another message from someone she barely remembered.

"Hey hun, just saw the news. Are you okay?"

She turned the screen face down.

Later that night, when Sara was in bed and the flat was dark and silent, Emily sat alone at the kitchen table. The police had told her they'd keep her updated. That they were working every lead. That they had a team dedicated to tracking him down.

She believed them. She also knew Daz wasn't stupid.

He'd planned this. He'd vanished like smoke. Left no trace. No phone. No cards. No car registered in his name. The kind of disappearance you didn't pull off unless you were desperate—or determined.

She stared out of the window, into the dark London street below. Somewhere out there, Daz was watching the news too. Or maybe he wasn't. Maybe he was holed up in a squat, or hiding in a caravan by the coast, or sleeping rough under a false name. Maybe he was gone forever.

The thought chilled her.

Not just because he might never be found. But because he might come back.

The next day was more of the same. She didn't go to work. Couldn't face it. Her boss had been understanding enough, though vague. "Take whatever time you need," they said. "We're here if you need support."

She opened her laptop but didn't type anything. She scrolled instead—mindlessly, through endless news pages and social feeds, looking for updates. There were none.

A knock at the door made her jump. Her heart jolted, irrationally, fearfully. For a second, she was back in that street—watching Daz from across the road, seeing him bolt when their eyes met. That expression on his face. Like a cornered animal.

She approached the door slowly, peeking through the spyhole.

It was Cynthia.

Emily sighed, unlocked the door, and opened it a crack.

"I just want to talk," Cynthia said quickly. "Please."

"I'm not in the mood."

"I know. But I'm scared too. I needed to see you."

Emily opened the door a little wider and stepped aside to let her sister in.

Cynthia looked tired. Pale. Her expression softer than usual.

"I saw the news," she said. "I… didn't think it was real at first. I thought maybe someone was winding me up."

"It's real."

"Why didn't you tell me you were involved?"

Emily's eyes narrowed. "I'm not involved."

"I didn't mean it like that," Cynthia said, backpedalling. "I just mean… you knew him. You *knew* him. Better than any of us. And I always thought something was off, but you defended him for years—"

"Because he *wasn't* always like this!" Emily snapped. "He protected me. He cared about me."

"And then he *killed our dad*."

Emily flinched. Cynthia softened.

"I'm sorry. I didn't come here to fight. I just… I'm trying to make sense of it too."

Emily let out a long, slow breath. "Yeah. Join the club."

That night, Sara offered to stay up with her, but Emily insisted she'd be fine. She wasn't. Her head was spinning with too many thoughts, too many memories. She kept replaying the moment she saw Daz in the street. The look in his eyes when she confronted him. That strange mix of guilt and conviction.

He thought he'd done the right thing. And maybe, in his twisted way, he *had* done it for her. But that didn't mean she could ever forgive it. Or him.

She didn't sleep much.

Two more days passed. The news was quiet. Still no confirmed sightings of Daz. Police were "following up on credible leads," but they hadn't said where. Or how close they might be.

Emily checked every update obsessively.

She'd already told the police everything she knew. She'd sat in the same small interview room twice now. Spoken to the same detective, who had a calm voice and kind eyes. "You've been brave," he said. "We're doing everything we can."

She wondered if Daz had seen her go into the station. If he knew. If he was watching her still.

Every time she left the flat, she scanned the street. Every reflection in a shop window, every parked car, every face in the crowd—she looked. She *searched*. Just in case.

Because if he did come back…

This time, she wouldn't be caught off guard.

Chapter Sixty-Four

In the dark

Daz hadn't slept properly in four days.

The floor beneath him was concrete, cold and cracked. The old shipping container behind the scrapyard was just as he remembered it from years ago when he'd helped out the owner for cash-in-hand work. It smelled like oil, rust, and rats. But no one asked questions here, and no one noticed one more shadow slipping in after dark.

He hadn't dared use the same place twice in a row until now. But he was running out of options. His legs ached from walking, hiding, doubling back. His eyes burned from lack of sleep. And still, every time he heard a siren in the distance or a car slowing down outside, he braced himself for the sound of boots, voices, the crackle of a radio.

But they hadn't found him. Not yet.

He'd seen his face on the news the first night, on a small TV mounted above a kebab shop counter. The owner had been too busy yelling in Turkish into the phone to notice Daz standing there, staring at the grainy CCTV footage. His heart had stopped for a beat. Then another. Then it had kicked in again, hard and fast, and he'd left without his food.

The phone was gone. He'd snapped the SIM, tossed the casing in a bin, the battery in another. He kept the charger cord, out of habit more than need. He texted Nan once, told her he was alright, told her not to worry. That was it.

Now, there was only movement. Constant movement.

The city was loud and indifferent, which helped. London didn't look too hard at people on the margins. Daz had perfected the art of disappearing. Hoodie up. Head down. Don't linger. Don't stare. Don't ask. He slept in bus shelters and under bridges. He stole food from shops and took clothes from washing lines. He'd done it before, years ago. It came back easily.

But it was different now.

Now he had a face. Now they were *looking*.

And through it all, he thought of Emily.

He'd seen her the day she went into the police station. Watched her leave Sara's flat, sit alone in that quiet coffee shop, then make her way toward the station. He hadn't followed her in. He didn't need to. He knew what was coming.

He felt it in his chest like a dull thud.

He wasn't angry. He didn't even blame her.

He had told her the truth. For once, he hadn't hidden behind stories or rage or bravado. He'd told her what he did. Why he did it. And she'd looked at him like she didn't know who he was anymore.

Maybe she didn't.

He barely knew himself.

In the silence of the container, he lay flat, staring at the rusted beams overhead. They looked like veins. Split and clogged. Like something broken inside a machine.

He'd been running his whole life. From homes, from schools, from jobs, from people. The only place he'd ever stayed still was with her. And now she'd become the one thing he couldn't run toward. Not without destroying them both.

He thought about going north. Maybe Scotland. Or across the Channel. But he didn't have contacts anymore. No one he trusted. No one that wouldn't sell him out for the reward.

He thought about his Nan. She wouldn't tell the police anything, he knew that. But she'd be scared. She'd already lost too much. He missed her. Missed the safety of her tiny house, her bitter tea, the scratch of her records in the background.

And Emily.

He missed her more than anything.

Not the way she looked at him now. But the way she used to.

That small, defiant girl with the scraped knees and angry eyes. The one who let him sit beside her in silence. Who didn't ask stupid questions. Who let him be.

He used to dream of the future. Not big dreams. Just small ones. Waking up somewhere warm. Making her laugh. Holding her hand. Not worrying if the door was going to get kicked in.

He never deserved that.

But he wanted it. For a long time, he wanted it more than he wanted revenge. More than he wanted anything.

Now all he wanted was an ending.

Not for her. For himself.

He couldn't keep running. Not forever. He didn't want to. Maybe the cops would catch him. Maybe someone would rat him out. Maybe it would end in blood. He didn't care.

But he needed to see her one last time.

He needed to say goodbye.

Not to fix anything. Not to ask for forgiveness.

Just to let her know he was going. That she wouldn't have to look over her shoulder. That she could live the life she was building without him clinging to the corners.

When he stepped outside, the night air was cold. The city buzzed like a living thing, and he melted into it again, invisible but watching.

He would find her.

And then he would disappear for good.

Chapter Sixty-Five

The Café

The nights were colder now, but Daz barely noticed. It wasn't the wind that chilled him—it was the waiting. The hiding. The wondering. Every time a siren wailed in the distance, he flinched. Every unfamiliar face in a crowd was a potential threat. But nothing unnerved him more than the thought of never seeing Emily again.

He knew he couldn't run forever. And deep down, he didn't want to. Not without making things right—or at least trying to. Closure. That was the word he kept turning over in his mind. He owed her that. He owed himself that.

She deserved to look him in the eyes. To scream. To cry. To walk away. Whatever she needed to do. He wouldn't stop her. He just had to see her one last time. Face to face.

But how do you approach someone who sees you as a monster?

For days, Daz observed from the shadows. He tracked Emily's routine, always careful to stay two steps behind. She hadn't changed her routes much. Still walked to work when the weather allowed. Still visited the same café on Sundays around three. He noted the way she paused before stepping into places, as if always checking for something—or someone. He wondered if she already knew.

She was with that lad sometimes. Alex. Daz hated how normal he looked. How safe. He hated how Emily laughed around him, that easy kind of laughter he hadn't heard in years. But he also felt something else—a strange sort of relief. She was surviving.

Still, he needed to talk to her. Not in the middle of the street. Not while she was surrounded. Somewhere private. Somewhere quiet.

The café came back to him like a vision. Tucked away on a side road near her flat, just out of view. He'd been there once before, during better days. Back then, the most serious thing on his mind had been how to ask her if she wanted to go halves on a sandwich. Now, he was plotting how to confront her with the truth.

He watched the café over several days. Learned its rhythm. Busy from noon until two. Then a lull. The back room was rarely used—sometimes left open, sometimes closed off with a curtain. It would do.

He didn't want to scare her. He wanted her to come willingly. But he knew that wouldn't happen. So he planned it carefully. He'd wait until she was inside, alone. Then he'd follow. Quietly. Just once. Just to talk.

He thought about what he'd say. Practiced the words over and over:

"I never meant to hurt you." "It was never about revenge." "He wasn't a father. Not really."

None of it sounded right.

He considered writing her a letter. Leaving it somewhere she'd find. But that felt like running. Like hiding. He needed to stand in front of her and say it. Accept the consequences.

The night before, he barely slept. He lay beneath an overpass wrapped in an old jacket, the concrete cold beneath him. He thought about their childhood. The summers spent climbing trees. The bruised knees. The pinky promises. Then the years between—the silence, the pain, the choices that changed everything.

He remembered her at the funeral. How she'd barely looked at him. How quickly she'd left. She had moved on, built something better. And now he was about to tear a hole in it again.

Still, he had to do it.

He woke early and washed in a public bathroom. Shaved with a disposable razor he'd nicked from a service station. Wore a plain black hoodie and jeans—nothing that stood out. He didn't want to look like a threat.

He arrived an hour early. Watched from across the road. At ten minutes to three, she appeared. Alone. Headphones in. Hands tucked in her coat pockets. She looked tired. A little thinner.

She stepped inside.

His heart thumped.

Daz counted to sixty. Then crossed the street.

The bell above the café door jingled as he entered. The warmth hit him first, then the smell of roasted coffee beans and cinnamon. The barista barely glanced at him.

Emily was seated in the back, alone, sipping from a small cup. Her eyes were on the window.

He approached slowly. Every step felt like a warning.

When he was close enough, he said her name.

"Emily."

She turned.

Shock. Recognition. Fear.

Their eyes locked.

She didn't scream. Didn't run.

He raised his hands slightly.

"I just want to talk. Please."

She stared at him. Motionless.

The noise of the café faded.

"Just five minutes," he said. "Somewhere private."

She stood slowly. Her hands trembled.

"ok" she whispered.

Chapter Sixty-Six

Clink

The morning light poured into the café through tall glass windows, casting soft reflections across the marble counter. The quiet clatter of cups and hum of low conversation filled the air, familiar and comforting. Emily stirred her oat latte, the creamy surface rippling beneath her spoon. No syrup today—she liked it plain now. Cleaner. Like her life.

Her phone buzzed on the table. A reminder about an upcoming meeting. She dismissed it with a swipe, taking a slow sip of her drink. The warmth of the coffee was grounding. This café had become a ritual, a sanctuary. She came every morning before work, claiming her corner seat by the window, where she could look out at the street and feel both part of the world and removed from it.

Since everything had happened—her father's murder, the investigation, Daz vanishing—she'd built her life carefully, piece by piece. Therapy twice a month. Journaling. Cooking for herself. Her and Sara had even painted the hallway last weekend. A calming grey-blue. She'd made peace with some things. Others remained... heavy.

She exhaled deeply. Her chest had felt tight all morning. An unspoken weight hung over her, and she couldn't place why. The sky was clear, her job secure, her relationships stable. She should feel okay. But the unease crept in anyway.

She heard the door as it opened, the little bell chiming.

And a few moment late a shadow grew over her.

She looked up.

Daz.

Her spoon slipped from her fingers, clinking into the cup. The noise was drowned out by the sudden roar in her ears. Her vision narrowed, like a tunnel. Her breathing hitched. Her body, once relaxed, turned to stone. Fight or flight. Or freeze.

His face was older. Drawn. His shoulders tense. He looked like a corpse who hadn't yet realised he was dead.

He walked toward her slowly. Each step echoed in her mind louder than the buzz of the café. Her fingers curled tightly around the edge of the table. She could run. She should run.

But her legs didn't move.

She wanted to scream, cry, shout, ask a thousand questions. But her voice was trapped behind the lump rising in her throat.

He reached the table. His eyes met hers. They weren't wild, not yet. They were... pleading.

"Emily," he said, quiet but firm. Like he'd practiced it.

She didn't reply. The room spun gently. She felt nausea rise, her mouth dry. Her fingers trembled on her cup.

"Just five minutes," he said. "Somewhere private."

No.

Her mind screamed the word, over and over again. This was madness. He was dangerous. He'd admitted to killing her father. He was being hunted. There was a warrant out. Her therapist had told her to protect herself. This wasn't protection.

And yet.

Here he was. Flesh and blood and fear and sadness. Daz. Not a ghost. Not a headline. Just a man standing before her.

Part of her wanted closure. An explanation. Another part wanted him arrested, locked away. But the most frightening part of all—the tiny voice, buried deep— wanted to understand him. Just one last time.

Her hand released the coffee cup. She wiped her palms on her trousers.

"Okay," she whispered, though it felt like the word belonged to someone else.

He nodded, once. No smile. No relief. Just seriousness.

She stood slowly, her legs shaky. Her heart thudded so hard it hurt. She couldn't look directly at him anymore.

"Go out the side," she murmured. "Wait five minutes, then follow. You know where my flat is. Sara's out."

He gave the faintest nod again, then stepped back.

She turned and left. The cold air outside smacked her in the face, a slap of reality. Her body moved on autopilot, putting one foot in front of the other, every nerve in her body screaming for sense, for safety.

As she rounded the corner, she looked over her shoulder once. He hadn't left the café yet.

She walked faster.

Back to her flat.

To face whatever was about to happen.

Chapter Sixty-Seven

Run

Emily unlocked the door to her flat with trembling hands. The click of the lock sounded louder than usual, echoing in the empty hallway like a warning bell. She stepped inside, closed the door behind her, and leaned against it for a moment. Her breath caught in her chest as if it refused to move past the rising tide of dread that swelled in her throat.

She slid the bolt across the door with a decisive snap, then turned and looked at the quiet familiarity of her space. The neatly arranged cushions, the half-drunk glass of water on the side table, the potted plants by the window that Sara insisted added life to the place—all of it felt surreal. She was home. Safe. But nothing felt safe.

She moved to the kitchen, poured herself a glass of water, and spilled half of it down her shirt as her hand shook. She didn't bother to wipe it off. Her mind was racing, skipping from thought to thought without ever settling.

Daz. Daz was back.

He had stood in front of her. He had spoken. She had let him.

What the hell was she thinking?

She set the glass down and paced across the room. Her feet moved in tight circles, looping across the rug as her heart pounded in her ears. A thousand thoughts fought for dominance.

Call the police. Run. Hide. Let him speak. Why did she tell him to come here? What had she been thinking?

Her phone was in her pocket. She pulled it out and opened it, her thumb hovering over Sara's name. She could tell her. She should tell someone. But no words came. What would she say?

"Hey, just invited the man who murdered my father into our flat The man on the run from the police."

Her hand dropped to her side.

The minutes ticked by like slow drips from a leaking tap. She stood at the window, peeking out through the curtain. The street below was quiet, but she knew he'd come. He said five minutes. Maybe more. Maybe he was already here, waiting for the right moment.

She checked the door again. Unbolted it. Bolted it back. Unbolted it. Bolted it back.

She couldn't keep still.

What did he want from her?

She ran through their conversation at the café, every word dissected and rearranged in her head. His face. His voice. The way he had looked at her, desperate and haunted. There had been no threat in his tone. Just sadness. Just...

Regret?

She didn't know. She didn't trust herself to know.

And then she heard it. A knock. Three soft, even taps on the door.

She froze. The air around her tightened. Her body went rigid, her heart thumping like a fly under a glass.

Another knock. Still soft. Still patient.

She didn't move. Not for a full ten seconds. Then, without quite knowing why, she walked to the door.

Her hand reached for the bolt. Slid it back. She hesitated, hand on the handle, then opened the door slowly.

Daz stood there.

He looked tired. Not the kind of tired that sleep could fix, but worn down to the soul. His hoodie was pulled up, shadows under his eyes. He didn't speak.

She stepped aside.

He entered.

She shut the door, not bothering with the bolt this time. The click echoed again.

They stood there in silence, the air thick between them.

Her fingers twisted in the hem of her sleeve. She watched him as he looked around, as if trying to remember her space, like someone walking through a memory.

"Sit," she said softly, though it sounded more like a question than a command.

He sat.

She stayed standing.

And then finally, after what felt like an hour inside of a minute, she said, "Why are you here, Daz?"

His eyes met hers. And she braced herself for the answer.

Chapter Sixty-Eight

Unresolved

The silence that stretched between them was unbearable. Emily stood by the window, her arms folded tightly across her chest, watching the shadow of Daz reflected faintly on the polished floor. He sat hunched at the edge of the sofa, elbows on knees, head bowed like he was praying.

She finally broke the stillness. "Why are you here, Daz?" She asked, firmer this time.

He looked up slowly. There were dark hollows under his eyes, his face was thinner than before, sunken almost, and his skin pale beneath the hood of his coat. But his eyes still carried that glint of obsession, of unresolved desperation.

"I needed to see you. I needed to explain."

"Explain what? That you killed my father? That you've been watching me for weeks, months? That you—" she stopped herself, voice faltering. Her throat was dry, and her hands trembled slightly at her sides. "That you're not the person I thought you were."

He flinched. "He was going to hurt you. Again. I saw it. I saw the way he treated people, the way he treated your sister in the shop—"

"You don't know what went on in that house! You weren't there!" Emily stepped forward, her voice rising. "You weren't even part of my life anymore. You lost that right!"

Daz stood, too quickly, the tension surging in his limbs. He stepped forward, voice strained. "I did it for you! Everything I did—losing sleep, hiding, the pain—it was all to keep you safe. You meant something to me, Em. You still do."

"Then why do I feel like I'm being stalked? Like I'm prey? You scare me, Daz." Her voice cracked. "And if you don't leave right now, I swear I'll call the police."

The words sent a shock through him. He looked stunned, betrayed. Then he snapped.

With sudden force, he lunged forward and snatched her phone from the table. Before she could react, he hurled it across the room. It clattered against the wall and shattered.

Emily gasped, stepping back instinctively. Her breath caught in her chest.

"Why are you doing this?" she said, eyes wide. "Why won't you let me go?"

"Because I can't!" he shouted. "You don't get to just walk away from me! After everything. After what I gave up. After what I did."

His hand drifted into his coat pocket, closing around the blade he had brought. Not to use—never to use. Just for protection. Just in case. But now, it burned in his palm.

Emily saw the movement. Her heart slammed against her ribs. "Daz. No."

He pulled the blade free, slowly, almost dazed, like he couldn't believe he was doing it. "What? Do I scare you now huh!?" "You said you'd always care about me. You said I mattered to you."

"You do! Or you did. But this isn't love, Daz. This is obsession. This is violence. This is madness."

"You think I'm mad?" He gave a dry, bitter laugh. "I did everything right. And you still turned away. You still looked at me like I was the villain."

"Because you killed people, Daz! You ended people's lives. My father or not, you don't get to choose who lives or dies."

He stepped closer, brandishing the blade without fully realising how tightly he held it. "I kept you safe. You don't even understand what I saved you from. I watched your life. I saw everything."

Emily backed away slowly, bumping against the counter. Her voice wavered. "Daz, please. Don't do this. You don't have to prove anything. You don't have to make it worse."

He reached for her. His hand brushed her arm, and she recoiled instinctively, shoving him back. He stumbled, his anger bursting free.

"You don't deserve me! You never did!"

And then, blind fury took him.

He lifted the blade.

Chapter Sixty-Nine

Polished

The blade shimmered in the low light of the apartment. Time seemed to slow.

Emily froze. Every nerve in her body screamed at her to run, to fight, to scream—but she couldn't move. The sharp glint of the metal stole all sense from her limbs.

"Please," she whispered. "Daz, don't."

Her voice cut through the fog in his mind. He blinked, his grip tightening, then loosening, then tightening again. The moment stretched, suspended between violence and retreat.

Emily's eyes shimmered with tears, but she didn't cry. Her voice, though shaking, stayed steady. "You don't want to do this. You're better than this. You have to believe that."

He faltered. A flicker of doubt, of humanity, passed through his face. His shoulders sagged.

Then he looked into her eyes and saw not fear—not only fear. He saw the disgust. The distance. The silent conclusion: you're a monster.

"You think I'm evil," he muttered. "You think I'm disgusting."

Emily didn't answer. Her silence was enough.

"All I ever did was love you," he said. "That's all I wanted. I just wanted to protect you."

"Then leave. Let me go, Daz. Let yourself go."

But it was too late.

His mind, spiralling now, refused to accept it. He couldn't let it end this way. Couldn't let her walk away with this final image of him.

He turned away, gripping the blade tightly. His breath came in ragged bursts. He paced in circles. Muttering to himself. Shaking. Unravelling.

Emily stayed by the counter. She scanned the room for a weapon, a phone, anything. Nothing was close enough. The walls felt like they were closing in.

"You took everything from me," he said, voice low. "Every time I got back on my feet, you were there. And now you're the one tearing me down."

"I never asked you to do any of this. I never wanted this."

"But I did! I wanted it all! I wanted you!"

His hand clenched. The blade shone.

She stepped forward, cautiously. "You don't have to do this, Daz. You can walk away. We both can."

He looked at her. And for a second, something soft returned to his eyes. The boy he once was, the boy who used to make her laugh, who used to walk her home and buy her sweets from the corner shop. But that boy was buried under years of pain.

"I just wanted to matter," he said quietly. "To someone. To you."

Her heart ached, twisted with grief and anger and fear. "You do matter. But not like this. This isn't love, Daz. This is a graveyard."

The silence returned. Emily could hear her heartbeat in her ears. A drip of the tap. The wind outside the window. Time slowed again.

Daz stared at the blade. Then back to her. Then to the blade.

He took one trembling step forward.

"Daz—"

Chapter Seventy

Pale

Emily didn't feel the pain at first. There was only a strange jolt, like someone had knocked the wind out of her. Then the warmth flooded over her abdomen—hot, sticky, too fast. She looked down slowly, blinking as if her mind couldn't catch up with what her eyes were showing her. The deep red spread across her jumper, soaking through the pale grey fabric.

Daz stood inches from her, hand still hovering in the air, the blade now lowered. It glinted faintly in the light from the kitchen window. His face had shifted. All rage had drained from it, replaced by something far worse: panic. Horror. Disbelief.

"No," he whispered, as if trying to rewind what had just happened. "No, no, no."

Emily dropped to her knees, her hands pressing instinctively against the wound. Her fingers were slick with blood. She gasped as the pain set in—sharp, raw, and deep. She felt dizzy. Her breaths were shallow, her ears ringing.

"Emily!" Daz cried, dropping beside her. He threw the blade across the room. It skidded under the radiator with a metallic clatter.

"I didn't mean to," he choked out, hands shaking as he reached for her. She recoiled slightly, her body tense, but she didn't have the strength to push him away.

Daz stood and grabbed a dishcloth from the kitchen side, then another. He stumbled back to her and pressed them against the wound. Blood quickly soaked through, but he kept pushing, his fingers trembling.

"Come on," he muttered, to her, to himself, to the universe. "Stay with me. Please stay with me."

Emily looked up at him. Her eyes were glazed but still alive, still present. She wanted to speak but couldn't find the words.

Daz fumbled with her phone. It was cracked from his earlier anger. His hands were slick with her blood, the screen smeared red as he dialled emergency services.

"Police and ambulance," he said breathlessly when the operator picked up. "Please. I've stabbed someone. It was an accident. I didn't mean to. She's bleeding badly. You have to come now. Please."

He gave the address, stammering through it, repeating it twice. Then he dropped the phone and crouched beside her again, clutching the cloth tighter.

"They're coming," he said. His voice cracked. "You're gonna be okay. You're going to be okay."

Emily's vision blurred. Her head swam. Everything felt heavy—her limbs, her eyelids, her thoughts.

She wanted to scream. Wanted to run. Wanted to tell him he was a coward. That he had ruined everything.

But mostly, she wanted to survive.

Her lips parted. "Daz..."

He leaned in close. "I'm here. I'm right here."

Tears streamed down his face. The blood on his hands had begun to dry in streaks. The flat was silent except for the low hum of the fridge and their uneven breathing. Outside, the world continued as normal. Inside, time had stopped.

The pool of blood beneath her was growing.

Daz tried to apply more pressure. He didn't know if he was helping or making it worse. He couldn't think straight. He couldn't remember anything he was taught in school or ever seen in films. Everything felt distant, surreal.

He leaned over her, forehead pressed to hers.

"I'm so sorry," he whispered. "I never wanted to hurt you. I just... I didn't know what else to do."

Emily blinked slowly. She was slipping.

Her flat blurred into a haze of lights and shadows. Daz's face became a smear of colours. Her chest rose and fell unsteadily.

Somewhere in the distance, there was a siren.

Daz lifted his head, listening. Then he stood, ran to the window, and flung it open.

"Up here!" he shouted. "She's up here!"

A voice called back from the street. Feet pounded up the stairs.

He ran back to Emily, dropping to his knees again. "They're here. Just hold on. Please. Hold on."

The front door burst open.

Two paramedics and a police officer rushed in. One of the medics dropped beside Emily, taking over the pressure on the wound. The other began unzipping bags, shouting instructions. The officer held Daz back, forcing him to sit against the wall.

"What happened?"

"It was me," he whispered, numb. "I stabbed her. I didn't mean to. It was an accident."

Emily moaned softly as they rolled her onto her side, attaching leads, checking vitals. A needle entered her arm. An oxygen mask went over her face. Daz watched, helpless.

The paramedic looked at his partner. "We need to go. Now."

They transferred her to a stretcher, blood still seeping through the cloths. As they wheeled her toward the door, Emily turned her head slightly. Her eyes flicked to Daz's. There was pain. Fear. But no forgiveness.

He stared after her, heart thudding in his ears.

The officer snapped handcuffs on his wrists.

"You have the right to remain silent..."

But Daz wasn't listening. His eyes stayed fixed on the empty doorway. On the red smears across the floor. On the broken pieces of something he couldn't name.

As they led him out, all he could think was:

What have I done?

Chapter Seventy-One

Red rivers

The walls were white. Not clinical, not bright. Just dull, tired white. The kind of white that had once held life but had been faded by years of waiting and watching, soaking up confessions, lies, rage, and despair. Daz sat slouched in a hard plastic chair, his arms cuffed behind him, and his head resting against the chipped corner of the interrogation table.

Time had stopped meaning anything. Maybe it had been two hours. Maybe ten. He couldn't tell. There was no clock. No sound but the soft hum of the strip lights above and the occasional creak of old pipes behind the walls. His eyes were open but not seeing. His brain was stuck in a carousel of memory—a looping film reel of blood, her eyes wide and glassy, his hands covered in red, her voice gasping something he couldn't even remember.

It wasn't supposed to go like that. It wasn't supposed to end.

The door opened once. Earlier. A young officer brought him a bottle of water. He hadn't touched it. The bottle just sat there now, sweating quietly onto the metal table like it was nervous too.

He didn't cry. Not anymore. The tears had dried up somewhere between the police car and this room. He had wailed then. Sobbed into the fabric of his hoodie like a child. Screamed into the darkness of the backseat, the sirens wailing overhead like a chorus of judgment.

But now? He was empty. Nothing but dust and echoes.

The door opened again.

Detective Walker stepped in. She looked tired, but not in a physically exhausted way. More like the tired that comes from seeing the same story played out a hundred times in different skin, with different faces.

She sat down across from him without saying anything at first. Pulled out a slim folder. Clicked a pen.

Daz blinked. The sound of the pen clicking felt like a firework.

"Darren Roberts," she began, voice measured. "Do you understand why you're here?"

He nodded, eyes locked on the scratches in the table.

"I stabbed her."

"Emily," she clarified, writing something. "And what about her Father? I believe there is a Warrant out for you Mr Roberts."

"Yes, I killed him."

"Can you tell me what happened?"

He swallowed. Tried to form the words. They caught in his throat like ash.

"I just… I needed to talk to her," he whispered. "To explain. I didn't mean for it to go like that. I never wanted to hurt her."

Walker nodded, but her face remained blank.

"You brought a weapon."

"For protection," he said, flinching. "Not from her. From whoever. I've been looking over my shoulder for months. I thought… I thought maybe someone would come for me. It wasn't for her."

"But you used it on her."

He pressed his forehead into the table.

"Yes."

There was a long silence.

"Tell me everything that happened today," she said, gently this time.

He spoke slowly, voice flat, the shame in each word dragging it down like an anchor. He told her about the café. Seeing her. Asking for five minutes. Her saying yes. The walk. The wait. Her flat. The arguing. Her threat to call the police.

"I panicked," he said. "I grabbed her phone. I didn't want to go to prison. I wasn't thinking straight."

"And the blade?"

He hesitated.

"It was in my pocket. I just… I didn't think. She pushed me away. She said things. I felt like everything was slipping away. Everything I did, all of it, it was for her."

Walker didn't write that part down. She just looked at him.

"She didn't want your protection, Darren."

He laughed, but it was hollow.

"I see that now."

They talked for twenty more minutes. Just questions and answers. Just facts. As if putting them into a neat list could make it logical, explainable.

Then a knock on the door.

Another officer, murmured something into Walker's ear.

She nodded slowly.

"Wait here," she said.

Daz slumped in the chair, face down again. The sound of the door closing echoed like a gunshot.

He waited.

Minutes ticked by. He stared at the bottle again. It was still sweating.

When she came back, something was different. Her jaw was tighter. Her eyes, dim.

She sat down and folded her hands.

"Darren," she said.

He looked up.

"Emily has been pronounced dead."

He blinked.

"I have to let you know that this is now a murder investigation."

"What?"

"They tried. Paramedics did everything they could. But the wound was too deep. She lost too much blood."

He stared. His mouth opened, but no sound came out.

"There was nothing they could do."

His whole body buckled inward.

It hit like a tsunami, like the air was sucked out of the room and all that was left was pressure. His knees hit the floor before he realised he'd even stood up. A choking sound escaped his throat. Something between a scream and a sob.

He rocked forward, head against the floor, sobbing now, wet and ragged. The sounds of true grief, raw and wild. He clawed at his hair, his skin, his arms.

"No," he whispered. "No, no, no, no. Please. No."

Walker didn't touch him. She let it happen. Let it break.

"I killed her," he wept. "I killed her. I… I didn't mean to. I just wanted her to see me. Just one more time. I didn't mean to do it. Not like that."

He curled into himself. Time stopped again.

Eventually, a medic came in to check on him. They gave him water. Tried to calm him. He didn't fight. He sat against the wall, arms around his knees.

His eyes were dead.

He said nothing more that day.

There was nothing left to say.

Chapter Seventy-Two

The secret garden

The sky was a pale, washed-out grey—the kind of sky that didn't cry but looked like it might at any moment. The air carried a heavy stillness as though the world, too, understood the weight of what this day meant. Emily's funeral had drawn a quiet crowd, the mourners filing into the church in solemn clusters, their voices hushed and footsteps soft against the stone floor.

Sara stood near the front, her eyes swollen and red, her hand wrapped tightly around a tissue that was already soaked through. The friends from Brighton—Sam, Nadia, Jess—sat quietly behind her, wearing black dresses and subdued expressions. Even in their youth and vibrance, the weight of the loss had settled onto them like a heavy coat.

Music from Emily's favourite film, *The Secret Garden*, played gently in the background. The melody, haunting and beautiful, carried through the air as the pallbearers—six solemn men from the funeral home—carried her in. People stood. Heads bowed. The silence deepened.

Emily's mother stood stiffly, her grief a strange mixture of regret and shock. Her posture was rigid, face unreadable, her hands tightly gripping the sides of her coat. Cynthia stood to her left, quieter still, her arms folded in front of her like she was holding herself together with sheer will.

Louise hadn't come. No one had expected her to, though the absence stung nonetheless.

The white coffin sat at the front of the chapel, layered with soft pink roses—Emily's favourite. The sight of it made Sara's breath hitch every time she looked up. It felt wrong. Emily had always been so full of life, laughter, and sharp wit. She didn't belong in a box. She didn't belong here at all.

Alex stood quietly at the back, half-shadowed by the doorway, in a black coat that hung too loose on his frame, as if the grief itself had worn him thinner. He didn't speak or move much—just watched, his eyes locked on the white coffin as though willing it to open and undo what had happened. He hadn't known Emily long, but she had lit something in him—a warmth he hadn't realised he was missing. And now, in her absence, that space felt hollow.

The vicar spoke gently, reading the familiar verses about peace and everlasting life. It all sounded so generic, so far away from the real girl who had lived and laughed and fought and tried. But no one interrupted. No one cried out. They just let the words wash over them, hoping they'd bring some comfort, some sense of order to the chaos that had shattered their lives. Alex reached for Sara's arm—not for her sake, but his own. A simple touch, just to remind himself he was still here, still breathing, in a world where Emily no longer was.

When it came time for the speeches, Cynthia stepped forward. Her voice was shaky, but she didn't falter. "Emily was complicated," she began. "She was bright. She was strong. She was the kind of person who wouldn't let anyone walk over her—not even when it might have been easier to let them. She made you think. She made you feel. And she made me proud every day, even when I didn't know how to show it."

There were tears in her eyes now, and she brushed them away quickly. "She deserved better. From all of us."

The words hung in the air like smoke.

As the service neared its end, the curtains began to close on Emily's coffin. Sara sobbed openly, her shoulders shaking, her cries unfiltered and raw. The others stood in silence, some dabbing eyes, some staring ahead, lost in their own grief.

And then it was over.

Outside, people lingered, the chill in the air biting through their dark coats. Condolences were exchanged in hushed tones. Hugs were offered. No one quite knew what to say.

Daz's Nan had come, her presence quiet but significant. She stood at the back, her hand resting on a cane, her expression tight with grief. She hadn't approached the family during the service, but now she stood near the church gates, waiting. Watching.

Cynthia noticed her. Their eyes met across the crowd.

Chapter Seventy-Three

Wake up

The wake was held in the function room of a local pub just down the road from the chapel. It was one of those old English pubs with low ceilings and carpeted floors, the kind that tried to strike a balance between cosy and slightly formal. A basic spread of sandwiches, sausage rolls, and quiche sat on a long table. The bar was open. People gathered in quiet groups, drinks in hand, sharing stories in hushed tones.

Sara sat at a table with Emily's work friends, picking at a corner of a ham sandwich she wasn't really eating. She'd cried all she could. Now she just felt hollow. Around her, the room buzzed with quiet memories, laughter that faded too quickly, tears that came in waves.

At the far end of the room, Daz's Nan approached Cynthia. It was an unlikely pairing, and yet they stood together like two women carrying invisible boulders on their backs.

"I'm sorry," Doreen said first, her voice gravelly but kind. "For everything."

Cynthia turned to face her, her expression unreadable. "How are you?"

"Getting on with it," Doreen replied, nodding slowly. "Trying to, anyway. He's got his trial date set. They say he'll likely spend the rest of his life in there."

Cynthia inhaled sharply but said nothing.

"I'm going to see him Monday," Doreen added, more quietly now. "He's just a broken boy. Always has been. Didn't know how to be anything else."

They stood there in silence for a moment.

"He loved her, you know," Doreen said finally. "In his own twisted, painful way. He really did."

"I know," Cynthia whispered. "But it wasn't enough to save her."

"No," Doreen agreed. "It wasn't."

They parted quietly, without ceremony, the weight of the moment settling into the carpet.

People started to leave shortly after. Goodbyes were exchanged, hugs given with promises to stay in touch that likely wouldn't be kept. Sara and the girls from work were the last to go, helping to tidy plates and pack away the few remaining uneaten pastries.

The pub emptied. The day ended.

And Emily's absence stretched on into the silence.

Chapter Seventy-Four

The beginning

The long corridor hummed with fluorescent light, flickering now and then like it resented its own existence. Doreen clutched her handbag tightly to her chest, her steps slow and deliberate as the prison guard led her through the secure wing. The buzz of each door unlocking made her flinch. She'd rehearsed this in her mind for days, maybe weeks, but none of it felt like preparation now.

They reached the visiting room. It was quieter than she expected. A few other inmates sat with their visitors—some crying, some talking low, some staring at the clock. The guard pointed to a table near the back, where Daz sat alone, his hands folded on the table, his eyes downcast.

He looked smaller somehow. Not just in the grey oversized tracksuit, but in the way he held himself, like something inside him had caved in. His hair was shorter now, his face pale. She hadn't seen him since the arrest. Seeing him now, the boy she'd raised, the boy who had broken, made her heart twist in a way she didn't think possible.

She approached slowly. He didn't look up until her chair scraped across the floor.

"Nan," he said quietly.

She nodded; her throat too thick with emotion to speak. She reached across the table, placing her hand over his. For a second, he didn't respond. Then his fingers curled around hers tightly.

"I didn't think you'd come," he whispered.

"Course I did," she said, voice trembling. "You're still my boy."

He blinked rapidly, eyes welling. "I'm sorry."

She didn't say anything to that, not at first. What could she say? That it was okay? That it didn't matter? None of that was true. She took a long breath, steadying herself.

"Why, Daz? Why did you do it?"

He looked away, ashamed. "I thought I was protecting her. Emily. From him. From everything. I thought... I don't know what I thought anymore. It just—it got out of control."

Doreen listened, watching the way his jaw trembled, the way he seemed to shrink deeper into himself. She remembered the boy he'd been. The quiet one, the one who tried so hard to be strong when his own parents had failed him. The one who never stopped looking for someone to protect, someone to love.

"You loved her," she said gently.

He nodded. "Too much. In the wrong way. I thought I was helping her. But I ruined everything."

They sat in silence for a while, the kind that pressed against your chest and made it hard to breathe. Doreen kept her hand on his. She could feel the tension in him, the guilt eating away at what was left.

"The girl you killed... she was good, wasn't she?"

"Yeah," he croaked. "She was kind. And strong. And smart. She saw me. Not like most people do. Not like I was just trash. And I threw it all away. I took her from the world."

"She didn't deserve it."

He shook his head violently. "No. God, no."

Tears spilled over now. His shoulders hunched, and he sobbed into the crook of his arm. Doreen watched him, tears in her own eyes. She didn't stop him. He needed to cry. He needed to feel it.

When he finally lifted his head again, he looked drained, hollowed out.

"They're going to keep me here forever, aren't they?"

Doreen's lips pressed into a thin line. "They might."

He nodded slowly. "I deserve that."

"Maybe. But you're still mine. I won't stop visiting."

That got him. A fresh round of tears welled up.

"I'm so sorry, Nan. I wish I could take it back. I wish I could swap places with her."

"Wishing doesn't change what's done. But maybe now, all you can do is be honest. Talk. Let yourself feel it."

He nodded. He looked up at her with red eyes. "Do you think... do you think she hated me at the end?"

Doreen swallowed the lump in her throat. "I think she was scared. But I think she also knew you were sick, not evil. That doesn't mean it's okay. But no, Daz. I don't think she hated you."

Silence fell again. The visiting time was almost up. A guard nearby gave a small nod—five more minutes.

"Tell me about her funeral," he said suddenly. "I—I want to know. Please."

Doreen smiled sadly. "It was beautiful. She had a white coffin. Pink flowers all over it. That song from the film she loved played. Her friend Sara cried like the world was ending. Her mum looked well. And Cynthia. Even Alex, her boyfriend, was there."

Daz closed his eyes. "I ruined everything."

"Yes," she said. "But it's not over for you. You still have time to learn. To make peace. To be something better. Even if it's in here."

He opened his eyes slowly. "Will you come back?"

"I will," she said firmly. "You're not alone. Not ever."

When the guard stepped forward and said time was up, Doreen stood, leaning forward to kiss the top of his head.

"I love you, Daz. I don't understand you. I don't forgive what you did. But I love you."

He clutched her hand one last time before letting go.

As she walked away, Daz stayed still, watching her retreat. The pain remained—sharp, endless. But her words echoed somewhere deep within the fractured parts of him. Not forgiveness. But love. A beginning, maybe, in the ruins of what he'd done.

Chapter Seventy-Five

Stillness

Louise stepped out of the car and into the pale hush of early evening, the air filled with the scent of cut grass and exhaust fumes. The car sat behind her, engine ticking, as she stood on the edge of the pavement and stared up at the house she hadn't seen in nearly a year. Her old house. Their old house. The place where everything began and unravelled.

She didn't need to go inside. That wasn't why she'd come.

She'd come because the silence in her own flat had become unbearable. The kind of silence that wasn't empty but loud. It had echoes. Breaths that weren't there. Laughter she remembered and couldn't forget. Arguments that returned with cruel clarity at four in the morning.

The front driveway was overgrown, a wild mess of grass and weeds pushing up through the paving. Someone had tried to trim the hedge at some point, but only half-finished the job. The house looked both abandoned and stubbornly alive, as if it had learned how to survive without them. Louise thought maybe that was what she'd done too.

She walked slowly past it, not daring to look into the windows. She wasn't ready for that. She climbed back into the car.

The pub was just down the road. A different one to the wake. One she remembered sneaking into with her friends back when she was fifteen and full of rage. She wasn't sure why she'd chosen it. Something about the smell. Dust and spilt lager and old regrets. It carried a weight to it.

Inside, the lights were low and the tables were half-empty. She ordered a gin and tonic without thinking, the words automatic on her tongue. She hadn't eaten, hadn't planned to. Her stomach was a fist.

She sat in a booth by the window, legs tucked up under the seat, her jacket pulled around her shoulders like armour. Outside, people walked past with bags of shopping, dogs on leads, children in arms. Everything so ordinary it hurt.

She hadn't spoken to her family when Emily died. Not a word. She'd read about it in a news article first. The headline had mentioned a body. She'd known immediately.

Somehow, she'd always known this was how it would end. Just not when.

She didn't cry. She'd done all her crying after Dad.

That day had split her open. She'd screamed in the bathroom until her throat bled. She'd thrown a mug at the mirror and watched her reflection crack down the centre. It hadn't made her feel better. Just different. Emptier.

After that, she couldn't go back.

To Mum, who drank herself into silence.

To Cynthia, who wore grief like a second skin.

To Emily.

Emily, who always wanted to fix what she didn't understand.

Louise sipped her drink and let the burn of the gin settle into her chest. The condensation from the glass left a wet ring on the table. She traced it with her fingertip.

She remembered the way Emily used to hum in the mornings. Always out of tune, always too cheerful. She remembered the way her dad would roll his eyes but secretly love it. The way he'd squeeze their shoulders as he passed, his own kind of affection.

She missed him. It came in waves, like nausea.

But she also felt something else. Something she hadn't been able to name until now.

Stillness.

Not peace. Not exactly.

But something that felt like the end of a long-held breath.

She was no longer waiting for the next explosion. The next slammed door. The next late-night argument echoing through the floorboards.

It was over. All of it.

And in the ashes, she was still here.

She drove home late, tipsy but steady. The streets were quiet, streetlamps humming. Her flat was small, always smelled faintly of toast and nail polish remover. She locked the door behind her and dropped her bag by the kitchen counter.

The photo of her and Emily sat on the windowsill. It was from years ago. Stood outside of the school gates. They were both grinning like idiots, arms around each other, their hair tangled by the wind. She'd meant to take it down a hundred times. But she never had.

She didn't cry.

She went to the bathroom and washed her face. Brushed her teeth. Took off her makeup like her skin depended on it.

When she lay in bed, the dark felt less like a weight and more like a comfort.

She closed her eyes and thought of Emily. Of her voice. Of her stupid jokes. Her fearlessness. Her softness. The way she always reached for other people first.

And then she thought of Dad.

And how the last words she said to him were shouted across a hallway. How she never told him she was sorry. That she loved him.

The guilt was there. Always. But it no longer strangled her.

Maybe that was what grief was. A long walk through fog until you stopped checking over your shoulder, and it began to clear ahead.

She didn't know if she'd ever speak to Cynthia again. Or Andrea. Or anyone from that life.

But she wasn't angry anymore.

She was tired.

And the world, for the first time, was quiet.

Morning came slowly. Pale blue and soft. She made coffee and drank it barefoot by the window. Her phone buzzed with a message from an unknown number:

"She would have wanted you there. - Cynthia."

Louise stared at it for a long time. She didn't reply.

She didn't go to the funeral.

She couldn't.

But she carried Emily with her.

She carried all of them.

And for the first time in a long time, she felt the weight shift. Not disappear. But change.

Not peace. But something like it.

Stillness.

End.

About the Author

Emilia G Collins

I grew up in a messy childhood, but these days, I'm exactly where I always hoped I'd be—normal, happy, and successful in my own way. I'm a mum to two brilliant boys, aged 10 and 6, who keep me on my toes, challenge me daily, and inspire me to keep learning and evolving.

I've always loved storytelling. English was my favourite subject at school, but I left education early, before sitting my GCSEs. Years later, while pregnant with my youngest, I returned and earned my GCSEs in English and maths. It was tough, but it reminded me how much I enjoy learning and pushing myself.

I'm a true-crime lover and have a soft spot for writing stories with suspense, though funnily enough, I can't stand watching horror or thrillers! I've always wanted to write a book, and I finally have.

Here's to messy beginnings, strong finishes, and making space for the things we've always wanted to do.

Emilia (right) and her sister Carmela (left).

Printed in Dunstable, United Kingdom